Horse's face was dark. "There is an uprising in Vreeport. Some civilians who found a cache of Inner Sphere weapons are shooting from the upper levels of buildings at passing warriors."

Aidan was shocked, and saw a similar expression on Joanna's face. "Civilians?" she repeated. "Are they mad?"

Horse nodded. "There seems to be only one course of action."

"Annihilation?" Aidan felt himself grow cold at the thought of it.

"Yes."

"Well, perhaps we can avoid that."

Joanna tilted her head slightly. "The general directive says to be merciless in dealing with uprisings."

"They are our enemies, yes." Aidan stared at her. "But that does not mean they are not humane. We must treat them with the same respect that we give our warrior foes."

"But we are not to annihilate them?"

"Only when we have to."

"I have never recognized any other choice."

Aidan looked at her for a long moment, and the cruelty she remembered came back into his eyes. "And look where it has gotten you, Star Commander Joanna."

BATTLETECH®

LEGEND OF THE JADE PHOENIX
VOLUME 3

FALCON GUARD

ROBERT THURSTON

A ROC BOOK

ROC
Published by the Penguin Group
Penguin Books USA Inc., 375 Hudson Street,
New York, New York 10014, U.S.A.
Penguin Books Ltd, 27 Wrights Lane,
London W8 5TZ, England
Penguin Books Australia Ltd, Ringwood,
Victoria, Australia
Penguin Books Canada Ltd, 10 Alcorn Avenue,
Toronto, Ontario, Canada M4V 3B2
Penguin Books (N.Z.) Ltd, 182–190 Wairau Road,
Auckland 10, New Zealand

Penguin Books Ltd, Registered Offices:
Harmondsworth, Middlesex, England

First published by Roc, an imprint of New American Library,
a division of Penguin Books USA Inc.

First Printing, December, 1991
10 9 8 7 6 5 4 3 2 1

Series editor: Donna Ippolito
Cover: Bruce Jensen
Interior illustrations: Jeff Laubenftein
Mechanical drawings: Steve Venters
Copyright © FASA, 1991
All rights reserved

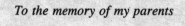

To the memory of my parents

Prologue

Star Captain Joanna, in her darkest fantasies, saw herself dying with a projectile ripping through her body, or incinerated in a BattleMech, or destroyed by a lucky shot from an enemy MechWarrior's weapon. In her wilder nightmares, she imagined being murdered in her bed by a vile freebirth, or mauled by a bloodthirsty creature on some planet where she was stranded, or perhaps ejecting successfully from the cockpit of her 'Mech only to drown in a deep lake before she could free herself from the restraints of her ejection seat. Once she had dreamed that the best death would come in heroic combat or even during a Trial of Bloodright, where she would meet her end in a ferocious final round of the competition for a Bloodname.

But now her dreams had faded, for she had become an old warrior. She still piloted a 'Mech as a warrior of Clan Jade Falcon, but no longer would any Bloodnamed warrior sponsor her for a slot in any Trial of Bloodright. Without a nomination, Joanna's only hope for eligibility was to take part in a Grand Melee, but to that she would never stoop. (Joanna knew of only one warrior who had eventually won his Bloodname via that route, and the man was high on the long list of people she despised.) Her best hope now was cremation after death so that her ashes would return to the same sibko system that had spawned her existence, to be blended with the amniotic fluid of the artificial wombs. Without a Bloodname, Star Captain Joanna could never achieve the ultimate goal of all Clan warriors, the inclusion of her genes in the sacred gene pool. Letting that dream die had been the most difficult of all, even after Joanna realized she would never win a Bloodname. Since then she had added an even more dread possibility to her fantasies about death, this one of surviving to the time when she would die in her bed either from disease or sheer old age. Of all the ends she could imagine, that was the most appalling.

Despite all the conjectures, Joanna had never foreseen being buried alive while trapped in the cockpit of her 'Mech, which was exactly where she was at this moment. The Clan invasion of the Inner Sphere had been going on for nine months now, and Joanna had just been assigned as a replacement to the Falcon Guards. Almost immediately after she had reported to the Cluster commander, Star Colonel Adler Malthus, the Cluster had been ordered to defend against an Inner Sphere counterattack on the planet Twycross.

The Falcon Guards had been traversing a pass called the Great Gash, when a single, battered Inner Sphere *Hatchetman* crested the ridge line. The BattleMech pilot identified himself as Kai Allard-Liao and issued a clumsy *batchall* for the pass. The enemy's bravery was admirable, but Star Colonel Adler Malthus went too far. Instead of simply refusing to grant Clan-warrior status to an Inner Sphere MechWarrior, he halted the Cluster's advance, and went out to finish off the Inner Sphere warrior alone. Star Colonel Malthus advanced and raised the arms of his *Summoner* to smash the Gash's defender into rubble, but before the blow could land, the *Hatchetman* exploded.

As though in sympathy, the Great Gash itself blew apart, sending rocks and dirt spouting and flying, boulders bouncing off the surface of Joanna's *Hellbringer* with a horrible clanging that nearly deafened her. Then another nearby 'Mech exploded, and before Joanna knew what had happened, she was staring through her viewport at a wall of geological debris. With enough air trapped in the *Hellbringer*'s cockpit to keep her going for awhile, she kept her panic at bay, using the 'Mech's still-functional computer to calculate the compartment's volume plus the amount of air that might still remain in the circulation system. It looked like it might be enough to survive for at least fifteen minutes, perhaps more. Who could be sure?

When it came to survival, the human organism sometimes went beyond its own limitations. Perhaps she had even more precious moments than she estimated.

Joanna briefly considered using some of the deep-concentration techniques she had learned during warrior training so long ago. By slowing her breathing profoundly, she might be able to remain alive even longer. Then she decided to hell with it. She needed her wits about her and did not particularly want to sink into some deep meditative funk. What she needed now was to keep her mind busy enough to figure a way out of here.

With so much of her *Hellbringer* apparently still operational, Joanna thought that perhaps she might still accomplish some miracle. Was she not a warrior, the product of a scientific program that engineered the production of superior humans by mating only the most superior genes? Add to that the abilities of the massive piece of fighting machinery called a BattleMech—and who knew what might be possible? Joanna had neither much faith nor liking for humanity in general, but she had confidence to spare in herself. As for 'Mechs—she respected them to the point of reverence.

She tried her communications system, which produced plenty of crackle and static, but no response from anyone on the line. Perhaps it was because fallen rock and dirt had cut off communications. Or perhaps all the other Jade Falcon warriors were as trapped in their 'Mechs as she was, but had not escaped death. Scanners proved inoperable also, so she could not tell how deep she and her machine were buried in the debris.

Staring at her secondary screen, Joanna tested other systems. It was immediately obvious that operating any of her weapon systems would be dangerous. If she tried to fire any of them, the weapon would simply explode and that would be the end of her. A mercifully quick end, to be sure, but not the one she craved.

Neither of the 'Mech's arms seemed functional, either, so she could not use them to dig herself out. Then she tried the right leg. Nothing.

The left leg, however, surprised her. She felt it strain at her attempts to move it, though that was about all. When she switched her concentration to the left foot, at first it failed to respond. With a little more effort, she felt it move, but ever so imperceptibly. Not much more than a twitch, but movement nonetheless. Pressing the foot pedal that operated the 'Mech's legs, Joanna tried again to move the left foot forward. This time it seemed to budge slightly. Not much, but enough to keep her trying.

Bit by bit, she kept at it until she had the left foot moving more freely. Now she made it slide from side to side, each time sensing its movement to be easier. If only her sensors were working, she could get an external view of the leg's movements and thus a clearer idea of its current mobility.

The air in the cockpit was getting hotter, the excess of carbon dioxide making her dizzy. No telling how much time she had left. But then, what did it matter when the time you had left was *all* the time you had left?

She decided to try to kick out with the *Hellbringer's* leg. A dumb maneuver in most battles, but one that might prove useful when buried alive. Working the foot pedal, she was pleased and astonished to feel the whole leg wrench free. Then she kicked again, laughing aloud just to feel the leg's freedom. With that kick, Joanna had a sense of the outward thrust dislodging even more rock and dirt. That was a start, she decided. With her next kick, she noticed a slight movement of the 'Mech at hip level. Perhaps it was the 'Mech's design that was working in her favor. The machine's wide shoulders might be blocking any further avalanche of debris from tumbling down to re-bury the 'Mech's leg, while the outward thrust of the hip was giving it sufficient leverage to escape from the trap.

Joanna was beginning to feel drowsy, her lids wanting to flutter shut. The air was very close. If only she could get the cleaner working again, it might be the difference between escape and death—a matter of minutes. She swallowed hard, with a sense that she might not ever be able to swallow again. Then she swallowed once more, just to prove it was not true. Joanna had always been stubborn, whether in jeopardy or at ease.

She realized now that she had no more time to wait through the minuscule gains won with each slight move of her 'Mech. She would be dead long before she could get to good air.

Setting the controls at high, Joanna attempted to maneuver the BattleMech forward with all the force the control systems could generate. At first nothing happened. The right side of the 'Mech seemed completely trapped, so she concentrated on its left. Urging the machine's left shoulder forward, she discovered that it would move slightly, no more than a mild spasm compared to a human shoulder's muscular convulsion. But when she repeated the action, the shoulder gave way more. In successive attempts, she sensed the shoulder's jerking motion, like a warrior punching in a hand-to-hand battle. The 'Mech's right side was still wedged too tightly for the whole machine to break free. Her only hope was in the jerky thrusts of the left side. Frantically, she continued to shove the left shoulder forward until finally she saw some of the debris in her viewport move. It was a slight shift, but enough to tell her she still had a chance.

Though the cockpit was stifling and almost airless, Joanna kept at her desperate actions until daylight suddenly showed through on the left side of the viewport. She could still not call up a computer diagnostic of the 'Mech's internal condition on her secondary screen, but she knew the odds were good that the area beyond the cockpit hatchway was now clear.

At the hatchway, she yanked on the manual release lever for the hatch, but the plate did not budge. The heat inside the cockpit was now almost unbearable. Forcing herself to calm, she tried once more to pop the hatch, which seemed to loosen but still did not open. With two hands now, first she pushed in on the control, hoping to release the pressure, then with a lifting motion, she pulled back once more. She tried this several more times, even though it took all her strength. Then came a sound that was music to her ears, a snap that might be the hatch lock releasing. Carefully now, gently, she continued to pull, side to side this time, gradually opening a crack wide enough through which she could wedge her body into the rocks and dirt beyond it. Some of the rocks fell inward, onto the cockpit's metal flooring, creating an odd clanging sound.

Wondering if she might have gotten enough movement from the 'Mech to free it from the heaviest layer of rocks and dirt, Joanna tried again to move the machine, but it did not budge. She was panting, the breathable air nearly gone. Clawing frantically at the rock wall in front of her, she dislodged rocks and flung them behind her, pushing dirt to either side of her.

Soon most of her torso was out the hatchway and into the tunnel she had dug. Instead of feeling exhilaration at the success, her body wanted to collapse, close its eyes, rest, and fall asleep. Fighting the urge to give up, she began to dig even more ferociously.

At just the moment when she might suddenly have tipped over the edge into unconsciousness, Joanna's left hand broke free into the hot, humid outside air. Knowing escape was so close, she rallied what little reserve energy still remained and frantically began to scratch, dig, and claw forward. Soon she had created a substantial hole. Air flooded in and she hungrily drew in a normal breath. Pushing herself headfirst, she forced her body through the opening, and emerged into the scorching air of Twycross. Joanna nearly collapsed just as she worked her legs out of the hole, rolling three or four meters down the slope of the rockfall. She landed on her back. Looking up, she saw the *Hellbringer's* shoulder, its launch mount bent backward, and a small part of the head. It seemed to peek out from beneath a rock pile.

With great effort, she hoisted herself to a sitting position and then looked around her. Various BattleMech parts were strewn all over the slope and down onto the floor of the pass. From what the wreckage showed, it looked as though the avalanche created by the explosions must have buried the entire unit. The *Hatchetman's* own fiery death must have set off the demolition charges buried in the sides of the Gash.

This Kai Allard-Liao was a courageous warrior, freebirth Inner Sphere pilot or not. The honor that should have gone to the Jade Falcons was now due him, whoever he was, wherever he was.

That grim thought was the last of which Joanna was conscious before passing out.

1

The *Summoner*, Aidan Pryde's 'Mech, lay on a plateau, looking for all the world as though it were merely resting, taking a breather before confronting another foe. Looks were deceiving, however. This 'Mech had met its fate in Clan Jade Falcon's battle to take the lush but undeveloped Inner Sphere world of Quarell. The enemy warriors left behind to defend Quarell had fought courageously, but Aidan's forces had overwhelmed them despite the low number of forces he had bid for the battle.

As for the *Summoner*, the BattleMech had been ripped apart. Its left arm lay elsewhere on the field, and its entire left side was a tangle of metal, wires, and other components. Aidan's chief tech, a grizzled old man named Lenk, reported severe damage to the fusion engine and that several other systems were inoperative. Lenk told him that any repairs would be makeshift, and so the 'Mech could not possibly operate at peak efficiency.

Aidan agreed, ordering Lenk to tag the spare parts that might still be useful to other 'Mechs, then assigned the rest of the *Summoner* for salvage. A good Clan officer always searched for the means to turn his defeats into virtues. A downed 'Mech, no matter how damaged, was never entirely scrapped. Someone somewhere would have a use for its remains. Nicholas Kerensky, he who had created the Clans, had instilled in his followers the absolute necessity for the severest economy measures. Nothing must be discarded until it had been squeezed dry of any possible new use. And, Aidan had noticed, there always seemed to be at least one more.

Warriors, too, wore out, for they were soon too old to fight. They often moved to support positions, training units, but failing that, these old warriors could still perform one more service for their Clan. In many battle situations the commander's only hope was to buy time by sending expendable troops into the fray. These warriors willingly sacrificed their lives. Aging warriors were often organized into such *solahma* units, then sent into the field for one last battle. Aidan thought of Ter Roshak, the training commander who had so changed the course of his life. Only weeks before, Roshak had given his life as a member of a *solahma* infantry unit.

A sad fate, thought Aidan, for a valorous warrior. Ter Roshak had survived heroically only to die as cannon fodder, an ignominious end. But perhaps survival had been the man's fatal mistake. Aidan would sooner die in battle, preferably in his BattleMech and while destroying both his enemy and his enemy's 'Mech, than live to see his worth as a warrior used up.

Having served for twenty years, he, too, was edging toward being an old warrior. Aidan was almost forty, an age when a warrior was supposed to be considering his options as an aging member of his Clan. Fortunately for him, however, there was a war on, a war the Clans had been living, dying, and preparing to fight for centuries, ever since the Exodus of their ancestors from the Inner Sphere after the fall of the once-glorious Star League. A Star Colonel now, Aidan could conceivably rise to high command levels, become part of the guiding forces of the long-awaited invasion of the Inner Sphere. That would certainly add a few years to his usefulness as a warrior.

But he knew such ideas were mere delusion. Though he had legitimately earned all his promotions to this point, including his Bloodname, he carried a taint as a warrior that would let him go only so far as a warrior. His codex showed too many black marks. There was, for one, the dark cloud over the means by which he had earned warrior status. After Aidan had failed his first Trial of Position, Ter Roshak had schemed, even murdered, to give him an unprecedented, and illegal, second chance at the trial to become a Clan warrior, one of the highest honors to which any eligible young trueborn could aspire. The second taint involved Aidan's posing as a freeborn, the false identity he'd assumed for his second trial. The freeborn stigma still clung to him even after he had confessed his true identity. The third black mark was that he had competed for a Bloodname despite his past record. Only a day before the Trial of Bloodright competitions began, he had been forced to fight a Trial of Refusal to protest his Clan's denial of his right to compete for a Bloodname. Only by winning that contest could he overrule the Clan's decision. He had won the Trial of Refusal through a combination of intelligence and skill, yet he had never escaped the taint of the accusations against him. Last, but hardly least, Aidan had won the Bloodname through a last-ditch maneuver that no one could have imagined would succeed. Until the last instant, Aidan's opponent seemed to be on the verge of crushing Aidan totally.

And yet, it was Aidan who had won the contest and his opponent who died. He recalled the moments immediately after winning the Bloodname. He had passed out and been rescued from Rhea, the moon over the planet Ironhold, where the final Bloodname combat had taken place. Upon recovering, he had expected that winning the Bloodname contest would also win the respect of his fellow warriors. Instead, they regarded him with more suspicion than ever. Even the official ceremonies seemed to smack of perfunctoriness rather than the usual solemn Clan ritual. Perhaps, Aidan thought, his life would never again be free of the stain of scandal no matter what Trials or battles he won or lost.

Even with a Bloodname, his warrior assignments had been not much better than his assignments as a ''freeborn'' warrior. Over the years, Aidan sometimes thought he must have served in every backwater military facility in the whole globular cluster that was the Clan empire.

''You're thinking bad thoughts again,'' Horse said, coming up alongside him. Aidan had qualified with Horse during his second warrior trial, and the two had served together ever since, with only three short interruptions. This time Aidan had specifically requested that Horse be assigned to his new command. Many of his trueborn officers grumbled secretly about that because Horse was a freeborn. Trueborns did not like serving with freeborns, especially within the same Star.

''I am famous for being unreadable, Horse. How can you know my thoughts?''

Horse stroked his new full beard, which he had recently grown. Freeborns often chose clothing or grooming styles in direct opposition to what the trues favored. Trueborn warriors were generally clean-shaven, and if they chose to be bearded, theirs tended toward thinner, less full growths. Horse's flowed outward like hairy flaps on either side of his jaw.

"I've known you for a long time. You're like an open book to me, one that I've read many times."

Aidan was so used to hearing Horse speak that by now he barely minded the man's excessive use of contractions—excessive even for a freeborn, who often used them out of defiance.

"How many books have you read many times?"

"More than you, especially since you made Star Colonel."

Horse was right. Lately Aidan had little time for his secret library, those paper books he had discovered so long ago in a Brian Cache. He had carried them hidden away and undiscovered from one assignment to the next. Now that he was a Star Colonel, he could read them openly, but no longer had the luxury of time.

"Well, what are you going to do now?" Horse said, pointing to Aidan's downed BattleMech. "We have no more *Summoner*s."

Aidan had fought almost exclusively in *Summoner* 'Mechs during his military career. He liked their tonnage, their various configurations, their jump capacity. Some warriors called him a "jumping fool" for the daring leaps he took with his 'Mech in battle. Yet there were few warriors who could attack while descending from a high jump as well as Aidan Pryde.

"I will take out MechWarrior Carmen's *Timber Wolf*."

"The *Timber Wolf*?" Horse's eyebrows went up in surprise. "That's a killer 'Mech."

"You should not call it that."

"Should I call it Deathtrap then? That's the name for it among the Elementals."

"Our Elementals have a morbid sense of humor, always have. But it is wrong to ascribe traits to a BattleMech. The fact that a few warriors have died piloting this particular—"

"A few? The Deathtrap has had more pilots than—"

"Stop, Horse! I need no statistics quoted at me. I know them as well as you. And the truth is that many pilots have survived this *Timber Wolf*."

"Most of them with crippling injuries or lost in madness."

"Now you exaggerate. At any rate, I will take the *Timber Wolf*, and that is the end of it."

The two fell silent as they watched the techs working around the *Summoner*. It reminded Aidan of a story from his secret collection, the book that told of a human who landed in a strange land peopled by beings so small that they could swarm like ants over the stranger's fallen body. The techs were larger in proportion than those lilliputian literary creatures, but the effect was similar.

"Oh," Horse said suddenly, threading his fingers through the beard, "I almost forgot the purpose that brought me here. The reinforcements we requested have arrived in-system and should be landing at first light this morning. Just in time to miss the battle, as it happens. Do you want to greet 'em and brief 'em, once they are down?"

Aidan felt weariness and pain all through his body, the typical aftermath of a fierce battle. He wanted to lie down, like the *Summoner*, and sleep straight through the next two days. But duty was always of the utmost importance to him, even routine duties like inspecting a new contingent of warriors.

"All right," he said, straightening his shoulders and lifting his head proudly. "Wake me two hours before their arrival. Shall I give them the abandon-hope speech?"

"I hope not. That might be like something you read, but it definitely would not be Clan."

"No it would not. Anything I should know about these reinforcements?" Aidan stopped suddenly, puzzled. "Why did your mouth fall open, Horse?"

"You are sometimes uncanny. It's not the first time you seem to read *my* mind. Yes, there are things you should know. First, a number of freeborns are in this lot."

Aidan shrugged. "No problem there. We are experts on freeborns, you and I."

"You speak of me as if I, too, were trueborn."

"I do forget. I do."

"Anyway, I know these freeborns will be trouble. A lot of anti-freeborn resentment has developed among our Cluster, and that could lead to disputes and fights. In a war zone, we cannot afford to lose personnel to stupidity."

Aidan nodded. "And if I seem to support the freeborns, the trues will be against me. If I support the trues, not only the frees, but you, will resent me. A dilemma, but I can handle it."

"I am sure you can," Horse said drily, "but I am not so sure you can deal with my other piece of information."

Aidan said nothing for a long moment, but let his gaze sweep the once-green Quarell landscape, which was now battle-scarred with scorched trees and long, deep gashes in the land. Then he turned to face Horse once more. "Well?" he said finally.

"It seems that this replacement pool includes a Star Commander. She is, well, an old warrior. She was one of the Falcon Guards who dishonored us on Twycross. In fact, this warrior is one of the few survivors of that debacle."

"I did not think you cared so much for abstractions like the honor of the Clan and such."

"I do not. I am merely presenting the situation the way most of your trashborn warriors will see it. The defeat on Twycross has shamed the Jade Falcons deeply. Anyhow, this new Star Commander carries that *dezgra* with her. She was formerly a Star Captain, but has been retested and reduced in rank to Star Commander."

"Ah, Horse, perhaps I understand you now. This *dezgra* warrior is none other than our very own Joanna, *quiaff?*"

"Aff."

Aidan frowned, the lines forcing his expression into something unfamiliar. The Star Colonel so rarely showed emotion that even a frown looked fresh on his skin.

"This is bad news, Horse," he said. "Very bad news indeed."

2

As always in battle, Diana faced her adversary with a stare as grim as it was threatening. It was a pose she had developed long, long ago, even before becoming a warrior. She had assumed this look in her early childhood games, which she had tried to model on her mother's tales of her warrior father. Diana always played her father's part, pretending pots and other utensils were parts of a BattleMech. Then, with proper battle shrieks, she would run after the other village children. Diana always won, for most of the children had neither her ambition nor, for that matter, her tenacity.

Those childhood games had borne significant fruit. Diana knew she would never be satisfied with any caste less than warrior. Even though she was not trueborn, she knew she must become a Clan warrior. It was that fierce conviction that had taken her with ease through training and her first warrior assignments. Unlike many other freeborns, she simply accepted her inferior rank in Clan society, easily ignoring the cruel remarks the trues often hurled at her. The word *freebirth*, a curse among warriors, did not ordinarily inspire her to seek retribution, as it did so many other freeborns.

She had two goals in life: to be a fine warrior and to find her father. Her skills in the first she had already proven time and again. As for the second, Diana was content that she would achieve it in time.

Now she stood poised in an improvised shipboard Circle of Equals, facing off against—of all people—another dedicated freeborn warrior. The several trueborns who had joined the observers at the outer rim of the circle seemed amused by the sight of two frees going at one another. They shouted encouragement now to one, now to the other warrior, always peppering their cheers with scornful insults. As usual, Diana noticed the condescension, but did not let it affect her. If she were a trueborn standing outside the circle, she would be shouting the same insulting remarks.

Her opponent, a stocky, muscular warrior named Trader (the nickname deriving from his origin as the son of a merchant), growled at her in the traditional manner of honor duels. His challenge had come over the right to pilot the *Warhawk* that had become available when its regular pilot took ill during the interstellar journey to the Jade Falcon corridor of the invasion of the Inner Sphere. The 'Mech assignment would normally have fallen to Diana because the Star's new commander had claimed her *Timber Wolf*.

After hearing the assignment, Trader had stepped forward to claim that his seniority and longer battle record made him more deserving to pilot the *Warhawk*. While acknowledging privately that Trader's fighting prowess was enviable, Diana could not, as a Clan warrior, merely acquiesce and back down. No, the two of them must battle it out for the 'Mech.

The new commander had insisted that the contestants bid their way into the Circle of Equals. Diana had cut off the batchall immediately with her bid that she would meet Trader with no other weapons but her gloved hands. The bid drew some admiration because the tall, slim Diana seemed no match for the shorter but definitely more muscular Trader.

At the signal to begin, Trader gave a great yell that seemed to bounce off the DropShip's walls, then charged like a wild boar straight for Diana. He landed the first two blows, one to Diana's midsection, knocking some of the wind out of her, and a punishing punch to the left side of her face. That one drew immediate blood and sent her reeling backward. Her low kick in response was ineffectual, connecting with nothing. If anything, the effect was comical.

Joanna watched with some pleasure the brawling between the two freeborn members of her new Star. Though she hated this new assignment, she had mellowed with the years and could accept it with more aplomb than she might have in the past. Yet the demotion to Star Commander had definitely raised her ire. It was like wearing the dark band, the special ribbon that denoted shame in Clan warrior culture. The lower rank was like an eternal dark band, for the shame would not end on any specified date, as did the punishment of the dark band. Her chances of ever climbing back up the ladder of rank were almost nil. Her chances of ever being a Star Captain again were remote. Reaching Star Colonel would be well-nigh impossible.

So what could Joanna do but perform her appointed task as well as possible? There was at least some service in it, especially the job of whipping into shape an undisciplined group like the new lot they had saddled her with this time. Like all Clan warriors, Joanna was committed to the goals of the Inner Sphere invasion, especially the dream of restoring the Star League. It was the Clans' almost sacred covenant that they would conquer and replace the corrupt, decadent governments that had destroyed the Star League centuries before. That was the word of the great Kerenskys, which was good enough for Joanna and nearly all the rest of the invading force.

She admired something about this Diana. Perhaps it was the pride showing in the young warrior's eyes, or her confident stance, or the fierceness of her demeanor. Joanna could not be sure, for it was so unusual for her not to roundly dislike the newer warriors.

As Clan warriors went, Diana was an impressive specimen, Joanna decided. She might also have been judged beautiful in those old cultures that cared for such rubbish. The young woman's olive skin was just dark enough to suggest mystery, while her dark eyes under strongly arched eyebrows said there would never be a solution to that mystery. Her black hair shone with red highlights, a subtlety like the dark red of her lips. A slight "flaw," a bump in her otherwise well-shaped nose seemed to add to the overall striking effect of her angular face.

Joanna was disappointed when the other warrior, a typically repulsive freeborn named Trader, took the immediate advantage in the Circle of Equals contest. He kept hitting Diana hard, at one point nearly sending her over the edge of the circle, which would have meant

Diana's instant defeat. Though Diana remained on her feet and within the Circle, the jabs she dispatched with her left hand were useless.

Joanna almost yelled to her to use her right, or at least to try for a harder punch. Instead Diana spun out of the way of Trader's new assault and rushed back to the center of the circle, where she turned to face the charging and ready-for-the-kill Trader. As he came up to her, gloved fists flailing, Diana knocked him off-balance with a hard jab to the center of his nose. Then, as he fought to regain his balance, she delivered a solid blow, finally using her right hand. There was a flash, something on the right-hand glove catching the light.

It was a good punch, Joanna thought, but hardly a disabling one. Yet Trader's eyes flickered, then closed, and he fell forward onto his face. Diana stood over him the requisite amount of time, then declared herself the victor before strolling to where Joanna stood at the edge of the Circle of Equals. At that moment, realizing the meaning of the flash of light during the punch, Joanna's expression was transforming from relative calm to pronounced anger.

Diana casually removed her gloves as she stepped over the circle and came to stand before Joanna, ready to accept the prize of the *Warhawk*, the final stage of the contest. Instead of beginning the ritual words, Joanna reached out and snatched the gloves from Diana's hands. The younger warrior did not so much as blink at her commander's actions.

Joanna examined the gloves. "I thought so," she said, holding up the right-hand glove. Those closest to her could see that the glove bore five metal studs arranged in a star pattern at the middle of the knuckle line. Joanna now recalled that Diana had not only connected with the side of Trader's face, she had seemed to rub the blow in, obviously to further punish with the studs. No wonder the man had gone unconscious.

Joanna pointed silently to the glove's enhancement, and Diana shrugged. "I bid gloves as the only requirement of the battle," she said. "No specifications were made about the gloves, nor was it in any way limited whose gloves I could use."

"But you stole these gloves from me, freebirth!"

Diana again showed not a flicker of reaction at the insulting term. "I return them to you now, as I intended. Whether or not I stole them, I leave to others to judge."

"You think you can get off with Trinary punishment?"

"That would seem proper under the circumstances, Star Commander Joanna."

"Yes, it would, but instead I invoke command privilege and will order the punishment here and now. The two of us will return to the circle now, and you will battle me, MechWarrior Diana. As in your bid, no weapons for this battle. And no gloves. Bare-handed. And we will dispense with the rule that makes any warrior who crosses the line of the circle the automatic loser. There will be no such rule. The winner in our battle will be the one who is left standing. Agreed, MechWarrior Diana?"

"Well-bargained and done, Star Commander."

As Joanna followed this graceful, seemingly unruffled warrior back in to the Circle of Equals, she wondered briefly whether challenging a strong young warrior barely out of the cadet ranks to an honor duel was the smartest thing for an old, and perhaps fading, warrior to do.

3

For the first time in Joanna's memory, the codex bracelet on her right wrist felt heavy. It was as if the combined weight of all her years of combat and 'Mech piloting had suddenly accumulated into the small circlet where a series of Oathmasters had recorded her achievements as well as her failures, like the shame of the Falcon Guard defeat on Twycross. Shame that she bore despite having been a member of the Guards for only twenty-four hours and without even a unit to command. Perhaps it was only the weight of Twycross, after all, that made her wrist feel as though the bracelet were made of solid lead.

The warriors around the circle buzzed with excitement. It was not often that a ranking officer went into the Circle of Equals with a new warrior. It was the regulars who usually fought these battles, with the few curious officers standing coolly outside the circle, making sure the rules were followed.

But this officer-MechWarrior battle was special. The Star Commander was new among them, and the fact that she had been demoted because of Twycross made her an unknown quantity. Would she display the ferocity of the reputation that had preceded her? Or had Twycross shaken her confidence, as defeat sometimes did to a warrior? In their minds this Circle of Equals conflict was a test for Joanna as well as Diana. A few of them sent each other the hand signals that signified discreet betting on the event's outcome. If Joanna had bothered to read the betting signs going around the circle, she would have seen that the odds favored her by about two-to-one. It was better that she took no note of it. Any odds that gave this inexperienced warrior a chance to beat her were an insult to Joanna.

"Are you ready, MechWarrior Diana?" Joanna asked.

"Yes."

"You do not wish to invoke *surkai*?"

"Neg."

"Good. Then prepare yourself for extreme pain."

Joanna spoke the last three words while leaping at Diana. Diana, accustomed to an opponent shuffling his feet, feinting, sending glares, or making some other slight move before going on the attack, was taken completely by surprise. Joanna had her tightly by the throat, choking off air for a moment, then sneeringly releasing her grip and hurling her sideways onto the ground. Diana landed on her side. As the Star Commander had promised, extreme pain surged through her body from the impact of her landing. Though she was up quickly, Diana felt a throbbing in her shoulder. Each throb made her want to flinch with pain, but she would show no sign to this arrogant officer.

Diana did not have much time to think about the pain, for Joanna was on her again, this time coming at her in a crouch, grabbing the younger warrior's midsection and wrestling her to the ground. Falling backward, Diana realized that Joanna was merely employing standard wrestling maneuvers, ones they taught in the first weeks of training. But *why* could she use them to such advantage? Moves that Diana might easily have countered in another young warrior became tricky when this old crone applied them.

The only good thing at the moment was that the pain in her stomach somewhat relieved that of her shoulder, or was she merely dividing the pain by dividing her concentration?

Joanna, holding down Diana's shoulders and staring into her eyes, could easily have declared victory because she had the young warrior pinned. Diana's legs thrust out futilely behind Joanna.

But before Joanna could speak, she saw something familiar in the struggling warrior's eyes. At first it was a flash, a sign that Diana would never capitulate, then Joanna saw another face, that of another young warrior from another time. It was something in this young woman's

eyes, and now that Joanna looked more carefully, it was in her facial features, too. This Diana, this freebirth, bore an uncanny resemblance to the warrior Joanna had defeated in his first day of training and whose life had become so intimately connected with hers at certain points. Then he had been cadet Aidan. Now he was Star Colonel Aidan Pryde.

The revelation made Joanna rise up, releasing Diana from the pin, but then she clasped her hands together and, in a harsh sweeping arc, swung them at Diana's head. The hands hit with a stunning impact, and Diana fell backward, dazed.

Joanna looked around at the spectators beyond the line. Though they tried, in the Clan manner, to seem detached, it was obvious that the sudden brutality of Joanna's blow shocked some of them.

Looking down at the fallen warrior, whose eyes were now shut, Joanna thought that except for the greater delicacy of the features, she might have been looking at Aidan.

Diana did not give away with the slightest premovement the blow she now delivered. Kicking upward, she caught Joanna between the legs, the force of the blow lifting the old warrior slightly. Diana scrambled away from Joanna, who leaped at her with a growl of fury. Her timing off, Joanna smashed her face against the hard metal DropShip flooring instead of connecting with her prey. Before Joanna could get up, Diana had jumped onto her back and pushed her back down. Again Joanna's head smashed against the floor, and she was nearly overcome with dizziness.

Most warriors would have given up at that moment, but Joanna never gave up, would never give up. Helpless, she could not stop Diana from grabbing her hair from behind and slamming her head down against the metal floor again. Then, sensing a slight relaxation in Diana's grip right after the impact, Joanna twisted her torso enough to throw her elbow back at Diana's lowered head. She made contact, which further loosened her opponent's grip. Bellowing her special battle cry, Joanna twisted her body around and, with a magnificent effort, dislodged Diana, who fell sideways, rolled, and was back on her feet again instantly.

Diana did not give Joanna a second to recover. She ran straight at her. Dizzied by the banging to her head, Joanna was not sure who was coming at her. At first it looked like Aidan—not Aidan as he had been the last time she had seen him, but Aidan as a young cadet. Then the image seemed to switch back to Diana. Then to Aidan. Then again to Diana.

Whoever it was, the warrior was upon her, trying to ram her backward. The shuffling of Joanna's feet as she tried to stay upright struck some of the spectators as comical. When they laughed, the sound made her furious.

She pushed what looked like Diana away, and what looked like Aidan did a little stumbling dance. Shaking her head in an effort to throw off her grogginess, Joanna charged what looked like Aidan, but it was Diana who sidestepped her. Joanna quickly adjusted to Diana's quick move, grabbing Aidan's arm and wrenching it toward her. Joanna seized the head, not sure whose head it was anymore, and twisted it violently. Not enough to kill, but enough to cause a pain that would linger for some time.

Yes, enough.

Her opponent fell, dazed again, but this time finally helpless.

Looking down at the fallen warrior, Joanna was again seeing a double exposure of Diana, Aidan, Diana, and again Aidan. It was all she could do to walk without stumbling out of the Circle of Equals, but walk she did past all those warriors who saw that their new commander might be old but could still outfight even the best of them.

4

"We are both pretty banged up, *quiaff*?" Joanna asked.

"Are we? I can see you are, Star Commander. I did not look into any reflective surface. I rarely do."

They were in Joanna's quarters. Diana's cheek showed a large, ugly bruise where Joanna had struck her, and along the other side of her face were a couple of cuts. Joanna had glanced in a mirror, and saw she was worse off than Diana. One eye was black and her forehead was both bruised and cut. One side of her upper lip was slightly swollen, and tiny spots of blood had dried and caked around her nostrils. Overall, not a good appearance at all for a commanding officer.

The quarters were like every room in which Joanna had ever lived. She had never seen much use for neatness, especially when the place to which she was assigned was only temporary, as were all places for warriors. And this one, after all, was only a DropShip compartment.

Clothing was strewn all over the room, which was stained and dirty. When Joanna nodded for Diana to take a seat, the young warrior had to remove a tunic and boots from the chair, and deposit them onto an already crowded table.

"Would you like a fusionnaire, MechWarrior Diana?"

"I doubt it. What is a fusionnaire?"

"A drink. Very potent. I do not know what is in it. I have it packaged and sent to me on a regular basis. Sure you would not like a dose of it?"

"I have no liking for any substance that calms, releases, allows for fantasies, or sends one into a stupor."

There was an arrogant stubbornness in the way Diana

held her head while giving her list of undesirable states that reminded Joanna of Aidan holding his head in the same way with the same boldness.

"I understand your feeling completely," Joanna said, "but I do not agree. I need to lose my awareness once in a while." She took a strong sip of the drink. "I wonder about what you said a moment ago—that you never look in a mirror."

"Not never. Sometimes we see ourselves when we do not intend to. I just never look by intention, unless of course there is a practical need."

"But why? It cannot be hard for you to examine yourself. By most standards I am aware of you would be considered beautiful."

"Would I? That is interesting, but ultimately useless to me."

"Useless?"

"I have always wanted to be a warrior. As a freeborn, that is not an easy goal. People often attempted to discourage me from it. But I continued, was accepted into training, qualified in the Trial, and am now serving. I have many skills, which I have demonstrated, plus others I am eager to test. There is not much need for beauty in all that, is there?"

Joanna took another sip of the fusionnaire. Tasting especially harsh, the drink was going to her head quicker than usual. The fight with Diana had undoubtedly weakened her resistance to the drink. She would have to settle for only one. But, she thought, staring down into the volatile liquid, she would make the most of the one.

"Truth to tell, Diana, you are quite right. There is not much need for beauty in the ranks of Clan warriors. Here your looks are no more than a painting in a museum or a statue in a square. We admire you, but ours is not the kind of culture that places emphasis on beauty, after all."

"I am glad of that."

"But I should tell you that beauty like yours does have its uses in some circles. In political ones particularly. Among Clansmen who have forgotten the meaning of their lives, and who encourage a certain decadence."

"That is detestable, and I do not believe it exists."

"I notice that you do not have the freeborn love of contractions."

"I have resolved to be a warrior and to speak like one as well. Star Commander, if I may speak frankly?"

"As a warrior would. Proceed, MechWarrior Diana."

"I have been told about my beauty before. There were some who, well, wanted things from me because of it. I am not as free with coupling as others. Even in my cadet days. The others in my training unit respected that. Out here in the war zone, there is not as much respect. Perhaps I would have more experience with coupling if the other did not always have to mention my looks beforehand. But once someone speaks to me of that, I wish only to hit that someone and certainly not do anything more."

"Your honor duel with Trader was about that, *quiaff*?"

"Neg. Trader is a fine warrior, too. He wanted the BattleMech assignment. He would always choose a 'Mech over a sexual partner. I like him. I was sorry to have to fight him."

Diana straightened her back, holding it stiffly away from the back of the chair. When the younger woman looked off to the side, Joanna recalled several moments when Aidan had glanced aside in the same way, with the same tilt of the head and a duplicate indifference in his eyes. Diana's words and her resemblance to Aidan made Joanna want to take a big swallow of her fusionnaire. So she did.

The drink was gone. She should not have a second one, not with her head spinning the way it was now. She poured the second one and took several guarded sips.

"Star Commander Joanna, did you call me to your quarters for this discussion?"

Joanna shook her head. The movement made it ache. She blinked a couple of times before responding. "I had no purpose in calling you here, except to praise your tenacity in battling me in the Circle of Equals."

"Your praise pleases me." Diana did not show a bit of pleasure in her face, although her voice was softer.

"And there is another reason, which I should keep secret, but this fusionnaire is doing its job. It often loosens tongues." She took another large swallow of the drink. "You look like someone I once knew. Another warrior."

Diana nodded. "And his name was Aidan."

The statement astonished Joanna, who was not an easy person to astonish.

"You know?"

"I have known since I was a small child. My mother told me his name. She held back much of my father's history, and hers, but she was honest in every other way."

An idea occurred to Joanna. "And what was *her* name, your mother?"

"Peri. She is a—"

"I know all about her, too. I was their falconer. I trained both of them."

Diana stood up suddenly, anger in the way she held her body if not in her face. "Then you are the one who came to Tokasha and took my father away, *quiaff*?"

"Aff. I was ordered to. Now you look as if you would like to fight me again."

Diana's body relaxed. "No, you are right, it is not worth fighting about. But you were part of the story my mother told me. She never mentioned your name."

"There have been times, MechWarrior Diana, when I wished I had not caught up with your father and brought him back. In some way that event has affected the course of my life, too. But that is irrelevant. Your father went on to become a warrior and a Bloodnamed officer. Do you seek him?"

"Once I intended to. But now I wish only to fight in this war."

"I know, I know. You are consistent, at least. If I were able to communicate with your father, would you want me to inform him about you?"

Diana seemed to consider the question for a moment. "No," she said. "If anyone tells him, it should be me."

Joanna toasted her with the fusionnaire, then drained it. "I salute you, MechWarrior Diana. I have to tell you that I despised your father, but I have seen him fight bravely and well. From what you showed today in the Circle of Equals, you may be quite like him. Now you must leave."

Diana obeyed the order without further comment. Once she was gone, Joanna allowed the darkness to overcome her. She fell, drunk, onto her bed, and passed out. In her frenetic dreams, images of Aidan and Diana kept flying toward her face and back and forth in front of it, sometimes one changing into the other, sometimes the two blending together. Several times she screamed out at the disembodied faces, cursing and vowing that she would kill both father and daughter.

5

For the next few minutes Aidan would be under more intense scrutiny than at any time outside of a Clan test or trial, and yet he would be unaware of most of it. He was, after all, merely performing the routine duty of a garrison commander.

As the DropShip descended, Horse studied the face of his Colonel with an almost scientific detachment. He hoped to see some telltale twitch or eyeblink, some slight twisting of the mouth that would reveal a reaction in this normally distant man. To Horse, Aidan Pryde represented all that was admirable in a Clan warrior, whether trueborn or free. Aidan held himself above mundane Clan conflicts, administered his command with fairness, fought with more skill than any two warriors, and was so imbued with the desire to succeed that he had often been criticized for overreaching himself. To Horse, it was exactly these qualities that made Aidan a superb Clan warrior, albeit one whose abilities were underused because of the taint that had plagued his career.

And perhaps, Horse thought, what he liked most about Aidan was that he might be the only trueborn Clan warrior who understood what it was to be a freeborn warrior. That insight came, of course, from having lived so long disguised as a freeborn. It was in one of Aidan's secret library books that Horse had read about men on Terra who had gone to live among peoples whose cultures were strange or even alien, but who had often been liberated from narrow preconceptions as a result. Sometimes these visitors were scientists, but just as often they were ordinary people thrown into unusual circumstances. Aidan was like that, one who had learned through the force of circumstance. It had made him someone different, someone special, in Horse's eyes. The one time he had tried to articulate all this to Aidan, however, his friend had scoffed gently, saying that his experiences had confused his understanding of life rather than enhanced it.

The DropShip landed in the field recently cleared for that purpose, disgorging a contingent of warriors. Horse would have recognized Joanna from any distance, even if she had been a pinpoint on the horizon. She wore the Clan trueborn haughtiness like a cloak, an aura as far removed from Aidan's empathy as the globular cluster was from the five original Clan worlds. Horse and Joanna did not like each other. Never had. Anytime they had been forced to work or fight together, Joanna had, it seemed, found every way possible to remind Horse of his "inferior" origins.

Now, Horse took care to stand to the side, wanting to see both warriors' faces as they came together. Aidan's was composed, for he knew that Joanna was among the reinforcements. Horse wondered if Joanna was prepared for Aidan's presence on Quarell.

When the meeting occurred, neither Aidan nor Joanna displayed the least sign, not the slightest recognition. Of the three, Horse was probably the only one whose reaction would show. He was surprised at how much Joanna had aged. How humiliating for her, he thought. Though he never understood why the Clans were so harsh on their old warriors, Horse was himself a Clansman who could not help but be appalled by the signs of age on a face. His own was not so young anymore, but having always looked older than his years, the erosions of age were less noticeable to others.

But Joanna's visage was a horror. Her eyes seemed even meaner now that they bulged out a bit, making her look fierce even when not angry. Her lips had somehow tightened, and gray streaked her hair. Some warriors disguised their gray, but others seemed not to mind it. With Joanna it had to be her natural indifference to triviality that prevented her from being vain about her graying hair. Also on her face were some cuts and several fading bruises.

But mere physical details were not the only difference.

She walked differently, carried herself in a new way. She might be just as self-assured, just as proud, but her pace was slower and the way she swung her arms and moved her legs lacked energy. In all the time Horse had known Joanna, she had never moved with anything less than agile athleticism.

She came directly up to Aidan. More than a head shorter, she nevertheless faced him as though they were equals. The changes in her seemed even more pronounced when compared with the vigor in Aidan's stance.

Joanna's head still hurt from the fight with Diana. When she looked into the familiar face of Aidan Pryde, she experienced the same phenomenon of double exposure that had struck her with Diana. First she saw Star Colonel Aidan Pryde, a proud and assured military man whose face showed the traces of age, but almost as though they had been delicately sketched in by the hand of a skilled craftsman. Then she saw the young Aidan who had tormented her since the day she had first laid eyes on him. When she had challenged him to a fight on his first training day, he had fought well, better than most trainees. And then, in one way or another, they had been fighting ever since.

"Star Commander Joanna and replacement troops reporting for duty, sir," she said with flat military intonation. She studied his face for a reaction to her new, reduced rank. Perhaps she was grateful to see none.

Joanna was not prepared for this meeting. No one had told her who was senior commanding officer here, and she was seeing Aidan for the first time as a Star Colonel. Her throat constricted as she considered the terrible moment when she must address him as Star Colonel Aidan Pryde. Not only had she trained him, but she had been one of his advisors when he won his Bloodname. That still galled her. Not only did he have the Bloodname, the honor she had always craved but failed to attain, but now the *stravag* even outranked her!

Joanna was, however, still a Clan warrior, taught to accept whatever the Clan required of her. She had no choice but to accept Aidan as a Pryde and as a Star Colonel. She did not have to like it, but she must accept it.

Then again, perhaps she would never accept it, not deep down, and that thought was strangely comforting.

Joanna lined up her charges. She had instructed them to stand at stiff attention, not slacking off as warriors sometimes did in war zones. No one in her command would be permitted to display anything less than correct military posture, she warned them.

As Aidan proceeded slowly from one MechWarrior to the next, Joanna studied him carefully. Diana was next to last in the line. Behind them, a few meters away, the BattleMechs were being unloaded from the DropShip. They made an impressive backdrop to the militarily correct line of warriors.

Joanna saw that Aidan had not looked down the line as he moved, so that when he reached Diana, he was seeing her for the first time. But Joanna knew Aidan would never react publicly, even if he did see a resemblance. The chances were that, like his daughter, he was not enamored of his reflected image and would see none of it in Diana.

Now that, was that a flicker of recognition in Diana's eyes? Or did Joanna merely imagine it? Because father and daughter shared the same cool stare, Joanna could not conclude much about the encounter. Aidan moved on to inspect the next and final warrior.

Diana was, of course, the only one on the field that day who also saw her mother when she looked at her father. It might not have been obvious to a casual observer, but Diana knew that Aidan and Peri had originated in the same sibko. Aidan had become a warrior, while Peri had flushed out of warrior training and entered the scientist caste instead. The resemblance was only slight, but Diana saw it nonetheless. It was so unexpected that she almost revealed her surprise in a slight widening of her eyes. Then her native reserve came to the rescue. The fact that the features of both Peri and Aidan were mixed in Diana's face did not interest her, only that she had seen her mother in her father's face. The recognition might have shocked anyone.

She did not know what to think. She had not expected to find her father so soon after discussing him with

Joanna. When much younger, Diana had wished so much to meet Aidan. When she had chosen the path of a warrior, it was because that had been his. Sometimes she had dreamed of their reunion. But now that the moment had come, Diana did not want her father to know her identity. Trueborn warriors scorned their freeborn children, so why should she expect him to behave any differently? No, he would never learn who she was. But she would study him and take pleasure in knowing who *he* was. There was something Clanlike about that decision. Indeed, the young warrior did not even watch her father, her Star Colonel, when a few moments later, he began to address the entire unit.

6

Clan commanders, when briefing a new officer, especially one accompanying reinforcement units, did not generally make a social occasion out of the meeting. For most the mere idea of a social occasion was foreign, but Aidan Pryde had a skewered view of almost everything, much of it derived from his extensive secret reading. He had been impressed by the way Terrans of past eras often combined social ritual with more formal activities.

To Joanna, who read only operational and artillery manuals, Aidan's offer of a drink of Quarell wine was surprising but welcome. She had been dreading this encounter ever since arriving on Quarell with the reinforcements, only to find Aidan Pryde calmly waiting to greet them. If Clan policy had made possible a request for immediate reassignment, Joanna would have asked for one the moment the formal rituals of greeting were over.

She took a sip of the wine, a rather thick brew with a woody and slightly sour taste, all the while trying to look as if her current predicament did not matter to her. Aidan either read her mind, or his thoughts were on a similar track. He came right to the point with typical Clan-warrior bluntness.

"You do not wish to be here, Star Commander Joanna."

"Permission to speak frankly, Star Colonel?"

"You have it now and from now on, unless you give me occasion to revoke it."

"If our past history is any proof, I probably will."

Aidan smiled. "You seem to have picked up a sense of humor since last I saw you, Joanna."

"Have I? If so, I am not aware of it." She took another sip of wine. This time it tasted better, which she thought must be a quality common to wines everywhere. "You are right, Aidan Pryde, I do not wish to be here. I would prefer going solahma toward the front lines, weaponless and seated on the shoulders of a dying Elemental, to serving in any command *under* you. Does that portray my attitude vividly enough? And, for the sake of Kerensky, must you grin? I do not remember you ever smiling when last we knew each other."

"You are right. I did smile rarely. But now I indulge occasionally."

"What an annoying trait. I hope I do not have to see your smile often for it makes your face look like the back end of a surat."

Aidan sipped from his own metal wine cup, then gave Joanna another smile as he returned to the subject on his mind. "I heard about what happened on Twycross, Star Commander. It is unfortunate that, in the Clans, we demote previously successful officers for blunders that are not really their fault. None of Malthus' unit could have anticipated the demolition charges."

"What you say comes close to treason, Aidan Pryde. The reasons for the loss are not relevant. The shame is in the loss itself. At any rate, you know I was not demoted merely because of that failure. What happened on Twycross demanded only that I be retested. When I did so, the outcome required a demotion in rank."

"Required?"

"Do not try to provoke me. Of course I do not enjoy being a mere Star Commander again, but I serve my Clan in any way that is ordained. It must give you great pleasure to outrank me now."

Aidan shook his head. "No, not at all, Joanna. I take no satisfaction from revenge."

"The Aidan Pryde I knew would have."

"You forget. I was not Aidan Pryde then. After my final Bloodname battle, I saw you again only long enough to hear you say that it was fate, and not my own skill, that won me the Bloodname. I have changed in some ways since that day when I became Aidan Pryde. My only aim now is to serve the Clan as both a valorous and loyal warrior."

"Strange."

"What? That I should have turned out to be a good Clan officer?"

"No. It is the curiosity of the name itself. When you were not Aidan Pryde, you were the most arrogant being I had ever observed. Except for me, that is. Now that you are Aidan Pryde, you seem to have lost that pridefulness. It is as if you are Aidan without Pryde instead of Aidan Pryde. Ah, but this wine is affecting my coherence, *quiaff*?"

"Aff. It has that property. But I have long wondered what you meant when you told me I owed my Bloodname victory more to fate than my abilities."

"The truth is I can no longer remember what I meant. I do not even recall saying that to you."

Aidan nodded. "A pity really. I have not stopped recalling that moment, and you have forgotten it." He could not tell Joanna, but he had once read a set of stories in which each character remembers the same events in slightly different ways. He had not understood the stories at the time. Now the meaning seemed a bit clearer.

"Think again," he said. "What *might* you have meant by attributing my victory to fate?"

Joanna shrugged. The movement shifted her tunic, giving Aidan a brief glimpse of a deep scar just below the collar line. "I do not know what I meant. We of the Clans put no store in fate. I do not even understand it. Are we not taught that we control our own destinies, that fate cannot affect our lives unless we let it?"

"And, if we let it, then we are still the masters of our fate, *quiaff*?"

"Aff. Or I suppose so. I have never cared much for any discussion beyond what I need to learn from the manuals and textbooks. Fate is fate. Keep it at the back door, and you do not have to worry about it."

"Maybe so. Maybe life is negotiation. Bidding against fate is what we do."

Joanna squinted at Aidan, then gulped down the rest of her wine. "You seem also to have picked up some strange ideas since I last saw you."

He had an urge to tell her about the secret library, but watching her stare somewhat longingly at the bottom of her cup, he knew that such a revelation would be unwise.

"Then enough of the past. The main reason I called

you here was to discuss the campaign,'' Aidan said. ''Would you care for more wine?''

''It is swill. But yes, I will have some more.''

''For the most part, our unit has not seen as much action as others,'' he said, refilling her cup. ''They usually hold us back in reserve, then send us in for mop-up.''

''Is that complaint I hear?''

Aidan looked away from her hard stare. ''Not complaint, but perhaps dissatisfaction. Do I have, well, permission to speak frankly?''

''You mean will I keep our conversation secret, *quiaff*?''

''Aff. I know how deeply your animosities run, but I also know you would never violate a vow.''

''Oh, come off the high-sounding drivel. Any Clan warrior can be trusted once he gives his *rede*. I give you my *rede* to guard whatever secrets you are harboring. It seems odd for a subordinate to say this to a commanding officer, but, yes, you have permission to speak freely, Aidan Pryde.''

Aidan put his cup down on the table and brought his hands together in front of his face in a gesture that looked to Joanna almost like praying. How many more oddities was this man going to spring on her? she wondered.

''It is about the campaign itself, its motives, its chances. When ilKhan Leo Showers was killed, I was called back to Strana Mechty with all the other Bloodnamed warriors. I have always done my duty toward attending councils and casting my vote when required. I have rarely participated much in the debates, however, for others often object to my viewpoint purely and simply because of the taint that still seems to hover over me. So I tend to hold my tongue.

''At this council, however, the stink of politics seemed to pervade every session. I came there excited, anticipating—''

''You? Excited?''

''As much as I get excited. You see, Joanna, this was the first election of an IlKhan in perhaps a hundred years. Not only were we participating in an historic event, but we had been forced to temporarily halt our invasion of the Inner Sphere in order to be there.

"But from the first I began to observe that the major leaders were attempting to manipulate matters. There were the two sides, the Crusaders and the Wardens, competing for support. Charges were hurled back and forth. The eventual selection of Ulric Kerensky as the new ilKhan seemed dominated by ulterior motives. What better advantage for the Crusaders than to place a Warden in power? It was a masterstroke for them to put the man prompting peace into the warlord's chair."

"Then the new ilKhan countered the Crusaders' plot by naming Natasha Kerensky to replace him as Khan of Clan Wolf. Finally he announced that the goal of the invasion was not to restore the Star League for the oppressed people of the Inner Sphere but to resurrect the League, with Clan leaders in the key seats of power."

"The difference seems insignificant to me. What is your objection?"

"I am not certain. But hearing that made me believe that the . . . idealism had gone out of the invasion. The invasion was suddenly about power, about us gaining more—"

"And I say, more power to us!" interrupted Joanna, raising her cup aloft.

"You do not see the difference?"

"Frankly, no."

"Looked at one way, the Clans are removing decadent and evil governments for the good of the people being crushed under these dictators. That is good. That is the reason for the existence of the Clans, I think. But if we are invading the Inner Sphere to take power for ourselves, to enlarge Clan domains, are we any better than the despots we conquer?"

Joanna growled and slammed her cup down on the table, which threatened to leap up even though secured to the flooring. She stood. The drink made her momentarily dizzy, but she took care not to show it.

"And you had to ask me to keep this secret? Even if you stood on top of a mountain and shouted this rot through a loudspeaker, who among Clan warriors would want to hear any of it? It has no relation to what we do, what we are. We fight, that is what we do. We are warriors, that is what we are. We do not worry about right and wrong. If we think, it is our hobby, and that is all. Permission to leave?''

Aidan nodded. Joanna stood up, none too gracefully. She turned a bit shakily toward the door, but Aidan was not done with her yet. ''Star Commander? I am wondering about your chief tech, Nomad. Is he still with you?''

''No.''

''He *did* look old the last I saw him.''

''It was not age that did him in. He was killed on Twycross, sometime during the Camora campaign. Blown up, I understand.''

''You understand?''

''He was not attached to my unit when it happened. The slimy freebirth, tricky as ever, transferred out just when I had given up asking him to.''

''He was a good tech, a—''

''He was a freebirth, and that is the end of it.''

As Joanna turned back toward the door, a sudden knock startled both warriors.

''Who is it?'' Joanna bellowed, forgetting for a moment that she was no longer in command. ''Speak immediately or go away.''

The responding voice was that of Horse, who entered when Aidan called out permission. He was carrying a sheaf of papers, which he handed to Aidan.

''There is an uprising in Vreeport,'' he said. ''Some citizens who have found a cache of Inner Sphere weapons are now perched on the city walls, shooting at any warrior who comes near. And there seems to be a Battle-Mech standing in the middle of the fortress. That's all I know so far.''

Aidan sighed. It was the normal kind of mop-up operation that had apparently become his specialty.

''Can we negotiate with them?''

''It has been tried, according to the report. There seems to be only one choice.''

''Annihilation?''

''Yes.''

''Well, perhaps that will not be necessary. Let us go. Star Commander Joanna, now may be a good time for your Star to get its feet wet on Quarell. This mission is yours.''

Joanna touched Aidan's arm as he walked by.

"We are eager for battle, Star Colonel, but the general directive says to be merciless in dealing with uprisings."

"That is true."

"So why not annihilation? This is apparently only a small guerrilla band."

"They are our enemy, yes, but that does not make them less human. We must treat them with the same respect we give our foes in BattleMechs."

"But do we not strive to annihilate *them*?"

"Only when we have to."

"I never strove for anything else."

Aidan stared at Joanna for a long moment, and the cruelty she remembered came back into his eyes. "And look where it has gotten you, Star Commander Joanna."

Warmed by the Quarell wine and Aidan's confidences, Joanna had momentarily forgotten the hatred she had felt for this man from the moment she laid eyes on him. Now it returned full force. Seething with anger, she followed him out of the room.

=7=

The small settlement of Vreeport was located in a clearing so surrounded by tall, leafy trees that it would easily have escaped the eyes of a 'Mech pilot operating exclusively on visuals. Believing visuals unreliable, Joanna vastly preferred to navigate relying solely on her 'Mech's inertial guidance system. She did not need to see the subtleties of color in the foliage, the deep brown of the ground, the strange gnarled patterns of tree bark, the quick moves of tiny animals away from the heavy tread of 'Mech feet—not when all she needed was available in its essential grid-and-line patterns. Knowing the coordinates of Vreeport, she found it easily, set off into its blueprint-like lines and shapes.

Stepping her *Mad Dog* out of the forest, she came upon Vreeport in its clearing. The rest of her Star, all BattleMechs, emerged just after she had guided her 'Mech through the last of the trees.

"Looks quiet," Joanna remarked to her team over the open channel. Among the various sounds of agreement, she heard Diana's voice: "Request permission to enter the settlement walls for recon."

"Request denied," Joanna said. "If anyone is there, let them see us first. Many a battle has been won merely through the intimidating presence of BattleMechs."

She switched to external speakers. "If any citizen still remains in Vreeport, it is my duty to inform you that our commander, Star Colonel Aidan Pryde, grants you immunity if you come out immediately. Whatever you have been told by the propagandists of the Inner Sphere, we of the Clan are not monsters who kill indiscriminately.

But neither do we have patience with lower-caste scum who dare take up the arms of a warrior.''

"But you are willing to make slaves of us!'' came a voice from inside the fortress, also amplified but without the resonance provided by a 'Mech's external speakers.

"What does he mean?'' Diana asked.

"That we shall find out,'' Joanna said as she opened up the communications link back to the Command Center and requested to speak to Star Colonel Aidan Pryde.

In the Command Center, Aidan sat with Demi-Precentor Melanie Truit, the ComStar representative charged with administration of the conquered population of Quarell. ComStar officials on Quarell, as on the other Clan-occupied planets of the Inner Sphere, were acting as a buffer between the planetary populations and their conquerors. He took Joanna's message, then turned to Melanie Truit.

"What do you know of this?''

Truit wrinkled her nose, a rather prominent one that looked out of place on her delicate face. "Less than you, I suspect. We of ComStar are only to administer and govern according to the rules of you, the Clan conquerors. You must realize, Colonel Pryde, that your bondsman custom goes against what any self-respecting Inner Sphere citizen can accept. The Clan custom of selecting a conquered people's finest mental and physical specimens to become bondsmen to warriors of Clan Jade Falcon is foreign to their way of thinking. Nor can they comprehend that the taking of bondsmen is a sign of respect by Clan warriors for those of their enemy who fought well.''

Aidan nodded. "I have selected several enemy warriors as bondsmen. Why would anyone protest? It is honorable to serve the Clan, even for a conquered enemy. They should be proud.''

Demi-Precentor Truit smiled, an attractive smile that revealed even white teeth. If she had been Clan instead of ComStar, Aidan might have asked her to accompany him to his quarters tonight.

"In the Inner Sphere we have no concept analogous to your bondsman custom,'' she said. "As the Vreeport man told you, to these people it is slavery, pure and simple.''

"Of course it is slavery, but being a bondsman and

becoming part of a Clan is better than being enslaved and with dim prospects on one's own planet, is it not?"

"You forget. I am not Clan either. I do not see the distinction. Nor need I, since I serve only ComStar." Despite Demi-Precentor Truit's politely neutral manner, Aidan sensed that she agreed with the insurgents that bondsman was not an honorable state.

"You seem to agree with this foul point of view."

"I am not permitted to say. As the ComStar representative on this planet, I am completely neutral. Do not grunt at me like that. It is quite true."

"I suppose I do not fully understand ComStar and its relationship with the Clans. Explain, Demi-Precentor."

Truit sighed, as if the question had come up too often for her liking. "Do you wish the lecture I give to school children?"

"No, the short version is fine. Give me, say, the kind of précis you deliver to your own superiors."

Truit nodded. "Centuries ago ComStar was founded as an administrative arm of the Star League to maintain the vast interstellar communications network that made it possible for a single government to rule over the three thousand inhabited worlds of the Inner Sphere. It was no more than a minor bureaucracy until the young First Lord Cameron died and the usurper Amaris claimed the mantle of First Lord of the Star League."

"And then the great Aleksandr Kerensky led the Star League Defense Forces to crush the usurper Stefan Amaris. You tell me nothing new, Demi-Precentor," Aidan interrupted.

Truit looked at him calmly. "If you are to understand ComStar, you must understand the conditions of our birth," she said. "And, yes, as you state, General Kerensky crushed Amaris, without the aid or support of the League's other High Council Lords. With Amaris out of the way, the Council Lords met to choose a new First Lord from among their number. As you might imagine, each believed that only he or she was the fittest to don the mantle of the First Lord's power. The only point on which they could agree was the decision for General Kerensky to disband the Star League Army."

"The unity of the Star League was destroyed by the avarice of the House Lords," Aidan intoned, almost on cue. "But its heart was protected by the Great Kerensky as he led his followers into the blackness beyond."

Truit looked surprised. "That was very poetic, Star Colonel."

"Those are lines from *The Remembrance,* the chronicle of our birth and life as Clans."

Truit smiled and continued. "Again, as you say, General Kerensky led the Star League Army, your ancestors, out from the Inner Sphere, escaping from the civil war that erupted between the Great Houses of Steiner, Marik, Liao, Davion, and Kurita. That conflict has lasted several hundred years—what we call the Succession Wars. Only ComStar remained faithful to the vision that shaped the Star League. In fact we are the last surviving remnants of the League government here in the Inner Sphere.

"Jerome Blake, our first Primus, realized that the undreamed-of ferocity of the Succession Wars threatened to destroy interstellar communications as well as the very existence of human civilization. And so he proclaimed ComStar's neutrality, offering all governments equal access to the hyperpulse communications network in exchange for the promise that our facilities would remain inviolate. Thus it was that for some three hundred years ComStar has served as the neutral arbitrator between the Great Houses of the Successor States, as well as maintaining and protecting the precious knowledge that stands between humanity and the abyss of barbarism."

"Now you wax poetic, Demi-Precentor," Aidan said. "But how does ComStar view the Clans' return? Some on Quarell brand ComStar a traitor to the Inner Sphere. Does that not concern you?"

"The primary concern of ComStar has always been the survival of human civilization."

"But you are more than mere bureaucrats and communications specialists. You have military troops, and your organization holds Terra."

Truit seemed offended by Aidan's comment. "The troops are trained merely to defend the integrity of our communications facilities and to serve as a deterrent against aggression. Twenty years ago the Fourth Succession War almost brought the Inner Sphere down in flames. The leaders of the Great Houses seized some of our stations, and we had reason to believe that House Davion was preparing to attack Terra. We only armed ourselves out of sheer necessity. Fortunately the Com Guards have admirably fulfilled their mission of deterrence. They have yet to fight a major battle.''

Aidan shook his head in puzzlement. ''A curious custom, that. Warriors who cannot war. It is unnatural.''

Truit's new smile was somewhat sly. ''There are those among ComStar's leaders who might just agree with you. Privately, of course.''

''And you are one of those, Melanie Truit?''

''I am not allowed to say, as you well know.''

''If ComStar is so neutral, why do you collect the bondsmen from the villages for us?''

''If I am ordered to obtain bondsmen, that is what I do,'' Truit said matter-of-factly. ''My work is to administer the planet's affairs, but I may not violate the customs and rules of those whom I serve, especially when I am doing my job for conquerors.''

''Conquerors who, from a certain point of view, are practicing a slave trade?''

''You must understand, Star Colonel, that some people would prefer not to be slaves. They might like to be a warrior, like you, but not a slave.''

''Most of them do not have the bloodlines to be good warriors,'' Aidan said. ''But as bondsmen, they would have a chance to prove their abilities, and some might actually achieve warrior status. It has happened that a freeborn bondsman has done exactly that.''

''I must accept your word on that, Star Colonel, for there is still much about the Clans that I do not know. All I am trying to explain is that it is not strange for the people of Quarell to object to being taken by force, thrown first into a DropShip and then into a JumpShip, to be taken away back to the Clan worlds, wherever that may be.''

Aidan knew that Melanie Truit was fishing for information on the location of the Clan worlds—a fact in which ComStar was very interested—but he made no reply. During this whole conversation, Horse had been providing him with updates on the Vreeport crisis, through messages transmitted onto the screen of Aidan's personal monitor. Seeing that events were heating up, he reopened communications with Joanna.

''Do you have a link with the insurgents?'' he asked.

"Well, one of them seems willing to talk to us. In fact, he has not stopped talking since we opened a line. He apparently has some kind of bullhorn."

"Patch me into your commline," Aidan said. "I will speak with him over your external speakers."

"Done, Star Colonel."

"Commtech Caton!"

"Sir?"

"Set the viewing holo for the scene at Vreeport, and enlarge it. I want to see the rebel to whom I am speaking. I want to see every pore, every drop of sweat."

"As you wish, sir."

In the viewing area above the array of control panels in the Command Center there suddenly appeared the face of a middle-aged man with excessively red skin and an expression of slight bewilderment. He was staring warily over the top of the city wall, apparently at the quintet of BattleMechs arrayed against Vreeport. Aidan thought the man's thin, unshaven face and narrow eyes made him resemble an ice ferret cub, a creature that sometimes ripped open the throat of its own mother. Not a good omen for negotiation. Aidan could also see the sweat on the man's face. Indeed, it was pouring off his forehead in rivulets.

"This is Star Colonel Aidan Pryde of the Nega Garrison Cluster," Aidan announced. He could see by the man's startled reaction that Joanna must have turned the speakers up to full volume so that his voice would no doubt resound across the clearing, shaking buildings and unsettling eardrums. It was a good ploy and might help achieve Aidan's goal of ending this uprising bloodlessly.

"Identify yourself, rebel!"

For a moment it looked like the unshaven ice ferret of a man was ready to disappear behind the wall, as people often did when confronted by ghostlike visitations. Then he seemed to get command of himself, slowing raising the bullhorn to his mouth. With his face so enlarged in the viewing area, it was disconcerting to hear the weak and tinny voice coming from it.

"I am Jared Mahoney. I am a survivor of the Vreeport militia and, as such, represent the community in dealings with oppressors like you."

Aidan winced, first at the fact that, like all Inner Sphere citizens, the man had a surname, one that was merely passed on through generations without being earned in a Bloodname battle. Though he realized that naming customs were different here, Aidan did not like to think of anyone other than a Bloodnamed warrior having a surname.

"Jared Mahoney, I order you to end this uprising and surrender to the BattleMech Star that you see near the walls of your city. Those five 'Mechs could level your small community in mere minutes. Your continued resistance is useless."

"But you are making slaves of us!"

"Bondsmen are not slaves. Their duty to us is only temporary. Slaves are purchased and are theoretically slaves for all their—"

Jared Mahoney's voice grew fierce. "Do not try to dazzle me with semantics!" he shouted. "We do not wish to leave Quarell, but you take us. That is slavery, no matter how you try to rationalize it."

"I am willing to discuss the matter with you, Jared Mahoney. However, I must remind you that we have the destructive power to make all negotiations meaningless. Surrender yourself and your people."

Inexplicably, Jared Mahoney did not reply immediately. While still trying to juggle the bullhorn with one hand, he reached down with the other arm to pick up two children, a boy and a girl. The children were as red-faced as the man.

"These are my children," he announced. "My son and my daughter. They are innocent. Would you kill them, merely to assert your authority?"

Aidan cut off communication and turned to Melanie Truit. "Why would he want us to kill his children?"

"He doesn't want you to kill them. He has no understanding of Clan concepts so he cannot understand that the innocence of his children is of no consequence to a Clan warrior. By displaying them, he thinks that you will back off and not kill anyone else in order to protect the children."

Aidan shook his head in puzzlement. "I do not wish to kill any of them, children or adult. But there is nothing in our Clan way that says I must have an emotional response to the idea of children as hostages, especially when they are merely the enemy's children."

"Sir, I am only a ComStar official and cannot hope to interpret any member of the Clan. I try merely to inform you of Jared Mahoney's probable state of mind."

Aidan could not comprehend the edge of frustration in Demi-Precentor Truit's voice, but he sensed that she somehow disapproved of his words. When he returned his attention to the Vreeport scene, he found Joanna addressing the settlement's representative.

"Put your children down," she was saying. "They are mere freebirth scum, like you. Killing freeborns is easy for us, even for the freeborns among us."

"That is enough, Star Commander Joanna," Aidan said over their private channel. "Nothing is gained by provoking them."

"And everything to be gained by putting Vreeport to flames or by marching through it to flatten its stupid citizens under our 'Mechs' feet."

"Patch me to the external speakers again."

When Aidan viewed the projected image of Jared Mahoney once more, the man was still—with effort—holding the two children while also clumsily gripping the bullhorn. The children looked at their father complacently. One of them smiled with what Aidan could only have interpreted as pride.

Aidan found the scene troubling. What was it all about, this relationship between freeborn parents and their children, he wondered, especially here in the Inner Sphere? Even on Clan worlds, Aidan had been equally disturbed by some of the parent-child situations he had observed. What did these children *feel* about their father, what did he *feel* about them? Though he had often read about parents and offspring in some of his secret books, the relationship had been just as mysterious to him then.

"Jared Mahoney! We are not impressed by this display of your children. The concept to which you attempt to appeal does not exist for us. Assemble your citizens and vacate Vreeport before any more harm is done."

Jared Mahoney set down his children carefully, then confidently raised the bullhorn to his lips. "We do not capitulate," he said. "If you insist on fighting us, we must fight back."

Aidan almost laughed. "You cannot fight Battle-

Mechs. Not without 'Mechs of your own. And every BattleMech on Quarell has been destroyed.''

"Not every one."

Before Aidan could put his question into words, he saw what was meant. Lumbering toward the city walls was a large walking machine that Aidan took to be a Battle-Mech until Commtech Caton got the image properly focused. Then he immediately saw that it was too small, too light. And it stood on four legs instead of two, with a small, merely protective cockpit on top.

"Are you insane, Jared Mahoney? That is merely an AgroMech."

"It is *our* BattleMech, Star Colonel. An agribot, to be sure, but one to which, as you can see, a pair of laser cannons has been added, plus a few other refinements. We have also attached explosives to almost every centimeter of its surface, with other explosives placed all around Vreeport—enough to blow up the whole settlement and any of your forces that come too close to the city walls. Perhaps you don't care about human life, Star Colonel, but our hostages also include several ComStar officials and Clan techs who were assigned to Vreeport. Perhaps you already knew about them."

Aidan sighed wearily before speaking. "Yes, I did," he said. "Now I demand you put down your arms and surrender Vreeport."

The demand, Aidan knew, was merely a gesture, and he was not surprised when Jared Mahoney laughed and shouted, "We would really like to see how you do not value human life, Star Colonel. We really would." With that, the red-faced man dropped from sight.

Aidan turned to Melanie Truit. "Do they have supplies enough to last awhile?"

"Yes. Does that matter to you?"

"Only for its logistical uses. I do not wish to destroy Vreeport, but if necessary I will."

Demi-Precentor Melanie Truit continued to regard him with puzzlement in her clear eyes, but Aidan returned his attention to the screen, which showed him that the transformed AgroMech, the makeshift BattleMech, had opened fire on Joanna's Star. His heart went to his throat as he heard her order to return fire.

8

Diana and Trader spoke over a private channel as they watched the exchange between Aidan and Jared Mahoney. This was the first civilian uprising they had ever observed, and they could not see the point of it.

"Why negotiate with this scum?" said Diana.

"I'm not sure. Clan policy on conquered worlds, I suppose."

"But these idiots would like to blow us up along with themselves. If I were in command, I would order our warriors to take up positions around the city walls, pouring shot in until Vreeport was leveled or they surrendered. Let us get to the real war, not waste time on this trivial bilge."

"What do you mean? Aren't we part of the real war?"

"No, this is backwater stuff, mop-up. I want to get to the forefront of the invasion, the front lines."

"Well, I were you, I would give up hope. You're in the wrong outfit for all that. Don't you know about Aidan Pryde's command?"

Trader did not know that Aidan Pryde was Diana's father, but she had no intention of telling him, or anybody, for that matter. She was satisfied merely to have found him. After having heard so much about him at her mother's knee, Diana now wanted only to observe him. Serving in his command was sufficient for her. She was a warrior now, and Clan warriors put no value on the parent-child relation. The very idea was abhorrent to them.

"What do you mean, Trader?"

Briefly he told her about Aidan's tainted Bloodname, then recounted the other rumors that were rife about him.

"They say he will never get an important command and that his genes will never be accepted in the gene pool."

What would Trader say, Diana wondered, if he knew that Aidan's genes were hers—well, half-hers, anyway.

"So you can see, Diana, that as long as we are part of Aidan Pryde's command, chances are we will see *only* backwater duty, will spend most of our time merely putting down minor uprisings, will only be—"

Trader stopped speaking as the challenges passing between Aidan and Jared Mahoney grew fiercer. Then suddenly the AgroMech's laser cannon shot outward, its beams passing between Joanna's *Timber Wolf* and the *Stormcrow* beside her.

"All 'Mechs, open fire!" Joanna shouted.

Diana, aiming her PPC at the city wall, quickly opened a massive hole there. Other 'Mechs connected with other targets. To her far left, she saw high flames erupt. The AgroMech took a hit to the shoulder, but no explosions followed. That made Diana wonder if the threat of explosives attached to the AgroMech was merely some cowardly terrorist bluff. She aimed for a new part of the city wall, but was stopped by Joanna's shouted, "Cease fire, all units."

Then Aidan Pryde addressed all the pilots. "We are not here to destroy Vreeport, whatever the provocation. We are to preserve civilian life wherever possible. That is the order of the ilKhan. Negotiations will continue. Star Commander Joanna."

"Sir?"

"Patch me into the speaker system again."

While listening to this, Diana watched as the Agro-Mech seemed to be preparing to fire again. She took a bead on it, just in case battle erupted once more.

"Jared Mahoney, this is Star Colonel Aidan Pryde again. Please come forward."

It was a long wait before the form of Jared Mahoney appeared atop one section of the city wall. He now had some kind of bandanna wrapped around his head and his face was smudged with dirt. A line of sweat darkened the rim of the bandanna.

"Jared Mahoney, our offer is simple. You will release all hostages, those from among your citizens as well as members of the Clan and ComStar. You will also surrender all your weapons and ammunition. Neither you nor your fellow insurgents will suffer repercussions. There will be no arrests, no punishments. We will leave you and your community in peace.''

Jared Mahoney raised the bullhorn to his mouth. ''And no more bondsman will be taken,'' he said. ''Not in Vreeport or in any other place on Orkney.''

''I am not authorized to revise Clan policy in this matter. To become a bondsman is an honor.''

''Go to hell, you bloody sons of bitches!''

Diana gasped in shock. Clan warriors rarely cursed, and when they did, they used epithets such as *freebirth* and *stravag*, both referring to the live-birth process of freeborns. Jared Mahoney's ill-chosen words would be disgusting to any Clansman or woman, no matter what his or her Clan.

The insurgent leader dropped suddenly from sight, then the AgroMech fired again. This time its beams hit the *Stormcrow* dead-center. The 'Mech rocked back slightly on its heels, but remained upright.

Diana awaited the order to demolish Vreeport, but only silence came over the commline.

After a moment, Joanna's voice clicked into the line. ''We have been ordered to withdraw,'' she said, sounding angry and bitter. ''Proceed into the forest in an orderly fashion. We will regroup twenty-five meters in.''

Diana was furious. ''Trader, what is happening here?''

''A strategic retreat, apparently. To protect us while the others arrive at a plan. I hope.''

''The Clans do not retreat before mere civilians. How could Star Commander Joanna order a retreat?''

''Weren't you listening, Diana? It wasn't she who ordered the retreat. It was our Star Colonel, watching from his safe haven at command center. He is the one behaving cautiously.''

''He must have some reason. I mean, a good, solid military reason,'' was what she said aloud. But in her thoughts, she told herself, he is my father and he cannot be a coward.

''He's protecting the lives of the hostages, I suppose.''

''You do not sound convinced, Trader.''

''I'm not. It may be unfortunate that ComStar people are involved, but they're not Clan. The Clan hostages will be proud to die. And the others, the native hostages, why should we be careful about their lives?''

"I do not know, Trader. I would just go ahead and annihilate Vreeport, make this place an example. Hostages are not important. It is wrong to permit scum like Jared Mahoney to use them against us. Wipe out this group of hostages along with the insurgents, and perhaps you will never have to deal with another group of either.''

"An interesting theory, Diana.''

"But you doubt it.''

"You know I do. I'll never be as bloodthirsty as you.''

"And that is why I deserve this *Warhawk*.''

"I know you think that.''

They had cleared the line of trees at the edge of the forest and were following Joanna's *Timber Wolf* to the rendezvous point.

There must be some strategy here, Diana thought, some trick that my father is planning. If not that, a respite until he can come up with a good scheme. It must be that. It has to be. He cannot be a coward. He will destroy Vreeport. It is the only way to handle the situation, and he will rise to the challenge.

As Diana considered the actions of Aidan Pryde, her commander as well as her father, doubts began to pull on her thoughts like weights. She hated the doubt. In this universe she had only one father. Whether or not he was aware of her existence, he had to be the father she had dreamt of so often, the father who had never been far from her thoughts.

9

To Diana, the rumbling sound of the ComStar helicopter seemed to slide toward the forest, then over it, shaking the branches and leaves with its vibrations. She and her *Warhawk* stood at the edge of the forest, where Star Commander Joanna had assigned her on orders from Command Center to post a 'Mech as scout. From her vantage point, Diana watched the large craft settle onto the ground in front of the city walls. Then Jared Mahoney's head reappeared above the main wall.

On the forest side of the aircraft, two people emerged from the open hatches. The first was a tall woman with broad shoulders and wide hips. If not for the ComStar insignia on the woman's white jumpsuit, Diana might easily have taken her for a Clan warrior, though she moved a bit clumsily for one. The second figure was her father, dressed in a simple green field uniform that showed no insignia of his rank.

Star Commander Joanna had told her that negotiators were coming from Command Center, but Diana suspected that even the hard-edged and confident old warrior would be surprised that Aidan Pryde had selected himself to negotiate with these vermin.

The moment his feet hit the ground, he looked around alertly. When he nodded in her direction, Diana thought he must have spotted her *Warhawk* lurking in the forest's shadows.

She studied his face, thinking it might solve the mysteries he had created for her. But there were no clues there, much less solutions. It was an impassive face, its skin rough from years in severe climates, yet generally untouched by age. The eyes seemed to shine in their sockets like jewels, giving off the same serene detachment. It was not a coward's face.

Diana worked her lips nervously, chewing on the bottom lip, rubbing the top one on her upper teeth. She was angry at feeling *anything* about this man. What did it matter that he was her father? Yet she knew that if Aidan Pryde brought even the mildest shame to his unit, it would bring deep shame to her. The thought was so unClanlike that she did not like admitting it even to herself. Freeborn warrior she might be, but Diana preferred to think like a trueborn one. Concepts like father should have no meaning to her, especially since Aidan had never been a father to her, nor was he even aware of their blood tie.

Aidan saw a flash of light off the BattleMech stationed at the forest edge. From what he could see of its configuration when he squinted, it was a *Warhawk*. He fervently hoped that neither Jared Mahoney nor any of his insurgents had spotted it, however. This was no time to provoke them, especially over a scout 'Mech.

The last thing Aidan wanted now was any provocation. As commander of the Quarell occupation forces, he wished to prevent the unnecessary slaughter of civilians. Despite Clan Smoke Jaguar's destruction of the city of Turtle Bay on Edo, Aidan intended to obey the ilKhan's directive specifically ordering that civilian casualties be kept to a minimum.

Melanie Truit had insisted on accompanying him to Vreeport, suggesting that it would be prudent to have at least two spokesmen when dealing with emotionally volatile rebels like Jared Mahoney. "Because I am not Clan, it may be easier for me to interpret ideas that now seem so unacceptable to him," she said.

"I insist on conducting the negotiations myself. This is not a team effort. Understood?"

"Understood, Star Colonel."

"But I will appreciate your contributions and insights, Melanie Truit."

"I thank you. You are unusually decorous for a warrior, particularly a Clan Jade Falcon officer."

"And have you observed so many Clan officers, Melanie Truit?"

"Not many, but enough. And you make me wish to be as direct as any Clan warrior. I wish to couple with you when all this is over."

Aidan's stride broke.

"You hesitate," she said, with an embarrassed laugh. "Is it that I have violated a taboo? Are you Clansmen so culturally primitive that a woman may not make such an overture to a man?"

"No. My Clan has no such taboo. But an individual from another caste or someone not of the Clans may not initiate the request to couple."

"And, as not-Clan, I am unacceptable to you?"

She was beginning to become angry, he could see.

"No, it is not that at all. I merely say that, as a Clan warrior, I must ask that you wait for me to make the offer."

"Then I will wait, Star Colonel. But do not ask me to wear caste-marks."

Was he mistaken or had her voice taken on a sarcastic edge?

"I assure you, Melanie Truit, that the offer will be made."

"I am pleased, I think."

A ComStar adept, a lower-class functionary in the Inner Sphere, climbed out of the VTOL after Aidan and Melanie Truit. He handed Aidan a bullhorn similar to the one the insurgent leader was using, but it was an upgraded model, easily operated by buttons next to his thumb. It was also much lighter.

Coming around the vehicle, with Melanie Truit just behind him, Aidan began immediately to address Jared Mahoney. "I am Star Colonel Aidan Pryde. I would speak with you, Jared Mahoney. Open your gates."

"What makes you think I wish to meet with you, Pryde!"

Aidan cringed at being addressed by his surname alone. That was never done within the Clans. A Bloodname was sacred, and no one would ever use it in any casual, pejorative, distorted, or demeaning way. And certainly not as a form of address without other names and titles.

But, as Melanie Truit had instructed him, it was essential in hostage negotiations to remain calm and to keep the rebels from controlling the discussions.

"If you wish to have your own people come out of this alive, you must deal with me, Mahoney."

Aidan used the rebel's surname with malice, but doubted that the man cared how he was addressed.

"All right. Are you armed? If so, drop whatever weapons you have."

"I am not armed."

"Who is that with you?"

Melanie Truit stepped forward. "I am Melanie Truit, ComStar Demi-Precentor for this sector of Quarell."

"So ComStar is frightened by us, too?"

"Do not become self-important, Jared Mahoney. It is only I who am interested. No official ComStar policy is to be inferred."

"Are you armed, Truit?"

"No."

"Then come forward, both of you."

Diana watched as her father and the ComStar representative went through the opened gates of Vreeport. She felt a catch in her throat as the gates closed behind them. It suddenly occurred to her that she might never see her father again. The regret aroused by that thought was as detestable as it was unbearable.

10

Jared Mahoney led them down a cluttered Vreeport street. Hardly a street, Aidan thought. More like a dirt path strewn with litter. The buildings, too, were battle-scarred, with doors hanging off hinges, windows broken, char marks on siding. The people seemed to hang back from them, their gestures nervous and agitated. Hostility hung over Vreeport like a corona around a moon.

The rebel leader pointed to a large building at the end of the street. "In there first," he said, an odd note of satisfaction in his voice.

The building turned out to be a warehouse full of weapons, ammunition, and boxes of explosives. "This is one of many filled with enough volatile material to create one damn big blast," Jared Mahoney said. "I show you this to prove that we're not bluffing."

Melanie Truit touched Aidan's arm. "This may still be bluff," she whispered. "Maybe this is their only ware-house, not 'one of many.' And how can we know what those boxes are filled with?"

"Do the people of the Inner Sphere employ so much deception?"

Melanie Truit smiled, and Aidan noted once more the evenness and brightness of her teeth. "Star Colonel, in some way you Clansmen are guileless. Don't you imag-ine that people with their backs to the wall would use any trick possible to get out alive?"

Aidan bristled at the allusion to naiveté, but all he said was, "You are right about the Clans, Precentor. We sometimes use bluff in our bidding procedures, but bla-tant lying is not our way. I suppose it is another aspect of the degeneration of the Inner Sphere."

"The Clans are skilled enough in warfare, Star Colonel, but the sophistication of Inner Sphere politics seems to elude you."

"You call it sophistication?"

She shrugged. "A word merely."

"Not merely, I think."

She smiled again and took his hand in hers, giving it a gentle squeeze before releasing it. No one had ever touched Aidan like that before, and the sensation gave him pleasure. He even looked forward to being with this woman later, once the negotiations were concluded. That anticipation perplexed him. He generally attended to any problem at hand without being distracted by thoughts of the future except as it related to the problem. Casual speculation about the future seemed unClanlike.

Jared Mahoney led them to what Aidan thought must be the town square, except that it had no real geometric definition. Viewed from above, it might have seemed more bloblike than anything. Standing roughly in the center was the AgroMech, with some vehicles haphazardly arranged around it.

If any doubts remained about the rebel claims, Aidan saw now that they were not lying about the explosives attached to the AgroMech. They had actually gone overboard, decorating the machine with enough charges to blow up ten AgroMechs and much of the surrounding area. And enough to set off the caches of explosives and ammunition in the warehouses.

Such a chain reaction would certainly destroy everyone in Vreeport. Jared Mahoney was definitely not bluffing.

After the rebel leader permitted Aidan and Melanie Truit to examine the AgroMech, he raised his right hand and waved it from side to side. At the signal, hundreds of people began pouring into the streets. Some climbed out from vehicles or through building windows or slipped through doorways. Soon the town square was filled with them, leaving space only for Jared Mahoney and his two visitors.

Aidan's throat constricted, not from fear, but from the sheer sensation of being surrounded by so many people. The air seemed to tighten, condense into compacted molecules that could be felt separately with each inhalation.

Jared Mahoney spread his arms expansively to take in

the crowd. "These are my people. All we ask is fair treatment." Some in the crowd echoed bits of his words. "And that includes our demand that the Clans cease taking our citizens as slaves." The crowd seconded him again, this time more angrily.

The rebel took a few steps toward one end of the open area. Standing there was a group of people being held by the arms.

"And these," Mahoney said, "are our hostages. Pryde, you may recognize some Clan tech insignia among the group."

One Clan tech pulled away from his captor and took a step into the circle and shouted, "Sir, I am Astech Trion. I was stationed here. Do not deal with these—"

Before the man could say more, Jared Mahoney struck him on the side of the head, instantly knocking him unconscious. A Vreeport citizen dragged Astech Trion back into the crowd.

Jared Mahoney walked back to the hostage area. "Truit, you, too, may recognize your ComStar people by their shoulder patches."

She nodded and turned to Aidan. "They are ComStar," she said, "and like all loyal members of our Blessed Order, they are prepared to die if duty requires it. However,"—and here she turned to address a section of the crowd, pointedly ignoring its leader—"if Jared Mahoney has his way in this issue, it will create needless slaughter, not honorable sacrifice. Agree to surrender, and I vow that ComStar will work to modify the policy that you now pro—"

"Keep quiet, woman!" Jared Mahoney shouted as he ran toward her.

She turned toward him, refusing to back down. She even managed to utter a few more words before the rebel leader hit her viciously across the face. The Precentor staggered back, but held her ground.

The violence took Aidan by surprise. Before Mahoney could hit Melanie Truit again, he stepped forward and grabbed the rebel leader in a bear hug. He squeezed fiercely, trying to kill the man. Before he could do that, some Vreeport citizens rushed up to seize Aidan by the arms. They managed, with some difficulty, to pull him away from Jared Mahoney. Then they threw him to the ground and began to kick at him until Jared Mahoney called out for them to stop.

Like robots, the attackers obeyed and faded back into the crowd. Mahoney extended a hand to help Aidan up.

"I apologize to both of you," he said. "Feelings are running high here, my own included. But the prospect of slavery would tend to make anyone a bit edgy. And yes, if you must know, I have already been selected as a bondsman, so my interest in this cause does have its personal, even selfish, ramifications.

"Do you see now, Star Colonel, why negotiation is useless? From our point of view, there is nothing to negotiate. We demand the release of all previously seized bondsmen and the cessation of all further attempts at enslavement. No compromise is possible. What could it be? That I say it is all right to you to have *some* slaves if you give up some others? No, such a deal would be reprehensible, unacceptable. The only *negotiation* is that you will accede to our demand. Do you?"

"I have told you that I cannot in any way—"

"Then the negotiations are over. Will your forces attack?"

"Eventually, yes."

"Then I wish you to see whom you will kill. Not only your hostages, not only our adult citizenry, but these—"

He gestured toward one side of the crowd, which parted to reveal an array of children, some gathered around the feet of the AgroMech, others underneath the machine, and a few of them sitting next to the cockpit. Inside the AgroMech, the female pilot gave Jared Mahoney a confident thumbs-up. There were children of all ages, all sizes. Scattered among them were some adults, presumably their parents.

Aidan had to look away, more from the sheer impact of all of these children and parents gathered together than from the dramatic scene Mahoney had thought to create. His confusion about parent and child relations made him feel sick in the pit of his stomach. This group represented all that he did not understand about the nature of the bond that apparently existed between parent and child, but it was not something he liked to think about.

"When your forces attack, these children will be the first to die. They are willing, but let me ask whether you truly wish to destroy those whose lives still lie ahead of them?''

Aidan did not know the answer. What was more, he did not want to consider the problem.

"We are serious, Pryde. Let me assure you of that.'' Mahoney gestured toward the hostage section of the crowd, where someone suddenly shoved Astech Trion out into the open area. The rebel leader walked slowly to the edge of the circle. One of his minions handed him a small laser pistol, which he placed against the back of Astech Trion's head. The next moment he triggered the weapon, killing Trion with a short blast. The astech, a man not much older than the oldest of the children gathered around the AgroMech, toppled quickly.

"Does that convince you, Star Colonel?''

Aidan resisted the urge to attack the rebel leader again. "There is no point in continuing this. The negotiations are closed. Take us back to the city gates.''

Jared Mahoney laughed. "Did you think I would allow you to return? No, not when I have the leader of the occupation forces and the chief ComStar representative as hostages.''

Aidan lunged forward, but the rebels yanked back on his arms. "You cannot violate the pact of truce that brought us here.''

"Can't I? I don't recall agreeing to it in the first place. You charged in here, Pryde, making your demands without hearing me. I did not invite you in under any flags, white or otherwise. No, you are my hostages now. Even if we had agreed to a truce, I would probably violate it. I am funny that way.''

Aidan realized that it was pointless to argue with this fanatic. "It does not matter,'' he told Jared Mahoney. "I am Clan, and we do not attach so much importance to a warrior's rank. Whether your hostage is a Star Colonel or a tech, our response to your stupidity will be the same. You have lost, Mahoney.''

"No,'' the rebel leader said, pointing toward the children, "but they have.''

═══ 11 ═══

Although electronic interference from Vreeport created occasional static, Joanna was able to monitor the events within the city walls because Aidan had assigned a pair of high-flying aerofighters to train video cameras down onto the settlement. He had ordered the fighters not to interfere, but only to record data about potential Vreeport defenses against an all-out attack.

She could see that the rebel leader had spoken true. They had the caches of explosives, the heavily mined agribot, the hostages, the angry rebel horde. When Jared Mahoney went after Aidan, she wanted to order her Star to attack the fortress, but Aidan had explicitly ordered her *not* to attack.

Then, when the rebels took Aidan and the ComStar representative, Joanna had burned up the commline with her curses. She ordered her Star forward, the four BattleMechs joining up with Diana and her *Warhawk* at the forest edge.

As Joanna briefed Diana on what had just occurred within the city walls, she saw that the young Mech-Warrior was just as ready as she was to charge forward on her own. Joanna wondered if this was the righteous fury of a dedicated new warrior or if it was motivated by some stupid freebirth concept of father.

She radioed back to the command center for orders. Aidan's second-in-command, a Star Captain named Haryn Crichell, merely backed up the specific written orders Aidan had left behind.

"But those orders do not reflect the situation where the leader of the occupation forces has been taken hostage himself."

"No, they do not. But the Star Colonel wrote that, under no circumstances, were we to attack Vreeport unless he gave the order or was dead."

"With all due respect, Star Captain, how can he give the order? He is captured."

"He has a tracer signal planted on him. If he activates it, he can order the attack. Until then, or until the situation changes, we will wait."

"Star Captain—"

"That will be enough, Star Commander Joanna. Remain in position. Another Star will arrive soon, one more familiar with the terrain."

Joanna resisted telling Crichell that knowledge of the terrain was not exactly essential in the small, uncomplicated area called Vreeport.

When Diana requested the visuals from the aerofighter cameras be transmitted onto her primary screen, she was appalled at the sheer mass of people crowded into the town square. Clanspeople of any caste did not often mingle closely together. Even when assembled for ceremonies or in council, each person made sure to leave sufficient space between his body and that of others. In some Clans one warrior approaching another too closely could be grounds for an honor duel.

"Stravag," she muttered several times as she focused on different sections of the scene. She was especially appalled by the children placed around the feet of the AgroMech. Growing up in a village, she knew how the lower castes cared for children, how her own mother had cared for her during her earliest years. As a trueborn and former warrior, Peri had not been as warm as other village mothers, but she had shown a bond with her child that most trueborns would never comprehend. Now that Diana had been a cadet and learned to think like a warrior, she despised such ties—but she understood them.

And understood them enough to also despise Jared Mahoney for his willingness to sacrifice innocents for a trivial and futile cause.

It took awhile to locate her father and Melanie Truit on her primary screen. They were seated in chairs and under heavy guard near the AgroMech, facing the machine and the children. Once, when Melanie Truit tried to look away, a rebel took her roughly by the chin and forced her to look back. At times Jared Mahoney came to speak to them at length, probably haranguing them to do his bidding. While he gestured in what seemed to be frustration and anger, Diana focused in on her father. His expression was unreadable, but the steeliness in his eyes showed that he was unmoved by the rebel leader's apparent arguments. The scene would go on this way for a bit before Jared Mahoney would walk away again, only to whirl around and return, more words coming rapidly out of his mouth.

Disgusted with the transmission, Diana cut it off, then looked out her viewport at what was still visible in the waning daylight. The VTOL was still there, never having been ordered away. It blocked the view of the city gate, but Diana could still see the hole she had blasted into the Vreeport wall.

It was then the idea struck her. The moment it did, she clicked onto the commline, requesting a private link with Joanna.

"All right, MechWarrior Diana, no one can hear us now," Joanna said. "I hope you have something worthwhile to say."

Diana swallowed hard before speaking. "I request permission to enter Vreeport, Star Commander."

"Why? So you can become a hostage too? Listen, Diana, I realize that Aidan Pryde is your—"

"I plan no empty gesture. No warrior relies on empty gestures. Even sacrifice is done for a—"

"Spare me the trainee litany. I was a falconer, remember? Are you planning to request permission to enter from Jared Mahoney?"

"No. As soon as it is dark enough, I can slip in through the hole I shot in the city wall. The VTOL will give me cover for most of the distance between the forest and the wall. And the hole is big enough for me to—"

"And what do you do if guards are posted there?"

"I can take care of that."

"And what about rebels in the streets?"

"I can take care of that."

"Sounds interesting. Perhaps I will accompany you."

"No."

"You would order me to stay behind, MechWarrior Diana? I am your commanding—"

"Yes, you are, but my plan has more to it. And it is important that everything be done before the other Star arrives, so that its officer cannot countermand your order."

"I do not know, MechWarrior Diana. Convince me."

Diana's argument was both hurried and terse, but she did just that.

12

It seemed to Aidan that Jared Mahoney could not stay still. He moved constantly, speaking in rhythm with his movements, his agitation so pronounced that Aidan could barely keep track of what the man was saying. When Mahoney walked too far away, the words got lost. When he was close, the words seemed to come out of nowhere, apparently based on that part of his discourse that had gone unheard.

"Can you understand him?" Aidan asked Demi-Precentor Truit.

"What is so hard to understand? He wants what he wants, and he listens to nothing else. That is the way of the fanatic everywhere, no matter what side he favors."

Aidan shrugged in agreement. "It does not matter anyway. I have given up listening to him."

"So then. We have two leaders not listening to one another. The way of politics everywhere, I suppose."

"Do you believe I should deal with him, Demi-Precentor? Agree to demands that I have no authority to honor?"

"No," she said. "That you cannot do. For the moment it is a stalemate. Either you or he can order the destruction of Vreeport. Either you or he can in some way surrender."

"You seem cynical."

"Perhaps. We of ComStar tend to be realistic about political matters. That is the way of ComStar."

"Politics or not," said Aidan, "something must be done soon. I can give the order for the Star outside the city walls to attack, or even have our aerofighters strafe the square."

"You can order that from here? How powerful. How is it done?"

Aidan knew that Melanie Truit thought him somewhat naive, but he was not so naive as to confide to a ComStar official about the tracer signal on his person.

"I can do it. That is all."

"Why do you hesitate then? I have heard that Clan warriors place little value on their own lives, so it cannot be fears for your own safety that prevent you from giving the order. Besides, I have seen enough of you to know that it is not cowardice or even indecision that hold you back either. What stays your hand, Aidan Pryde?"

"First of all, the destruction of this place would serve no purpose, so all other methods must be tested first."

"Oh?" said Truit. "I know the Clan does not believe in waste, but that pertains only to Clan matters, Clan people, Clan property, does it not? Do you mean to say that it is the Clan way to protect the enemy from waste? I would like to know the real reason for your hesitation, Aidan Pryde."

For all Melanie Truit's plain-speaking ways, Aidan was not so inclined to speak frankly with her. He knew how devious ComStar officials were reputed to be. Then he realized that it made little difference here and now. With the two of them held captive in a rebel community, and with no present possibility of escape, what did it matter if the Demi-Precentor were devious?

"It is the children," he said, pointing to the now-restless young ones gathered around and beneath the legs of the AgroMech. Some of them whined, others cried, a few only whimpered complaints. The silent child was the rarity.

"The children? But haven't you told me that the Clans have no special feeling for children, their own or anyone else's?"

He nodded. "Yes, but it is not that simple. We are children, of course, in the sibko."

"Sibko?"

"Sibling company. The warrior caste is, as you know, genetically engineered. A number of young are born at one time and are raised together in early childhood. As we demonstrate our specific abilities, the weaker members of the sibko are weeded out, assigned roles in other castes. The sibkin who survive the warrior training are considered the fittest to become Clan warriors. But even among those survivors, more will fail and flush out of the sibko at various points along the way of training. Only a few of us make it to the Trial of Position, where we qualify or do not qualify as warriors.''

It was politic, he decided, not to tell her about his own failure in the Trial of Position. It was not so much to keep it a secret, but to avoid the complicated task of explaining his years of posing as a freeborn after he had qualified in his second Trial. The story was so long and involved that Jared Mahoney would probably have blown up the town square and them with it long before Aidan could conclude the tale.

"I have heard something of your customs," Melanie Truit said, "but not about the impersonality of your childhoods."

"Impersonality?"

"You say you are children in the sibko. Yet it sounds as though these sibkin are so dedicated to warrior goals that they experience little or no life as real children. You are so, well, *controlled* that you could never imagine what it means to be a child, much less what it means to know the bond with a parent."

"The warriors of the Clans regard parenthood and the terms related to it as near-obscenities. Why would one want to be a child like those huddled around the AgroMech? Look how much they whine and cry. They seem to be continually complaining."

"You too would complain, Star Colonel, if you were held captive but had no understanding of why or what it meant. You must at least admit that this situation is a stressful one for these children."

"That may be so, but I have seen lower-caste Clan young as well as Inner Sphere children under somewhat better conditions, and have been appalled by them also. What good is a childhood without purpose, one spent whimpering at the mother's knee?"

"The purpose of childhood, Aidan Pryde, is to be a child. The Inner Sphere has its own militaristic societies, but none of them operates on a stratified caste system that places a child on a single-minded path to a warrior destiny, whether or not he or she chooses it."

"There is never a question of choice. Of course we want to be warriors."

"I would much prefer the life of any of these ordinary children to being a child in one of your sibkos."

Aidan was shocked by her words. But Melanie Truit was not Clan, so how could she understand what it meant to him? How could he convey to someone outside the Clans what it meant to be a member of one?

"Do you understand the sentiments that pass between these children and these adults?" he asked.

"Yes. Yes, I do. I have a child, though he is almost grown now. He lives on Terra. Unfortunately, he hopes to become a MechWarrior. He might still outgrow the desire, and I sincerely hope he does."

"Are you trying to provoke me, Melanie Truit?"

"A bit."

"You seem to hate war."

"What sensible person would favor war?"

"Is there nothing for which you would fight? Your child, perhaps?"

"If attacked, yes. But I would not be an aggressor."

"And is your pacifism an expression of the philosophy of ComStar?"

"I cannot speak for the others. We are not exactly like the Clans, where one can speak for all."

"I find ComStar a puzzle. Neutral, with a powerful army. Pacifistic, with military preparedness."

"Recall that I told you what I would do. ComStar is a vast network with its own rites and rituals."

"Do you hate the Clans the way the people of Vreeport do?"

"I am neutral here also."

"But what are your personal sentiments?"

"The Clans seemed hateful when I first encountered them. You, however, are an exception."

"Perhaps we can discuss this more, after we return from here. Tonight."

"I will be happy to. And does that satisfy your need to take the initiative?"

"In truth, yes."

Jared Mahoney, who had been conferring with some of his subordinates, was approaching them again. He had changed weapons and was now carrying a small automatic rifle. He cradled it in his arms lovingly, almost the way some of the adults about the AgroMech were holding their children.

"Our patience is running thin, Pryde. Have you made up your mind to honor our demands?"

"No."

"Then it is time to kill another hostage." Mahoney glanced toward the group of Clan and ComStar hostages, then shook his head and turned toward the AgroMech.

"Some of the children are from Clan tech families," he said softly. "Perhaps it is time to kill one of them."

He gestured toward the AgroMech, and one of the rebels grabbed a tow-headed boy and dragged him forward. Tears edged from the boy's eyes, but he stood silent and defiant before the barrel of Jared Mahoney's rifle.

"It will not disturb you to see a child killed?" the rebel leader demanded, glancing back at Aidan.

Aidan refused to answer, but Demi-Precentor Truit rose from her chair. "You bastard!" she screamed. "You can't—"

Before she could finish her thought, Jared Mahoney had whirled around, raising the automatic rifle, pointing it at her. The next instant he coolly squeezed the trigger and let off a round at Melanie Truit. Her face seemed to explode outward with blood and bone, then she dropped in a heap to the ground.

Too late, Aidan jumped to his feet, his arms thrust out in a motion he could not stop.

Jared Mahoney strode over to the corpse and turned it over with his foot so that it faced upward. Beneath the blood there was no clue to the kind of face that had been there.

"Does that make you feel anything, Pryde?"

"It makes me feel that you have committed a stupid error, Mahoney."

Jared Mahoney rammed the rifle into Aidan's stomach. "Perhaps you are next, Clan-scum."

"No. I am your chief hostage, your best hope for negotiation. You would not kill me until your cause is hopeless."

Jared Mahoney removed the rifle barrel from Aidan's stomach and took a few steps backward. He looked down at Demi-Precentor Truit's corpse and clucked his tongue.

"You two seemed so very chummy. Do you feel no regret at her death, Star Colonel?"

Aidan could barely hide his contempt for this fool. "I wish you had not been so stupid as to kill the chief ComStar official at Quarell. Now you have ComStar as well as Clan against you."

"I know that. It is a calculated risk, actually. I had intended all along to kill Truit so there would be no doubt about the seriousness of our intentions, but I had not planned to do it so soon. But that is not what I asked. Are you like the others of your kind, these Clan monsters for whom a human life has no value? You feel no sadness for the death of Melanie Truit?"

"No sadness," Aidan said. "It should not have happened, but it did. What more is there?"

"Your indifference appalls me."

What a strange thing for a murderer to say, Aidan thought, as he watched Jared Mahoney swagger away.

13

Running barefoot, Diana quickly made her way from the edge of the forest to the helicopter. She always went shoeless any time there was a need to run. Dressed in the shorts and cooling vest that were standard cockpit garb for a 'Mech pilot, she could feel the cold night air raising goose bumps on her bare arms.

Reaching the helicopter, she went up to the hatch and knocked lightly. It opened immediately to reveal the face of the Comstar adept within. "I saw you coming," he said.

"One bad mark for me. I hope those vermin in the city did not spot me as well."

"Why didn't you radio ahead?"

"We were not sure if the rebels were monitoring transmissions. I plan to enter Vreeport, and I do not want to run into any welcoming committees."

She explained to the adept that Aidan Pryde and Melanie Truit had been taken hostage inside Vreeport. The man immediately volunteered to do anything to help rescue the Demi-Precentor, impressing Diana with his loyalty.

"What do you need?" he asked.

"A weapon heavier than this pistol. What have you got?"

Without another word, the adept went to a storage bin at the rear of the craft. He pulled out a submachine gun and handed it to Diana. "You can have this," he said.

Diana sneered at the weapon. "Is that the best you have?"

"I'm a ComStar helicopter pilot, not a member of the Com Guards. Besides, that submachine gun could be very useful. It has great range for a small-bore weapon. If your aim is good, what difference does it make whether a weapon is low caliber, right?''

''Aff.''

Rummaging further into the locker, he pulled out a sheathed knife.

He held it up triumphantly. ''And here's a survival knife. Never been used. Should also be useful in there. You going in by yourself?''

''By myself.''

''You have my admiration, beauty.''

''Do not call me that.''

Her voice was low and menacing, and the tech got the point. She hated the man for his impertinent Inner Sphere manner, but she suppressed her rage, knowing she needed his help.

''Sorry,'' he said. ''Didn't mean to scorch your armor. But you're quite a looker, you know.''

''My looks are of no importance,'' Diana said irritably. ''I am going to enter Vreeport by that hole in the city wall. Can you create a diversion for me?''

''Glad to. I'll make a flyby, then come back here. That should grab their attention. You can hide in that small clump of bushes just outside until I've passed over the city walls.''

''Right.'' She moved toward the spot he indicated, then settled down among the shrubs while the helicopter revved up, rose, and then soared low over the city wall.

She was up and running as soon as it disappeared. At the wall she pressed herself against the area just alongside the hole, listening for movement on the other side. Then she glanced quickly through the gap in the wall, the next moment diving through. Coming out the other side, she somersaulted and came up with the knife ready in her left hand. But there was no one near. Diana ran for the shadows of the nearest building, stopping for a moment under an overhang, listening to the sound of the helicopter going away from her. She could also hear a commotion, the sound of angry shouts, no doubt directed at the aircraft.

Aidan wanted to wave the helicopter away. Who had authorized such a foolhardy maneuver? These rebels were already so wound up that they might commit any kind of violence, including blowing up the AgroMech in a mass suicide. Indeed, Jared Mahoney was running around like an animal whose head had just been chopped off as he tried to rally some response from his astonished cohorts.

Finally, the rebel leader grabbed a pulse laser rifle from one of his supporters and aimed it skyward, firing wildly. His reckless act inspired others, and soon many of them were shooting at the aircraft.

What fools they were, thought Aidan. Did they not see how easily their fire could hit the wrong target and create a chain reaction that would destroy all of Vreeport?

Most of the shots went wild, until one hit the side of the helicopter, loosing tongues of flame from the side of the aircraft. As the copter began to go out of control, spinning first to the right, then to the left, it looked as though it would come down right in the middle of the town square, directly on top of the AgroMech.

Aidan held his breath as he watched the pilot regain control of the helicopter, which now hovered shakily in the sky over Vreeport. The pilot's attempts to control his craft were only partially successful, however. The next moment it began to slide downward toward the square.

Aidan braced for the expected crash, but somehow the pilot lifted just enough to clear a building on one side of the square. The helicopter continued onward, dipping a bit, then rose and leveled off. The pilot must have used up the last of either his luck or his skill, however, for the craft crashed to the ground just after clearing the city walls. The explosion sent up a flame that rose above the treetops of the forest, then disappeared.

Aidan stared at the wall, then at the bodies of Astech Trion and Melanie Truit, lying nearby but covered now with blankets. He wondered how many more would die.

Perhaps all, he thought, perhaps all.

Diana did not see the crash, but she heard it and the gunfire that preceded it. She did not have time to speculate on the crash or the death of the ComStar adept who had helped her, because she saw, in a building across the way, one of the rebels. The man was so amazed at her presence that he forgot to raise the automatic weapon held casually at his side. That moment of hesitation let

Diana draw her own submachine gun and burn a scorching hole between the man's eyes.

When she was sure he was dead, she stripped him of his tunic and loose trousers, slipping them over her shorts and vest. Then she went searching for the mob itself, the man's automatic weapon replacing the submachine gun in her arsenal.

14

"All right, Pryde, what is this offer you wish to make?" Jared Mahoney said, speaking loudly, making a play for audience attention.

"You and I, Mahoney, on a field of battle. I will grant you warrior status and the right to choose both weapons and the site. The winner will decide all issues. I win, you and your mob give up. You win, I find a way to stop the claiming of your people as bondsmen."

Jared Mahoney stared at Aidan for a long moment, then laughed harshly. "I have heard about your Clan battles. What is it you call them? Trials? And what you said to me, was that your bid?"

"Not exactly. But close enough, I suppose. For these circumstances, at least."

"And I have also heard that such bidding does not consist of idle challenges. It is based on strategy, the attempt to achieve the best possible results with a low bid of personnel and weaponry. If I understand the process correctly, it is strategic for the bidder to make his bid from a presumed stance of victory. And I submit to you, Pryde, that that is what you are doing. You make the challenge sound even, knowing that you, as a trained warrior, have advantages that I, as a barely trained militiaman, could not match. Don't speak to me of an even match between us. It cannot be."

Aidan nodded. The man was right. The bid was not legitimate. It was against warrior custom to make the kind of bid that Jared Mahoney suggested, one that would allow for differences between true warriors and hastily trained rabble.

"Sit down, Pryde."

"I wish to stand."

Jared Mahoney pushed Aidan roughly, with unexpected strength, back into the chair. Then, surprisingly, the man sat down in the other one, the chair so recently occupied by the ComStar Demi-Precentor.

"I have lived all my life on Quarell," he said suddenly. He looked away from Aidan, obviously not expecting a response. "The Free Rasalhague Republic never considered this world to be of much value, even though the reason for its underdevelopment is the years, centuries, of war. But we who live here like it that way. We like living in what is considered a frontier existence. We know of the luxuries available on so-called civilized worlds, but they do not interest us. Hell, we would not even use Agro-Mechs if it were not necessary. We like getting out into the fields and working with our hands.

"But we are loyal subjects, too. When General Craigh called us to defend Quarell against your Clan, we mustered the militia and fought, despite the futility of the effort. We did not want to see our home world violated. You swept over us as if we were not there. Your forces occupied the planet, ComStar representatives replaced our elected leaders, and then we returned to our homes. Yet for many of us it was only to find that we would not be resuming our lives, rejoining our families, enjoying our children, returning to the joy of working with our hands."

Aidan, a man with no home and who had never known parents, could not easily understand what Jared Mahoney was trying to tell him. Could it be, Aidan wondered, that the concept of family superseded the ideals of service and achievement for these people? Aidan would give up anything, sacrifice any part of himself, to serve the Clan, to achieve such glory that his genes would be passed on in the sacred gene pool. Then it occurred to him that the transmission of one's genetic legacy did have at least one correspondence with these people's values. In the Clan genetics program, the parent was transmitted through generations via his children and their children. The Clan way was similar but, because there were no social entanglements, better. Still, for the first time he almost understood something that had filled many of the pages of the books in his secret library.

Just then, he glanced up and saw a familiar face staring at him from the first rank of the crowd. For a moment he thought of Marthe, who had been so close to him during their days in the sibko, then he realized that this face was younger than hers would be now. Now he recognized the woman, and wondered how he could have confused her with Marthe. It was one of the new warriors from Joanna's Star. He could not recall her name, nor did that matter. The main puzzlement was, what in the blessed name of the Kerenskys was she doing here now?

Their eyes met for the briefest moment, then she edged backward into the crowd and vanished, leaving him wondering if it were only some hallucination created by the strain of being held captive.

"I want you to understand this, Pryde," Jared Mahoney was saying. "I have nothing against any of you. You are the conquerors and we can accept that."

"Then you must accept our rule."

"But when a rule is immoral or unethical or unnecessarily cruel, must we allow you to rape us with it? I think not. It is wrong to make slaves of us, and that is all there is to it. Slavery is your way of life, how could you understand? But we must make our stand and fight for it."

"Why do you say that slavery is our way of life?" Aidan asked, though a bit distractedly. He was still busy scanning the crowd for another sign of the young Clan warrior he had just glimpsed.

"You are a bondsman, too, Pryde. You are a slave of your system, bound to the ideas of war and caste. If you succeed in making me a bondsman, I will still be freer than you."

"This is mere rhetoric," Aidan said, turning his gaze back to the rebel.

Jared Mahoney's eyes widened. "I didn't know you Clanfolk had a sense of rhetoric."

Aidan shrugged. How could he reason with this man? At any rate, he was too preoccupied with the presence of the warrior from Joanna's Star. Where was she now? What was she up to? What kind of crackpot strategy motivated her?

Jared Mahoney was still going on with his fanatical talk, when one of his subordinates rushed over.

"The BattleMechs have moved out of the forest again," the man shouted. "They are advancing on the city."

"Man your posts," Jared Mahoney roared, springing out of the chair. He gestured toward one of the other rebels, then pointed toward Aidan. "Hold a gun on his head," he said. "Anything happens, kill him."

Aidan was aware again of that face in the crowd. The young woman's head turned in his direction, concern in her expression.

If there was going to be some kind of attack by his people, Aidan would have liked to get out of this chair and lead it. A rescue attempt by Joanna's Star might not be the best strategy under the circumstances, but Aidan was beginning to believe there might be no other way to subdue this rebel group. Jared Mahoney was too fixed in his ideas, too obsessed. Better to wipe them out, rebels, innocents, and hostages, than let such ideas fester and spread.

The young warrior looked away from him and began to walk toward the AgroMech, away from the flow of the rest of the crowd, which was readying for battle. In the AgroMech, the pilot gave Jared Mahoney another thumbs-up gesture, then fired off a series of pulses from her pair of lasers. It was immediately obvious that the woman had no idea how to pilot a 'Mech, much less an agribot with weapons on makeshift mounts.

The children and their parents still huddled together, not having budged from under or near the AgroMech's legs. They all seemed full of fear, but the adults clutched the children protectively, as though to shield them from harm.

Then Aidan saw the young warrior again. She was standing now next to one of the AgroMech's giant rear legs.

15

As Diana stared down at the confused and restless children, she wondered whether to just abandon her plan and only mutilate Jared Mahoney instead. What kind of person would use non-combatants as a buffer between himself and the enemy? It was true that the Clans often used old warriors in that way, but for useful strategic purposes, for the good of the battle or the campaign, ultimately for the good of the Clan itself. Besides, they were *old* warriors, all of whom had served well and lived a useful life; they were not *children* whose chances were yet to come. Jared Mahoney's words were meaningless if he must use children to die for them. If he had substituted all the old people of Vreeport for the children, Diana would have understood.

From her present vantage point, she could see the tops of four BattleMechs. They advanced without firing, all part of the plan Diana had suggested to Joanna. There was no point in an accidental shot setting off an explosive chain. The AgroMech pilot must have been getting better at handling her weaponry, for one of her shots chipped off some bits of ferroceramic armor from Joanna's *Timber Wolf*.

The 'Mechs came near the city walls, then stopped and seemed to wait there briefly. The next moment they turned and headed back toward the forest.

Guards standing atop the Vreeport walls shouted back that the enemy was retreating. Some desultory cheers rose from the crowd, and the people in the square seemed to visibly relax, especially those actively with the rebels. They lowered their weapons slightly.

Diana, however, tensed, watching the cockpit of the

AgroMech. Her hope had been that the pilot would come out of the cockpit at the sight of the Clan 'Mechs' retreat, if only for a breath of air. When she did not, Diana shifted to her alternate tactic.

Trying to look joyful, an emotion that a Clan warrior could summon only with difficulty even when genuine, she scrambled up the AgroMech's leg and leaped onto the level area next to the cockpit. Smiling and waving wildly to the pilot, she gestured that she had a message.

The pilot flipped up the cockpit canopy. "They're truly afraid of us, aren't they?" she said with a laugh.

"They truly are," Diana replied as she reached into the cockpit and grabbed the woman by the neck. With the twisting movement she had practised so often on dummies during cadet training, she snapped the pilot's neck and quickly yanked her out of the cockpit. Lifting the body up, Diana flung the woman down into the surprised arms of a rebel warrior, who fell clumsily to the ground when the weight of the body hit him.

Diana did not stop to watch the fall. Jumping into the cockpit and snapping the canopy shut, she grabbed the joystick and stepped the machine several meters away from where the children had been crouching beneath it. Taking the gunnery controls, she whirled the AgroMech around and started to direct fire against those rebels with weapons. She raked a group of them with fire. At least two fell dead, while three others squirmed on the ground, wounded.

Next, she looked around for Jared Mahoney, knowing that his followers might quickly surrender if their leader were killed. Not seeing him, Diana blasted another group of rebels, killing several instantly. Then she felt the AgroMech suddenly rocked by a successful hit to its right foreleg. It wavered a bit, but Diana was able to keep the machine upright and still shooting. What she could not do was move it further forward.

Where in the name of the great Kerenskys was Jared Mahoney? she thought frantically as she saw the first of her two laser weapons overheating.

Aidan witnessed the young warrior's acts from his uncomfortable sitting position, the barrel of the guard's weapon still pressed against his neck. But when she turned the AgroMech to fire on the rebels, with the children and their parents now scattering through the square, the astonished guard released the gun's pressure ever so slightly. Aidan reacted immediately. He knocked the weapon completely away with the back of his hand, then grabbed the guard by the waist, ramming his shoulder into his stomach. The man went limp immediately, and Aidan hurled him to the ground. He stepped on the wrist of the hand holding the weapon, then wrenched the light laser pistol out of the man's grasp. The weapon had probably come from the Vreeport arsenal. It felt cold and probably had never been fired. He fired it now, killing his former guard with a single shot through the temple.

Aidan had no time for further weaponry analysis. Looking around, he saw that everyone was so panicked by the AgroMech that his escape had gone unnoticed. Moving through the crowd, he headed toward the big machine.

The young warrior was on a suicide mission, he thought. There were too many rebels, too great an arsenal of weapons aligned against her, for her to succeed for long. Only concern for their own personal safety kept the rebels from simply blowing up the AgroMech with a well-placed shot or grenade. He had to get her out of that cockpit. The two of them had a better chance of shooting their way out of the settlement on foot. That strategy was perhaps as suicidal as hers, but no better alternative occurred to him.

Nearing the AgroMech, Aidan saw someone climbing its left rear leg. The red skin of the man's neck told Aidan it was Jared Mahoney. He stopped, set his feet, and fired, but the shot went wide. The sights in the pistol must be off. Well, there was no time to work out its adjustments now. Aidan picked up his pace and reached the AgroMech, where Jared Mahoney had climbed higher up the machine's left rear leg. It would not take much for him to reach the cockpit.

Aidan had no choice but to imitate Jared Mahoney's action by climbing the damaged left front leg. Halfway up, he clutched a section so red-hot that it burned the palm of his hand. He hardly felt it as he continued to scramble upward.

Pulling himself onto the top level of the AgroMech,

Aidan saw that Jared Mahoney had yet to notice him. He was too intent on firing his submachine gun toward the cockpit. Flecks of canopy were breaking off. Aidan could still see the warrior in the cockpit, however. One of her laser weapons had fused from excessive heat buildup and the other was now firing sporadically, about to go.

Diving, he grabbed Jared Mahoney by the ankles and flipped him down. There was no time to grapple, so he merely seized the man's gun arm and wrenched it backward. The gun went flying off the agribot. Giving the arm another twist, Aidan felt a bone breaking as Jared Mahoney screamed in pain. Aidan pulled at the arm, and the rebel leader's screaming became choked and pitiful.

Aidan released the arm and pulled Mahoney to his feet. Holding the laser pistol to the man's head, Aidan let the pose say everything for him. Mahoney's legs buckled. Aidan grabbed him with his free hand and held him up.

Looking around the town square, he saw rebels dropping their weapons and edging away from the AgroMech. Some stood mute and helpless, still holding onto their rifles and pistols, but obviously unwilling to use them.

The young warrior emerged from the cockpit. She held an automatic rifle. Turning toward the forest, she waved and the four BattleMechs reappeared and began to advance toward Vreeport.

"I think the rebellion is over," the young warrior said. She was looking at Aidan with an expression he could not interpret.

"What is your name, MechWarrior?" he said.

He might have been mistaken, but was that a flicker of disappointment in her eyes? "I am MechWarrior Diana, Star Colonel."

"Your name will go on report, MechWarrior Diana. Your actions were brave but foolish. Too much could have gone wrong. You overreached yourself. You interfered in a hostage situation. Though the outcome has been successful, I would not have approved the action. No, do not speak. I have had enough protest for awhile."

The danger now over, Aidan released Jared Mahoney. The man dropped to his knees. Shaking his head, apparently to clear it, he spoke in a low growl, "I will not be a bondsman."

"No," Aidan said, "you will be no one's bondsman."

Lowering the laser pistol to the man's head, he shot Jared Mahoney, changing his redskinned face into a mass of blood and bone. Aidan killed Jared Mahoney in exactly the same way that the rebel leader had killed Melanie Truit.

16

"No, Diana, it would not be a good move to challenge your commanding officer to an honor duel in the Circle of Equals. This is not even a matter for a Trial of Refusal. Anyway, Aidan Pryde is a skilled fighter, and your youth would be *no* advantage. He would probably kill you. He *would* kill you."

Diana leaned sullenly against the outer wall of a supply hut, staring with unseeing eyes at the activity around her. The people of Vreeport had been transported to the occupation forces' stronghold. Many of them were being herded into various temporary buildings, to be classified and reassigned. Aidan Pryde had ruled that the Vreeport rebels would be separated from the rest of the citizens and sent to other settlements.

After evacuating Freeport, the conquerors' last sight of the city was the massive explosion that destroyed it, sending up a huge mushroom cloud. Though Aidan thought it wasteful to leave behind Vreeport's arsenal of weapons and ammo, he knew that reprisal against the uprising was imperative, and he wanted the act to stand as an unforgettable symbol of Clan dominance. The leveling of Vreeport, like the devastation of cities and countries throughout history, would be a dramatic lesson for everyone on Quarell.

Joanna's dry comment on the matter was that so few people lived on this underpopulated planet that Aidan's grand symbol might not have all the impact he hoped.

Diana pulled away from her position by the wall. "I cannot put into words how I felt when he chastised me after I had saved him and the hostages and—"

Joanna took Diana by the shoulders and shook her

lightly. "Do not let your anger run away with you, MechWarrior. We have all experienced the disapproval of a commanding officer. We all know what it is to make a supreme effort, only to be criticized for it later by the one person whose approval might mean something. I grew up in a sibko, Diana, so anything to do with family feeling simply escapes my understanding. Perhaps being disciplined by a disapproving commander who is also one's father is—"

"I am not looking for *approval* from anyone. I wish to avenge an insult, an undeserved one."

"Was it really undeserved? There were standing orders and we ignored them. That is why you have no valid grounds for an honor duel, Diana. And that should be the end of it, *quiaff*?"

Diana nodded her agreement, but the look on her face was as sullen and unconvinced as before.

As the two of them crossed the parade ground, Joanna detected some excited movement among the techs, a scurrying back and forth, a hum of agitated talk. She stopped one and asked her what was going on.

"There's a DropShip arriving in this sector. They say it is traveling under order from Khan Chistu himself."

What in the name of Kerensky, Joanna wondered, would Khan Chistu want with a mop-up unit on one of the already-conquered planets? Nothing good that she could think of.

Aidan received the news of the DropShip's arrival from Horse.

"I tried to contact them," Horse said, "but they refuse all messages. All I got was a voice-only from the DropShip commander saying that a representative of Khan Chistu would pay you a visit later today."

Aidan looked across the parade ground where some of the Vreeport citizens were being processed. Crossing his line of vision were Joanna and the feisty MechWarrior, Diana.

For a moment he forgot about the Khan's representative and wondered if he had been too hard on Diana. She had been brave and saved not only his life, but who knew how many others? He had noted those facts for her codex even while recording the violation of standing orders.

Who should understand better than Aidan Pryde, something of a hothead during his own military career? His codex recorded the many times when he had followed his own instincts and urges in combat situations, those many times when his valiant efforts had been rewarded only by reprimands. Now that he was the commander, he saw the need for careful evaluation of all warriors, but was often uncomfortable with the duty.

Anyway, this Diana would survive, he was sure. And from what he had seen of her so far, he was sure she would do more than survive. She would excel.

He turned away from the window, these thoughts still on his mind. "What do you think, Horse? Should I have gone in and razed Vreeport the moment the people rebelled?"

"That is what I would have done. But that is all past. Why do you still think of it now?"

"I am wondering about Khan Chistu's representative. Why send someone here? Does it have to do with some policy of mine for which I am to be reprimanded? It is a long trip to take for a simple bureaucratic censure, after all."

"Now that I have had a chance to study you trueborns up close for so long, nothing surprises me in what *any* of you do."

Aidan merely nodded and went back to his duties, oblivious to Horse's sarcasm regarding trueborns after all these years.

It was several hours later when Horse returned. "The shuttle from the DropShip has landed. I would have come for you sooner, but they gave us no advance warning. The Khan's representative is on his way here in a VTOL."

Aidan left his office and walked to the parade ground to await the tilt-rotor craft. It appeared in the west, above some trees, and gently settled onto the landing platform. An aide assisted the Khan's representative from the VTOL, for the latter seemed barely in one piece. He limped and one of his arms was held stiffly at his side, as though useless. A half-mask covered one side of his face. Many Clan warriors used such half-masks to cover disfiguring injuries.

Aidan did not recognize the Khan's representative until

he was only a few steps away. He might have noticed something familiar in the man's posture or bearing, but that would have been all.

He recognized him well enough now. No matter how disfigured, here was Kael Pershaw, a man Aidan could never forget. Years ago, when Aidan was still posing as a freeborn, Kael Pershaw had been his commanding officer on a backwater planet named Glory. Though that world did not live up to its name, it was the place where Aidan had first found his own glory as a warrior. The Glory Station battle over Kael Pershaw's genetic legacy had put Aidan on a direct line to winning his Bloodname.

He and Kael Pershaw had hated each other almost on sight. And if the steady glare in the man's visible eye was any indication, Aidan guessed that Kael Pershaw's sentiments had not changed much.

Looking at him, remembering him, Aidan discovered that his own sentiments were equally unchanged after all these years. From the moment he recognized his former commander, Aidan despised him all over again.

17

"**M**ay I offer you a drink?" Aidan said, once he and Kael Pershaw were settled in his office.

"You can offer, but there is no point in my accepting. My stomach is, well, reconstructed, and my sense of taste is useless now. I am completely sustained by pill and injection. When I have thirst, I merely suck on a wet cloth, and it does all I need. But go ahead and serve yourself."

"No. I have only occasional use for spirits. Now, seeing you again, I prefer to remain cold sober. I notice you are a Star Colonel."

Pershaw's eyebrows rose. "A *mere* Star Colonel, do you mean? Yes, if I were still in command of a fighting unit, I would have a higher rank. But age, as well as"—he made a head gesture that seemed to take in the game leg, the stiff arm, and the damage to his face—"injuries have made me unfit for command. Officers of advisory capacity may not outrank commanding officers still in the field. Thus, I am demoted to Star Colonel, the rank, I believe, I held when we last encountered each other."

"That is correct. In a way, I have you to thank for my present success."

Grimacing, Pershaw shifted uneasily in his chair, his deformities obviously making all movement painful. "You are being ironic, I trust. Do you credit me for my disciplinary treatment of you?"

"I *do* remember the dark band," Aidan said. The dark band was an emblem of shame that Pershaw had forced him to wear for the killing of another Clan officer.

"I wished at the time to crush you; instead, you became a hero. I wonder, too, at your allusion to your present success. *Success?* Your career is a history of unfavorable assignments, of minor battles, of garrison duties. Even your experience here on Quarell has taint to it. Other units are presently engaging in more important battles on more important planets.'' Pershaw cocked his head inquisitively. ''You are silent. Unwilling to make excuses, are you?''

''Clan warriors do not make excuses.''

Pershaw laughed abruptly, the sound having lost no cruelty over the years. ''Oh, spend some time with the Jade Falcon command group and you will hear excuses enough. When circumstances are extreme, Clan tradition sometimes suffers. Our warriors, however, perform consistently with our virtues and ideals. They are honorable. And you are one of them, *quiaff*?''

''It is my hope,'' Aidan said. ''But you have spoken truly. I have not had key assignments in this invasion or in preceding duties. And I am aware of the taint that has accompanied my career. I have tried to wipe it out by— well, it does not matter to you what I have tried. The taint remains.''

Pershaw's eyes narrowed. ''Perhaps if you had beaten Megasa differently in your final Bloodright battle . . . Then again, perhaps not. With your history, the taint would have remained, no matter what. We of the Clan are an unforgiving lot, *quiaff*?''

Aidan shrugged. He was finding it difficult to look steadily at Kael Pershaw. The man's deformities, especially the half-face, were disconcerting. On the visible facial skin was a trio of deep scars running from the edge of the half-mask, over his nose and across his cheek, disappearing into his hairline.

Like all Clan warriors, Aidan dreaded becoming old. Yet his worst fears had never envisioned this kind of old warrior, one so damaged by battle that he had become at least half-monster.

Pershaw, perhaps sensing some of Aidan's reaction, carefully rearranged himself on his chair, using his good hand to settle his bad leg into a more upright position. He lifted the shoulder of his stiff arm so that the limb did not seem to hang as a weight.

''I can do nothing to remove this taint, Aidan Pryde, and I am here to convey a decision that will no doubt add to it. As you know, the Falcon Guards Cluster was nearly demolished by the action in the Great Gash on Twycross. This is the only major defeat Clan Jade Falcon has suffered in this invasion, and it has tainted the Falcon Guards, just as you are tainted. *Dezgra* is the word.''

"Yes, but were the Guards not the victims of secretly planted demolition charges and—''

Pershaw nearly rose out of his chair in anger. "You do not make excuses for yourself, nor do you make excuses for the Falcon Guards! Adler Malthus was too arrogant. He should have scouted the pass properly before leading so many 'Mechs into a confined area. He should not have accepted an honor duel with an Inner Sphere freebirth nor stopped his command in the middle of the Great Gash."

"Kael Pershaw, who knows what command decision another commander—myself included—might have made in the same circumstances, with the same intelligence data."

Pershaw's visible eye blazed with fury. "Good! Good! Then perhaps, in your own arrogance, you *are* the proper choice to command the new Falcon Guards!" He was almost shouting.

This time Pershaw did attempt to rise out of the chair, but unable to achieve the proper balance, he fell right back into it. Despite Aidan's intense dislike of the man, he was saddened to see the former superb warrior in such a diminished physical state. He was a rare specimen, so debilitated as to be unsuitable even for one of the old-warrior units often sacrificed as a delaying tactic in battle. Again he saw his own future as an old warrior, and he did not want to reach it. He would also hate to become such a physical wreck.

Then the meaning of what Pershaw had just said hit Aidan like a projectile with a delayed charge.

"I am to command the new Falcon Guards, Kael Pershaw?"

Pershaw's new laughter was low-down, mean. "That is the gist of the message for which I am messenger. All survivors of the former Falcon Guards will be transferred out and a completely new contingent will be formed, with you at its head. Do you see, Aidan Pryde, what I meant about taint? You are the only available officer who would not be insulted by such a command. And I can see in your eyes that you are not.''

"The assignment means front-line duty, does it not?"

"Even more than you anticipate."

"That more than compensates for any taint."

"And that is why I chose you, Aidan Pryde. I knew you would feel no shame at the assignment."

"*You* chose me? You are now a Khan?"

"And not just his messenger? You are right, Aidan Pryde, quite right. I was the only one, in fact, who could convey this message. Khan Chistu is busy at the moment, as you might imagine. To forestall any further questions, let me say that I am among the highest-placed advisors to our Khan. He selected me, even though I am a crippled old man."

"That is logical, given Vandervahn Chistu's reputation as an intelligent and crafty warrior. You were always known as a supreme military strategist, Kael Pershaw."

"I should say that you flatter me, but I cannot for it is true. If the Khan had not rescued me from mere bureaucratic duty, I would be buried alive somewhere. At any rate, I cannot talk further about my role in the present invasion. Let us just say that I chose you, Aidan Pryde, because your tenacity and uncommon skill at sometimes audacious maneuvers have the best chance of reviving the Falcon Guards. If you do not, nothing is lost. No shame you might bring to the role of unit commander could bring the Falcon Guards down any further."

"It is strange, Kael Pershaw. I should be wounded by your words, but instead I am eager to take the command you offer me."

"Just as I suspected. Make no mistake, you will start this new assignment with several disadvantages. In addition to the stained reputation of the Guards, you are being assigned subordinate officers and warriors who are not, may I say, among the best Clan Jade Falcon has to offer. Like you, each of them has some mark against him, some blemish to his codex. Many of them you would best eliminate immediately by putting them in your front lines against formidable odds.

"But how you handle this new duty is your responsibility. My task is merely to inform you that you are detached from your present duty to meet with your new, uh, warriors. They will be assembling on Orkney's southern hemisphere, at a training field called Mudd Station. You will not have much time to form up your Falcon Guards and whip them into any kind of shape. You will soon go into battle."

"How soon?"

"That has not yet been decided. The Khan has authorized me to brief you, but until all announcements are official, you must regard our conversation as secret. I have your *rede*, *quiaff*?"

"Aff."

"ComStar is no longer neutral. The ilKhan has informed them that our objective is Terra, and they refuse to allow us to occupy their home planet."

"Then we must be concerned about the ComStar administrators on our planets rising up against us."

"No. The ComStar Precentor Martial has issued a *batchall* to ilKhan Kerensky, which has been accepted. ComStar has arranged with ilKhan Kerensky for a single battle between the Clans and the ComStar military forces on a planet named Tukayyid. A Clan victory will mean that the prize of Terra is ours. But if we lose, the ilKhan has agreed that our forces will not advance for a period of fifteen years. And during all that time we must be content merely holding and administering the planets we have already conquered."

"The Khans of the other Clans have accepted this?" Aidan was a bit incredulous.

"Yes. IlKhan Kerensky has called a *kurultai* of Clans Jade Falcon, Smoke Jaguar, Steel Viper, Ghost Bear, Diamond Shark, and Wolf. The terms of the *batchall* were ratified. In the bidding for objectives, Khan Chistu offered to use the Falcon Guards. That reduction in our forces earns our Clan the right to land on the first day."

As Kael Pershaw continued the briefing, it was all Aidan could do to concentrate. Already he was speculating on what he might do as commander of the new Falcon Guards.

18

Nobody knew the origin of the name Mudd Station. Before the Jade Falcons had taken it over, it was little more than an outpost constructed for some now-abandoned scientific study. Presently it served the Clan invaders' strategic purposes, with the addition of new landing areas, buildings, and the installation of a defense system.

Despite the improvements, Mudd Station was no more desirable a place than before. Every afternoon it was battered by a heavy rainstorm, whose downpour could knock to the ground anyone foolish enough to be out in it. The storm usually damaged some item whose repair took techs away from their main labors. Slogging around in the mud afterward, Aidan often wondered if the station's nearly continual ground condition had inspired someone to give the place its name.

The discomforts of Mudd Station did not, however, dampen his spirits. Each day brought new contingents for the Falcon Guards, new challenges, and new complications. DropShips seemed to transport as many problems as they did personnel. Not the least of these, in fact, was the personnel.

"Star Colonel, these are among the worst specimens of Clan warrior I have ever seen," Horse complained, as he and Aidan made their daily tour of Mudd Station. Their boots squished loudly with each step. "I wonder how anyone could ever justify the trashborn genetic programs with this bunch."

"Be careful, Horse," Aidan warned. "Let no one else hear your slurs. You are, after all, only here on my sufferance. You are the only freeborn in the Falcon Guards, and Kael Pershaw only made an exception when I referred him to your codex. That means you will have to toe the line even more than normal.''

''Oh, I'll be your good little warrior, Aidan Pryde. But, to be effective, I must be honest with you.''

''Please do. Just be sure that no one overhears. And I would suggest dropping the contractions. We need no unnecessary reminder of your origins among these warriors. We want to whip them into shape, not distract them with matters of less importance. They are already aggressive enough among themselves, but perhaps we can channel that energy into useful acts to restore the honor of the Falcon Guards.''

Horse stared intently at Aidan. ''This assignment has addled your brain. This unit is condemned, can't—cannot you see that?''

''Condemned to what?''

''I do not know what lies Kael Pershaw has poured into your head, but the scuttlebutt among the warriors and techs is clear enough. We all know that we are merely filling a slot here. There has to be a Falcon Guards, so there is one. But do not delude yourself into believing that we have some honorable goal before us. Have you not noticed the great number of old warriors assigned to us, individuals on the verge of ending their careers? That is your clue.''

''You speak in riddles,'' Aidan said impatiently. ''We are getting older warriors for one simple reason: they are among the few warriors available for reassignment.''

''Is that what Kael Pershaw told you? He masks at least half his motives in the same way that he does his face. We are getting older warriors because Khan Chistu is not really concerned with our fate. If any unit was formed to be cannon fodder, *solahma,* it is the present Falcon Guards. They expect little of us, we are considered a *dezgra* unit, don't—do you not see that?''

Aidan stopped in his tracks, glanced around, then signaled to Horse to follow him to where no other Clan warrior could hear them. ''Of course I know Khan Chistu is willing to write us off, Horse. He would not intentionally send us to our deaths, but he would not mourn us as trothkin lost if it happened. But you know as well as I that this is my only chance to achieve something as a

Clan warrior. The Falcon Guards have been promised front-line duty. Kael Pershaw even put it in writing, and for all his devious qualities, you can trust Kael Pershaw's word. We are included in the bidding for Tukayyid. We will fight there.''

"Is that what all this is about for you? Personal glory? All that contribution to the gene pool bilge that you and your—"

Aidan grabbed Horse by the shoulders. "I know what you think about Clan ways, Horse." Aidan's voice was unusually tense. "But yes, I do seek personal glory. Yes, I do wish my legacy to pass into the gene pool. Yes, I want my contribution to this invasion and the Clan goals to be both exceptional and honorable. Whatever errors my nature has led me to commit in the past, I am a Clan warrior and intend to do my part to help the Clans gain dominion over the worlds and people of the Inner Sphere. If you cannot understand because you are freebirth, then try to—"

Horse broke Aidan's grip and returned his stare with equal intensity. "What is happening to you, old friend?" he said softly. "You never call me freebirth. And you are the only trueborn I have known who never has."

"I am sorry, Horse. A slip. I was one of you once, remember."

"No, you posed as freeborn. But you were never one of us."

Aidan heard the touch of scorn in Horse's voice. "I do not wish to offend you, Horse. There has been too much between us over the years. My only wish is to succeed as commander of the Falcon Guards. If you can try to understand that, perhaps you will be able to forgive the means I use to achieve my aim."

Horse nodded. "Of course I do."

"As for the freebirth business, need I remind you that you call me trashborn on a fairly regular basis?"

Horse shook his head. "No. I call your caste trashborn. Not you. There is a difference."

"Maybe, maybe not. Let us leave it at that. As you say, our task is to make good warriors of those who are not exactly the best specimens of the type. And, Horse, I appreciate your struggle not to use contractions. Keep at it."

As they walked toward the others, Aidan thought of the many passages he had read in books in his secret library. So many stories of friendship, comradeship, between two individuals fighting for the same side. The way of the Clan, however, put service to the group above individual alliances. Yet Aidan had always known that he and Horse were just like the characters in those old tales of the Inner Sphere.

19

The codex of Star Commander Summer Mandaka was filled with notations of insubordination. How she had survived this far without some commander simply shooting her to get rid of her was a mystery to her new commanding officer. When Aidan observed her skills at manipulating a BattleMech and the growling, rude way she whipped her Star—like all the new Falcon Guards, a collection of misfits, lowlifes, and aged warriors—into shape, he realized that her bad manners disguised a supreme officer.

That did not make her any easier to take.

Summer Mandaka was of average height, with short chunky arms and a thick neck bulging with thick veins. She was fair-haired, with chiseled features and a permanently angry expression in her eyes.

Now she stood before Aidan, her body trembling visibly with anger, if that was the right word. Wrath or fury might better describe her defiant stance.

"Star Colonel, I must speak with you."

"Speak your piece, Star Commander."

"I realize that I am now a member of the Falcon Guards because I have erred in the past. The worst of my errors is having lost a string of BattleMechs in recent battles. You have seen my codex. I have been chastised for a tendency toward waste. But if so, it is waste in the service of the Clan."

"Most Clansmen would not accept your reasoning, Star Commander."

"I realize that. I have vowed never to lose another 'Mech, unless I lose my own life with it. For that reason, I have disabled the ejection seat of my *Hellbringer*."

"That is allowed, though I must advise you that I do not consider it a wise move."

"I take the implied criticism as well-intended, Star Colonel, but the reason I tell you of my vow is that I fear I cannot successfully live up to it with my present Star. Each one of them is sorely lacking in skill, yet not willing to train for their betterment. I have never viewed such insubordination."

How ironic, Aidan thought, that a warrior famed for her own intransigence should grouse at the same characteristic in others. He must conclude that either she was turning over a new leaf or that her crew of misfits was extraordinarily incompetent.

"Insubordination is a problem for officers at every level, Star Commander. Why do you speak to me about it?"

"Sir, I know that personnel is stretched thin in the Falcon Guards. The pool of warriors for reassignment to a new unit is not wide. And no untainted warrior would ever volunteer for duty with the Falcon Guards."

It was all Aidan could do to keep himself from wincing at her use of the word *untainted*. Taint was the one concept he wanted to purge from the Falcon Guards, yet it seemed to be the one word none of them could escape.

"I must declare a Trial of Grievance with Mech-Warrior Rollan. He has agreed. His anger is equal to mine. You must serve as Oathmaster."

Aidan racked his mind for the proper Trial of Grievance procedures. In his previous commands such disputes had been handled without formalities.

"It is my duty to hear arguments from both of you about why the Trial of Grievance must take place."

"Of course, Star Colonel. MechWarrior Rollan and I await only your word about when the interrogation will take place."

"I gather that the two of you are already avoiding contact, as dictated by Clan tradition."

"That is correct, sir."

"And you have decided the nature of the trial?"

"We have agreed on BattleMech combat in a properly defined Circle of Equals. No bidding was necessary."

"All right then. We will begin procedures immediately."

Mandaka made to leave, then turned back again. "Actually, sir, there is little point in going through the procedures. The trial will take place."

Aidan sighed. "I am sure it will, Star Commander. I am sure it will."

Aidan soon learned that, as Star Commander Summer Mandaka had said, no peaceful resolution to the dispute was possible. MechWarrior Rollan was just as adamant as his superior officer about the need for a Trial of Grievance. During the interrogation, each responded to Aidan's questions with terse but polite answers. Aidan then ordered the Circle of Equals drawn in a clearing outside of Mudd Station.

As Oathmaster, he gave final instructions to the two combatants, who glared fiercely at one another throughout the ritual. When he gave the order for them to mount their 'Mechs, the eagerness of their response would have honored any warrior in battle.

Before engaging in combat, each combatant had to take a position equidistant from the other on the borders of the circle. In fact, they would be so far apart at the start that neither could gain a visual on the other.

Horse joined Aidan in the command post's upper levels. Arrayed around them were instrument panels and monitors for viewing the combat.

The other Falcon Guards arrayed themselves around a central holotank in the lower level of the command post. Battle cameras from an overhead aerospace fighter beamed a direct transmission to the tank. When the two 'Mechs reached the approximate center of the Circle, the spectators would have a god-like view of the battle.

While waiting for the two 'Mechs to engage, Aidan looked down at those Falcon Guards he could see. The sight gave him an overpowering urge to close his eyes. What he saw were surly so-called warriors whose uniforms were mud-spattered despite Aidan's regulation that they must wear clean uniforms except during exercises.

How did he imagine ever accomplishing anything significant or honorable with this bunch of misfits and *chalcas*? Kael Pershaw had been right about the formidableness of the task. Perhaps Horse had also been correct that they were doomed from the start. Perhaps this was a military unit not intended to succeed.

No, that made no sense. What kind of high command would order the reformation of a unit merely to kill it off? Even the Clan's use of old warriors as *solahma* did not justify the trouble his leaders were taking to revive the Falcon Guards. Aidan Pryde might be dispensable, but the Falcon Guards were not.

When Summer Mandaka's *Hellbringer* was the first 'Mech sighted, a desultory cheer went up from the spectators. One warrior, whose patch showed him to be a member of Mandaka's Star, reached out his arm to display a thumbs-down gesture. Well, Aidan thought, that tends to verify her claim that her Star is insubordinate. Her BattleMech was shiny and well-kept, except for the gobs of mud that had already collected on its feet.

When MechWarrior Rollan's 'Mech, less pristine, more muddy, came over a hill, Aidan reflected that it was a *Timber Wolf*, like his own, but with no curse attached. So far, though, Aidan had piloted his *Timber Wolf* without incident. Perhaps whatever jinx was on it would not affect him.

Aidan did not believe in jinxes. It was a pilot's skill, or lack of it, that counted. He liked his *Timber Wolf* already and longed to take it into battle. After so many years of garrison assignments, he anticipated frontline duty with more eagerness than some young warrior who had just won his Trial of Position.

Aidan had known many Trials of Grievance in his career—as supervising officer, as spectator, as combatant—but rarely had he seen one as quick or fierce as this between Star Commander Summer Mandaka and MechWarrior Rollan.

Summer Mandaka took the initiative, her *Hellbringer* coming at MechWarrior Rollan's *Timber Wolf* with a determination that looked almost as mean as its pilot. Firing the pair of large lasers in her 'Mech's left arm, she stitched a precise pattern on the *Timber Wolf*'s chest, the deep lines crossing other deep lines in its armor. The MechWarriors standing around the holotank looked at each other with a bit of surprise. It seemed that the Star Commander had chosen a non-standard configuration of weapons for her *Hellbringer,* one that Rollan might not be ready for.

But MechWarrior Rollan was quick to respond. The first cluster of long-range missiles from his left-torso mount went in high and a bit off, doing no more than chip off a big piece of the *Hellbringer's* searchlight. He was luckier with a second salvo, the missiles going in low to completely disable the knee of Mandaka's 'Mech.

Grinding her 'Mech to a halt, Summer Mandaka did not let up for an instant on her attack. Aidan saw now that she had reconfigured her 'Mech's right arm, replacing the *Hellbringer's* usual PPC or autocannon with a Gauss rifle. Firing the weapons, she hit her opponent's chest with the silver streaks of the Gauss projectiles. The *Timber Wolf* moved forward, but uncertainly. Its movements reminded Aidan of staggering.

With one 'Mech unmoving because of the lucky leg hit, and the other severely damaged and progressing in fits and starts, it was obvious that it was only a matter of time before one or the other would fall.

For the next several minutes the two BattleMechs went at each other with all they had, neither one able to finish off the other, all the while inflicting brutal damage with an almost continual exchange of fire. At one point it looked as if the *Hellbringer* must surely fall as the *Timber Wolf's* last missile salvo nearly exposed the other 'Mech's fusion engine. Still using both her Gauss rifle and her large lasers, Mandaka suddenly forced the *Timber Wolf* to retreat a few steps. Aidan wondered if she knew what she was doing. Her heat levels had to be approaching the limit.

Then the battle was over almost before anyone knew it. What Aidan thought was probably the last of Mandaka's Gauss projectiles must have made a critical hit against the *Timber Wolf.* The *Wolf* had begun to tilt over backward, but the 'Mech did not quite fall.

Aidan was ready to intervene using his right to end the combat and declare Summer Mandaka the victor, when he realized that she was not yet out of Gauss ammo.

As the *Timber Wolf* swayed on its feet, its remaining weapons firing wildly, ineffectively, Mandaka fired one more time, the shot from the twin lasers hitting her op-

ponent's cockpit dead-center. Its canopy exploded outward, instantly killing the pilot.

Then the *Hellbringer*, its heat capacity overextended, also exploded. Flames leaped to the sky from the specially designed blowout panels in the back of the 'Mech as the missiles stored in the right and left torso went up. The force of the explosion rammed the 'Mech face-down to the ground, crushing the cockpit and Summer Mandaka.

Beside Aidan, Horse remained for a moment, still staring ahead in disbelief. "Was it suicide?" he said. "She had to know she was overheating when she fired that last shot. Why did not the autoeject mechanism function—"

"She could not eject," Aidan told Horse, then explained that Mandaka had disabled her ejection seat. "She said she could not survive one more lost 'Mech. She meant it."

"So it seems."

"At any rate, we are now short a Star Commander and a MechWarrior, with no pool of unit reserves from which to draw. I believe it is my privilege to request replacements from what is available on Quarell. I do not care how you do it, Horse, but I want Star Commander Joanna and that other MechWarrior—I think her name is Diana, the one from the Vreeport debacle—transferred to the Falcon Guards immediately."

"Are you sure?"

"Yes."

Horse walked away, muttering. Aidan knew what his friend was thinking. It was enough that they must somehow form up a band of misfits, warriors who could barely get along with one another, and now Aidan was asking for more trouble. No love had ever been lost between Joanna and Horse, but he knew Joanna was good. Horse had to give her that. Joanna was good.

=== 20 ===

Joanna hated the idea. "Consider my position," she said. "I was transferred from the Falcon Guards as one of the marks of the unit's failure, and then I was demoted, which I thought was the worst thing that could ever happen to me as a Clan warrior. Even worse than being a falconer wiping the backsides of your *stravag* sibko. Now I am back in the Falcon Guards, and it is worse than leaving it."

"But will you become the Guards' falconer?" Aidan asked.

"Do I have a choice, Star Colonel? If I remember correctly, you are the commanding officer. I must follow your orders, *quiaff*?"

"Not in this case. I am asking you to volunteer."

Joanna stood at the window of Aidan's office, looking out at the drilling catastrophe that was the Falcon Guards' calisthenics. She turned and twisted her face into what was perhaps intended as a smile. In a flash of memory, Aidan recalled seeing her in just such a pose when she had been a falconer years before. Time had not been kind to Joanna, but her poise and posture were as youthful as ever.

"I volunteer, Star Colonel. We old warriors are grateful for any kind of assignment, you know. When do I start?"

"How about immediately? Start with the calisthenics, if you wish."

She nodded. "Good a place as any, I expect. Dismissed?"

"Dismissed."

At the door she stopped. "Oh. Your permission to assign MechWarrior Diana as my, well, aide in this. Nobody out there knows either of us, so there will be no past histories to interfere.''

''She is inexperienced and a freeborn.''

''But she is as tough as fusion-engine shielding. You will see.''

''You may use any personnel in any way you wish, Star Commander Joanna.''

After she was gone, Horse pushed away from the wall, where he had been observing the encounter.

''What was that all about?'' he asked. ''Do I detect some clever strategy on your part?''

Aidan cleared away a pile of papers at the corner of his desk, then sat down on the clean spot. Looking at his friend, he saw that Horse, too, was beginning to show age. In any other unit, the two of them would have been the old warriors. But compared to the overage warriors they had been sent for the Falcon Guards, Aidan and Horse were still young.

''If I have a strategy, it is simply that I need someone who can whip these malcontents into shape. That is Joanna's special talent, and I intend to use it. That is what leadership is all about, Horse, using one's personnel effectively.''

Horse opened his mouth to retort, but they were interrupted by the sounds of a scuffle outside. Aidan moved quickly to the window, with Horse close behind. The sight that greeted them was one of their malcontent warriors on the ground a few meters from the window, grimacing as he rubbed his jaw. Joanna stood over him. Several warriors looked on, various degrees of surprise on their faces.

''Looks to me like Star Commander Joanna has begun her task,'' Horse commented drily.

For the next hour Aidan abandoned command duty for the sheer pleasure of watching from his window as Joanna conducted the drill session. She and MechWarrior Diana weaved among the warriors, prodding them to speed up or to better execution or to simply remain standing when they looked ready to drop from exhaustion. Several instances of defiance occurred during the first few minutes of the exercise, but the pair of drill instructors had countered each incident with a physical response. Several old warriors were easily decked; others had to be fought more craftily. But in each case Joanna or Diana prevailed. They had the advantage of determination as well as of having maintained their own regimens; they were simply in much better shape than any of these aging or scruffy warrior-misfits. By the end of the hour, this particular Trinary of Falcon Guards was actually beginning to show some precision in its group movements. Joanna immediately ordered another Trinary to assemble in the drill zone.

Satisfied that Joanna was carrying out her mission efficiently, Aidan began to study MechWarrior Diana more intently. Something about this young woman, who reminded him more and more of Marthe, intrigued him. It made no sense, of course. He must certainly be turning a slight resemblance into something more. But it was not only that the young warrior looked like Marthe; she moved a bit like her, too. What's more, she showed exactly the kind of skills that had been Marthe's specialty. Only her recklessness was a contrast. Marthe had been methodical, meticulous. Diana's hotheadedness was more like Aidan than Marthe.

Well, he thought, Clanspeople of all castes could resemble one another. Was there not a saying that everyone had his or her twin on some Clan world? Sometimes it seemed quite possible.

Joanna felt exhilarated for the first time in years.

"You know what it is?" she said to Diana. "It is power. I have always craved power. I was meant to be at the highest levels of command. Only circumstance has kept me from it. Your father has given me a chance to—"

"Please. Never refer to him as my father. If anyone heard—"

"If anyone heard, they would not care, nor would they believe it. Why be so obsessed by the fact? No one else would. Your father himself would probably treat the information as no more than a curiosity. It is not as a daughter that you must strive to impress him. Impress him as a *warrior*. And now be silent. I have much work to do."

As ordered, Diana spoke no more.

* * *

Over the next days, Joanna began to post so many rules about nearly everything that the grumbling from the barracks seemed to became part of the night sounds of Mudd Station.

But her rules brought results. Formerly filthy MechWarriors suddenly began to appear at musters clean and in immaculate outfits. Personal weapons drills led to high scores. In marches, left feet tended uniformly to contact ground followed by the simultaneous movement of right feet. Aidan knew from watching the marching drills that Joanna's success was phenomenal. None of the warriors had been in a close-order march since cadet training. How she had terrorized them into it he did not know, nor did he care.

Her real triumph, however, was the 'Mech drills.

At the beginning of them, she had delivered a long, scathing oration on how most of the warriors had lost sight of their place in the Clan and what the Clan should mean to them.

"Individuality, that is your curse," she screamed at them. By this time, they were surprisingly docile whenever she raised her voice. "You know who believes in the promotion of the individual at all costs? The warriors of the Inner Sphere, that is who. They have weakened themselves with just that sort of degeneracy. They scheme. They employ vicious trickery. They believe in personal glory. Heroes are valued. And do you know what happens? They become reluctant to take the necessary risks, the ones that might endanger their lives, because they have begun to think their personal existence matters more than the goal for which they are fighting.

"Their kind of hero separates himself from the others and attempts to prevent any tarnish to his reputation. Suddenly it is better to hold back and let someone else fight the battle. Suddenly there are more heroes in the rear than at the front. Is that the kind of hero you all want to be?

"No? Yet each of you seems to have developed personal styles, quirks, and idiocies. But it is not differences, individuals, that are the way of the Clan. Do you forget the cause that has governed our lives since any of us emerged from the iron womb? It is the cause that must be our beacon. In this war with the Inner Sphere, it is the Clan that must prevail, not the individual in battle. Each time you destroy an enemy 'Mech, it is for the Clan, not for your personal glory. Anyone who is not willing to die for the Clan is not truly a warrior.

"You have transformed yourselves into individuals. I intend to make you Clan warriors again. Do you wish to be Clan warriors?"

"Seyla!"

"Ah, I thought so. Then get off your spreading behinds and do as I tell you. *Exactly* as I tell you."

If a few recalcitrant warriors still resented Joanna, the others brought them back into the fold. Soon the Falcon Guards were operating with more precision. But Joanna insisted on more, and she got it. And what Joanna could not get, Diana did. The two warriors savaged the new Falcon Guards and then revived them. Which was exactly what Aidan had ordered them to do.

Joanna came into Aidan's office one day. "Go to your window, Star Colonel," she said.

Looking out, he saw the entire Falcon Guards on the field, all the pilots in their 'Mechs, all the Elementals in their battle armor. MechWarrior Diana stood on a recently constructed platform. At a signal from Joanna, she gestured toward the assembled troops.

In almost a single precise movement, all the BattleMechs, all the Elementals, raised their left arms to a chest-high position. This was followed by the right arms, which went past the chest position and raised up, stopping at an oblique angle, all of them in approximately the same position. Then each arm was lowered separately.

At the next signal from Diana, each of the BattleMech torsos inclined first to the right, stopped simultaneously, then in synchronization, inclined to the left. After holding the pose for a moment, all the BattleMechs returned to the upright position.

These were just the beginning of nearly an hour of precise drills, sometimes just the BattleMechs, sometimes just the Elementals. At the end, they formed into marching units and left the field in a precision drill.

Aidan, who had been spellbound by the demonstration, finally turned to Joanna and said, "I am impressed. But just what in the name of Kerensky was happening there?"

"Well, in one sense, you have just witnessed the universe's first BattleMech calisthenic drill. In another, you have seen I have done my job. You can go into battle with some confidence in the Falcon Guards. They are still a bunch of aging or eccentric warriors, but they are now a unit. Sir."

"I have seen your work over the last two weeks, Star Commander. I have known for some time that your mission was a success. And in good time, it seems. Our orders are to proceed to Tukayyid in two days. I appreciate what you have done, Joanna."

Joanna did not acknowledge either the credit or the familiar use of her name. As usual, Aidan could not be sure what she was thinking. She probably hated him as much as ever.

"At the beginning of this," he said, "you did not think much of my plan. What do you say now?"

"The plan was chancy, but it worked."

"Thanks to you, Star Commander."

"That is also true."

21

Kael Pershaw came to the DropShip *Raptor* early the night the Jade Falcons were to drop onto Tukayyid's Prezno Plain. He visited several of the DropShips that night, his stiff, useless arm and half-mask making a strong impression on the Jade Falcon troops. Later, they would call him "The Specter of Tukayyid."

On this night, though, he seemed blessed with an added vitality. When he spoke, his voice was unusually excited. He walked briskly, somewhat overcoming the limp, and a glow of eager anticipation showed in his visible eye. Perhaps it was this look that accounted for the legend. Never before in his life had Kael Pershaw looked this way, and even those who knew him well found it eerie.

Those like Aidan Pryde.

Aidan was glad to be sitting when Pershaw strode into his cramped DropShip quarters. He had been reflecting deeply about what to say to the Falcon Guards before they dropped for battle. No one had reported to him that Pershaw was aboard.

"You are to be praised, Aidan Pryde," Pershaw said after they had exchanged greetings. He stood just inside the doorway, and the only illumination in the room, a desk lamp to one side of Aidan's desk, shot light up at him. The effect only added to the eeriness of his appearance. A glow seemed to project from the scars on his face, the half-mask transformed into a dark hole on one side, the visible eye seeming to drift in front of the face. Aidan, not normally affected by supernatural suggestion, felt a shudder run up and down his spine.

"Praised? A strange word coming from you, Kael Pershaw. For what, may I ask?"

"In assigning you the Falcon Guards, I believed that I was prematurely destroying your career. That was not my intention, mind you, just my interpretation. But I planted a spy among your techs and—"

"A spy? That is troubling. Do we of the Clan now stoop to an Inner Sphere style of deception?"

Pershaw nodded briskly. "You are correct to be concerned. Our Clan, indeed all the Clans, seem to be subtly changing the deeper we penetrate into the Inner Sphere. We should imitate Clan Wolf, whose line of supply leads back to the Clan worlds. We should keep the lines of our heritage firmly tied to our own worlds. In some ways we are losing that. Perhaps no one expects any interference with the advance of our juggernaut. But that is neither here nor there. When we have captured Terra, there will be time enough to restore any lost values. I am merely here to tell you that the Falcon Guards will play a more important part in the fight for Tukayyid. We need your daring, Aidan Pryde."

"The Falcon Guards will serve wherever assigned, sir. As you know, we are ready. Much of the credit for that goes to Star Commander Joanna. I have, in fact, given her a field promotion to Star Captain for the campaign."

"A field promotion will not stick for her, I am afraid. She is too old, and there is the Twycross—"

"She knows the promotion is temporary. But the Falcon Guards respect her, and the rank will only enhance their respect."

Kael Pershaw moved to the right side of the doorway, out of the light cast by the desk lamp. Though Aidan could still see him, the details of his features and uniform were less clear. His voice also sounded disembodied, as though coming from another part of the small room's darkness.

"I must tell you, Aidan Pryde, that the struggle for Tukayyid is not going well. Two weeks ago, when the bidding took place to determine the order of the various Clans' landings on planet and what targets would go to the winners of each bid, we believed we would not need all our Clan forces in the fight for Tukayyid. Khan Chistu included the Falcon Guards in the Jade Falcon bid to win a favorable target. That was why so much fierce maneuvering took place to keep Clan Wolf off Tukayyid until it was almost over. It was believed that if the Wolves landed last and had only two relatively minor targets, they would have no opportunity to win any major advantages. We were confident the battle would be over by the time they arrived, making Clan Wolf a significant loser. The fact that the Clan Wolf Khan offered no significant protest to the blatant plotting against them puzzled me at first. I had thought that the ilKhan, himself a member of the Wolf Clan, favored his former Clan. He has told me that he wishes Clan Wolf to be the ilClan, the Clan that first gains control of Terra.

"Nevertheless, the Wolf Khan seemed content with the outcome of the bidding. Now I see that perhaps his bid was far-seeing. The landings early this morning have not gone well for the Clans, and it is possible that Clan Wolf will go in at the right time to gain all the spoils. At the moment, Clan Jade Falcon stands in the way of Clan Wolf. It is essential that we prevail."

"I understand that. And you must understand that I do not intend for the Falcon Guards to reap any more shame. If we go down, it will only be because we die."

"I am glad to hear that, Aidan Pryde. However, my fears are not only for the shrewdness of Clan Wolf. They are for all the Clans. We deserve to conquer the Inner Sphere. It is a matter of good defeating evil, after all. The people of the Inner Sphere do not, of course, see it that way. They complicate issues and ideas so much that they drain them of all meaning. An Inner Sphere concept is like a law made by some village council. The council members argue so many local trivialities that the law comes out meaningless. So it is with the Inner Sphere. That is another reason why the Clans must prevail. It is for the good of humanity. Once we have eliminated the deviousness of the Inner Sphere way, we will easily restore the glory of the Star League.

"Aidan Pryde, no one knows which Clan will become the ilClan or indeed how the selection will be determined—whether the prize should go to the best warriors on Tukayyid or to the first Clan to actually set foot on Terra. The important consideration for Clan Jade Falcon is that its predecessors have failed, whether they know it or not. The Smoke Jaguars, the Steel Vipers, the Nova Cats—all have become bogged down. I do not see any of them succeeding. Only the Ghost Bears have made any significant progress.

"Not only do the Jade Falcons stand a good chance of winning the honor of ilClan, but they are needed to turn the tide of battle. Khan Vandervahn Chistu has sent me with your operations orders. You and your Falcon Guards are detached from direct Galaxy control. You are to break through and bypass any ComStar resistance and take either the city of Humptulips or Olalla. You will not follow a set battle plan, but will improvise. Is that acceptable, Aidan Pryde?"

"It is."

Pershaw nodded, then turned toward the door, the half-mask side of his face toward Aidan. It was like watching a puppet moving without strings.

At the door, Kael Pershaw said, "I hated you once, Aidan Pryde. Now I admire you, though I cannot say when one thing changed to another. Fight well on Tukayyid. These new orders are just right for you. They incorporate your fine skill at improvising. They even allow for the kind of overreaching so typical of you. I believe you will do well."

Before Aidan could respond, Kael Pershaw had vanished through the doorway. He shuddered again. For all Pershaw's praise, any visit from him still felt like a visit from the lord of death.

A few minutes later, Horse appeared with the news that the Falcon Guards were assembled and awaiting their commander in the 'Mech bay.

Entering the bay, Aidan saw that the new Star Captain, Joanna, had been addressing the Guards. The eyes of many warriors showed excitement and anticipation, a shuffling of feet indicating their eagerness to mount their 'Mechs and begin immediately to meet the Com Guards in battle.

Aidan took his place before them to give his troops their new orders. "You see, Khan Chistu believes again in the Falcon Guards. We must be worthy of that confidence. I once heard of some ancient Terran legends, stories in which a hero must redeem himself after failing in some way. In every legend the hero wins that redemption through valorous actions. Now the Falcon Guards have such an opportunity to redeem the disgrace of Twycross or to erase any stains in our codexes. And it is on the battlefields of Tukayyid that we will do so. Those of us who are here simply because we are older warriors can renew our youth. Those of us whose characters have made us seem unClanlike, *chalcas,* can show that we are, after all, of the Clan. I tell you now that we are ready. The Jade Falcons are ready and we are the best of the Jade Falcons, *quiaff?*"

"Aff," the warriors shouted, almost in unison.

Horse, standing near Aidan, leaned toward Joanna. "Did you notice?" he whispered. "He is all three categories of the warriors he mentioned. His must be one of the strangest codexes in Clan history. He has been accused of being *chalcas.* He is reaching the age when warriors are considered old and useless."

Joanna, older than Aidan, an old warrior herself, sneered at Horse. "Shut up, warrior. Your commander is speaking."

Hearing the affirmation from these eager warriors, Aidan decided to say no more. He had learned that when the bid was right, one need bid no further.

The ceremony broke up after Joanna, acting as Loremaster for the unit, led them in some traditional Clan rituals. Aidan walked to the observation post from which he would supervise the descent of Trinary Alpha to the surface of Tukayyid, where its mission was to establish a secure landing zone so that the DropShip could transport the rest of the Falcon Guards to the battlefield.

MechWarrior Diana touched his arm. "If so many of the Falcon Guards are here because they are aged, insubordinate, or misfit, then why am I here?" she asked. "I am young, loyal, a good Clan warrior. Why am I here?"

Aidan nearly smiled at her. Perhaps it was her resemblance to Marthe, perhaps it was the sympathy he felt for her warrior style. Whatever it was, Aidan felt right about this young woman. It was not a sexual feeling, but much more like the bond between him and his old friend, Horse.

"Why am I here?" she asked again.

"Because I want you here," he said and walked away.

Diana looked after him. Aidan could not know that she felt for him much the same as he did for her. In that instant all her doubts about him faded. Now she felt right about him. Diana felt right about her father.

22

In final assault orbit the Jade Falcon DropShip *Raptor* sped through the blackness of space. Aboard her, Star Colonel Aidan Pryde looked out the observation port and surveyed the planet where the fate of the Clans' return to the Inner Sphere would be decided, the planet Tukayyid.

In the officer briefings he had learned that Tukayyid was primarily an agricultural world. Orbital recon sweeps displayed rich fields intricately patterned with varying crops, dense orchards of fruit trees, mountainsides covered with wild berries. Well, neither the Clans nor ComStar would lose the battle because of hunger, that was for certain.

The *Raptor* now moved from the sunlit day side to the shrouded night side of Tukayyid, the site of the Falcon Guards landing zone. Meteorological reports indicated that the ground temperature was pleasant, a comfortable 38 degrees C. Aidan could imagine himself standing on one of the rich fields, cooled by a gentle breeze and smelling the grain-scented air. Part of him thought it might be pleasant to shuck off the shell of war and find peace in a pastoral kind of life. Though he had not the slightest interest in the work of farming, the peacefulness of the image was what fed his fantasies of a life in which the machines of war would pass by overhead without touching his countryside.

But Aidan could not remain long in mere daydreams. He knew how unsuited he would be to a pastoral existence. When he tried to imagine himself milking whatever creatures might need it on this planet, the image was so absurd that the longing for the quiet life deserted him like a stray animal striking out on its own.

Almost at the same moment, Horse came up beside him. "The DropShip commander reports that the pathfinding Trinary will begin launch operations in two minutes. Joanna's Trinary reports that they are secure in their pods and ready. Do you wish to oversee the drop?"

"I will watch the descent of Joanna's Trinary, but she will have operational control of both the drop and the landing of the *Raptor.* Why do you smile, Horse?"

"Your delegation of duties. I like it."

"You get older, you learn."

"You get older, you die, too. Either way, there is a mighty accomplishment."

Aidan shook his head. "I should never have allowed you access to my books. You are showing a dangerous fondness for epigrammatic speech."

While they spoke, a rumble began to reverberate through the floors of the DropShip as the fifteen BattleMechs of Joanna's Trinary were launched into space. He watched the ablative cocoons containing 'Mechs and their pilots descend from the *Raptor* and enter Tukayyid's atmosphere. The drop had a certain beauty to it, especially in the darkness. What little light there was reflected off the underside of the *Raptor* as its main engine continued to burn to allow it to follow the flashes of light that was Alpha Trinary. In fact, an uninformed observer on the ground might have mistaken the flashes for flickering stars instead of the potent Stars they actually were. More flashes came from the several squadrons of aerospace fighters that darted, it seemed, from point to point in a precise pattern—keeping a close guard on the descending pods. Within a minute's time Aidan had lost sight of the Trinary. Within ten Joanna reported.

"Falcon Guard Trinary Alpha has landed, sir. Area is secured, and marker beacons are up. Your orders."

Aidan could feel the *Raptor* buffet a bit as it entered the thick lower atmosphere of Tukayyid.

"Star Captain Joanna, maintain security around the landing zone. After the *Raptor* has landed, your orders are to supervise the offloading of the Cluster. Assemble them in Sector VI-C, and I will join you there."

"Yes, sir. Bravo and Charlie Stars, I want a three-kilometer security zone set up around the LZ. Bravo, prepare to assist in disembarking the incoming BattleMechs. I will transmit deployment patterns shortly.''

Knowing the landing was in good hands, Aidan ordered Horse to his 'Mech in the hold of the ship. Aidan walked alone to his machine.

Entering the *Raptor*'s 'Mech bay, Aidan approached his own 'Mech, his *Timber Wolf*. He slowly scrutinized the BattleMech, his attention falling for a moment on its large swooping-falcon insignia. He had ordered that the design be repainted to add an almost luminescent green to the fierce gaze of the falcon's eyes. Its lines had been streamlined, too, according to his orders. The silver paint on the sword the falcon held between its sharp-clawed talons was also designed to gleam. The same image had been duplicated in cloth patches on all the Falcon Guard uniforms.

Aidan liked the falcon's new look. The legendary bird was revived, like the Falcon Guards themselves. He wanted every Com Guard warrior who went down to go with the falcon image in his mind. He wanted survivors to talk about the image as they limped off the battlefield. He wanted the image of the swooping falcon to represent the combat skills of the Falcon Guards. It was a large order, he knew, but he was more and more confident that the Falcon Guards would show their mettle in the battle that loomed so near.

Aidan thought of how Marthe had called him the jade phoenix after his final Bloodright Trial. She had been trying to say that, like the mythical bird, Aidan kept falling into the fires of failure, then reemerging in strength, a new creature who soared high for a long while before falling again.

''You see,'' she had said, ''the mythical phoenix had only one chance to rise from the flames; it seems that you, the jade phoenix, continually fall into the flames and reemerge. You failed in your Trial of Position, then were renewed as a freeborn who succeeded. You received poor and insulting assignments, then proved your worth in the Glory Station battle, then you became the phoenix again here in the Trial of Bloodright. Who knows how many times you can fly out from that mythic conflagration?''

What would she say to his new jade phoenix revival?

Perhaps Aidan would find out, for Marthe would be commanding one of the Jade Falcon Clusters on Tukayyid.

With that thought in mind, he let the howdah carry him up to the *Timber Wolf*'s cockpit, where he relieved the tech. Settling into the command couch, easing the neurohelmet onto his head, testing the controls, looking out the viewport at the darkened 'Mech bay and the rest of the silent Falcon Guard BattleMechs, Aidan felt as if everything in his life were right. No jinxed *Timber Wolf* could prevent another rise of the jade phoenix.

= 23 =

The Falcon Guards were deployed for an advance across a wide expanse of flatland free of the strange thorny grasses that covered much of Prezno Plain. Aidan was impressed, never in memory having seen a BattleMech mustering as clean-lined and militarily correct as this one. Though Summer Mandaka's death had been unfortunate and wasteful, it had given him the opportunity to reassign Joanna to the Cluster, something he had intended to do from the moment he took command of the Falcon Guards. The job she had accomplished in shaping up the Falcon Guards in so little time was probably just short of a miracle.

After years as a warrior who sometimes forgot that he was not alone in the field, Aidan had finally learned that delegation was the key to command. The thought made him smile inwardly. The young Aidan would never have considered assigning someone else to conduct training. He would have done it himself—and likely have been less successful. Joanna, whose natural antipathy toward almost everyone she met kept her from becoming entangled in inconvenient alliances, could stir up experienced warriors with the same methods she had used to turn cadets into warriors.

He recalled his own cadet days. Back then, how many times he would gladly have murdered Joanna in her sleep had he been given the chance. Joanna never let up or relented. And the cadets she rode the hardest and for whom she reserved her most priceless invective were the ones with the best chance of succeeding.

The 'Mech Stars were lined up in two echelons, the advance guard and the main body. The mixed 'Mech and

Elemental Trinary Delta was in front, dispersed as skirmishers. Next came the Stars of Trinary Alpha, Bravo, and Charlie, formed up as a column with the single Nova Star of Trinary Echo, whose remaining Elementals were arranged in Star formation on each of the column's flanks. To the rear of the main column was the one remaining Star of Trinary Alpha 'Mechs, commanded by Star Captain Joanna. With her were the four 'Mechs of Aidan's Falcon Guard Command. In the darkness of the plain, the Elementals were like tall stalks of grass rising around the feet of the assembled 'Mechs. All told, 60 Battle-Mechs and 150 Elementals waited for Aidan to give the order to advance.

Their objective cities were Olalla and Humptulips, and they would begin their march toward them the moment the rest of the Jade Falcon Clusters and the command group had formed up. The Clan Command Center had planned a rather straightforward march to the Prezno River, where they expected to engage the Com Guards. Beyond the river were the two cities that would decide the battle, Olalla about twenty kilometers to the north-east, Humptulips a few kilometers northwest of the river.

The operation looked simple enough on the battle charts and plans, the kind of direct engagement the Clans favored. Yet Aidan knew that the Inner Sphere forces had at times won battles against the Clans precisely because they were specialists at indirect engagement. They could employ the kind of sly, tricky strategies that Clan warriors scorned and therefore did not expect. Yet in the battle for Glory Station, Aidan had borrowed the same kind of hit-and-run tactics that Clan warriors usually considered dishonorable, and they had won the day. It may have been just such an improvisation that had persuaded Khan Chistu to give Aidan and the Falcon Guards free reign in the coming battle. Aidan's success with deceptive tactics, especially when the odds were hopelessly against him, was unusual among Clan commanders.

It was time to join his Cluster. Leaning slightly toward his headphone, and shaping its flexible metal cord to draw the mike closer to his mouth, he radioed Joanna. "Relieving you, Star Captain," he said.

"Sir, your transmission was disrupted. Some kind of static. Adjust. Repeat."

Aidan touched the microphone. Twisting the head, he tightened it. "Any better, Star Captain?"

"Aff. No glitches."

"I am taking command of the Guards."

"Roger, Star Colonel."

Aidan began his *Timber Wolf* moving forward. Was he mistaken, or did he detect a small, almost infinitesimal, delay in the response of the 'Mech's right leg when he depressed the right-foot pedal to turn the 'Mech toward the command lineup? Probably his imagination, he thought.

Coming up beside Joanna and her *Mad Dog,* he ordered everyone to review the terrain between here and the Prezno River on their primary screens. When he punched up his own data, however, the logistical charts came onscreen instead.

"Is something wrong, Star Colonel?" Joanna asked.

"I must have entered the wrong code." He punched the code once more. "There, that is better."

As he instructed his Cluster on the terrain, reviewing combat opportunities and ambush threats, the entire left side of the primary-screen image flashed on and off in an irregular rhythm. The distortion did not interfere with his briefing, but it made him uneasy.

After the briefing, Aidan began a normal checkoff on all controls. Nothing unusual until he pressed the button to display his armor status on his secondary screen. What he saw made Aidan draw in his breath so sharply that Joanna must have heard him over the commline.

"Is everything all right, Star Colonel?" Joanna asked again.

"Everything except that my display is saying that most of my torso armor has been blasted away. Red spots all over the chest and flashing. I may be down before we proceed from muster. Let me check again." When he touched the button once more, the onscreen information showed the proper prebattle armor configurations. "All right. My 'Mech is still functional, after all."

"It is that *Timber Wolf.*" Horse broke in. "The jinx. I told you about it."

"What is wrong with the commander's *Timber Wolf?*" Joanna asked.

Aidan did not let Horse explain about the legends attached to this 'Mech that had changed pilots so many times in recent years.

"That is all superstition," he said abruptly. "And this is no time for talk of tales and legends. Any 'Mech can have a glitch or two, and these are probably not even glitches. I am a bit eager for battle, that is all. My fingers hurry too much. The techs have checked out this 'Mech without finding anything wrong. It will be fine once we get into battle. Now, let us check the internal-damage screen."

As the rest of the checkoff went without a hitch, Aidan wondered if there was something to what Horse said about the bad luck this BattleMech could bring. On the other hand, how could it bring him luck any worse than he had already experienced in his career as a Clan warrior? Its defects, if they could be called that, were merely mechanical. No MechWarrior worth his salt was fazed by mechanical defects. In a BattleMech, the pilot had either an alternate control or configuration for any malfunctioning unit.

It was foolishness to attribute the *Timber Wolf*'s mechanical oddities to some eerie expression of the 'Mech's personality. 'Mechs had only what their pilots gave them. And, Aidan vowed, he would get this one under control if it killed him. Then he shuddered at his own thought. What a weird idea—as if a 'Mech could turn on its pilot. He had to purge such superstitions. There was no point to them, especially with an important battle waiting to be fought.

The city of Olalla, or at least those parts of it for which Aidan had been able to obtain intelligence, wavered on his main screen. This time it was not a 'Mech deficiency; the image was wavering on the screens of all the Falcon Guard pilots. The data was insufficient, creating gaps that in turn made the image unsteady. Pieces of the city seemed to want to close with other sections, as if the computer denied the missing parts. The projection for Humptulips was even less informative.

All briefings complete, the Falcon Guards could only sit and wait for the operation to begin. The last Drop-Ships had deposited their valuable cargo onto Prezno Plain, and all battle Clusters were assembled. Even the night seemed in readiness, darker than before. Yet the command to move did not come.

"Is there some sign of battle activity?" Joanna asked. "Is that why we are standing here like metal vegetables?"

"I have been informed of no enemy activity," Aidan said. "None of my sensors indicate activity of any kind. I think we merely await the order from Galaxy Commander Mar Helmer."

"I hope it comes before moss starts to grow up the legs of my 'Mech."

Aidan chose not to respond, not to express his worries. He had been in on all the command conferences. His superiors had rejected his battle-strategy proposal for its high element of risk. He did not mind that, yet it did seem that the Clan's high command had become surprisingly cautious. He believed they were placing too much emphasis on the Jade Falcons' superior recon capabilities.

Aidan knew that Prezno Plain offered few hiding places, while the rest of the battle terrain consisted of a river and then more relative flatland leading to the two objective cities. Reconnaissance did not seem truly vital to the campaign.

Then all further speculation became pointless. The order came for the Falcon Guards to move forward.

Aidan turned control over to Star Captain Joanna, who would coordinate the style and rhythm of the march. He had already instructed the Falcon Guards that he expected them to move in a controlled and even manner. The skirmishing 'Mechs and Elementals of the advance guard were to move swiftly forward to find, contact, and fix in place any ComStar units to their front. The mainbody 'Mechs were assigned interlocking fire zones to the flanks, to cover any potential ambush sites as well as to engage any ComStar forces that the advance guard encountered.

When Aidan had submitted his marching orders to Star Captain Joanna, she gave him a rare half-smile. "You have changed, Aidan Pryde. Once you were virtually a rebel, and now you have become nearly a martinet. Not quite, though. You still stitch your patches too high on your uniform."

Aidan shook his head. "I am but a Clan warrior, Star Captain Joanna."

"No, it is more than that."

He raised his brows interrogatively.

"It is not only the taint from the Falcon Guards that you wish to remove. You wish to remove the taint from Aidan Pryde. I respect your goal, but let us hope that this new caution does not make you stay your hand at a key moment."

"What kind of key moment?"

"Truthfully, I do not know *what* I mean. I am just trying to work out the new Aidan Pryde, even as I work out the new Falcon Guards. A formidable task, in either case."

It astonished Aidan to think that Joanna had spoken to him of his own caution, especially now that he was critical of the same tendency he perceived in his superiors.

As he took his rightful position at the head of the Falcon Guards, he wondered if there was something to what Joanna had said. It was true that he had craved this command, craved to be a commander on the front, craved to become a Clan warrior glorious enough to contribute his genes to the gene pool. He felt a definite thrill at the thought of his genes spawning generations of sibkos. He had sacrificed much to win this chance. Had he given up too much? Then, in typical Clan warrior fashion, in typical Aidan Pryde fashion, he shrugged off such thoughts in the face of more real concerns.

"Ready to move out, Star Colonel," Joanna informed him. He gave the command to march.

Once on the move, Aidan called up a visual from the small camera he had set on the *Timber Wolf*'s shoulders. Rotating it to capture a view of his warriors behind him, he brought the image as much into focus as possible, adding the infrared component to get more detail.

The Falcon Guards were spread across the landscape, the warriors strictly maintaining the space between themselves. Aidan could, in fact, eavesdrop on Joanna's regulating of the march. He could hear her tell a *Stormcrow* pilot to recalibrate his leg progress, then order a pilot in a *Summoner* to straighten the 'Mech's back because it was five degrees off angle and created a dead zone in the fire pattern of this Star. A *Warhawk* pilot, perhaps even MechWarrior Diana, was told to close the gap with another BattleMech. Joanna never stopped talking, never stopped revising the line, pattern, and rhythm of march.

All in all, the Falcon Guard advance was impressive, the massive fighting machines creating a pattern suggesting not only discipline but controlled force and power. It was exactly the look Aidan had wanted to achieve. That the other Jade Falcon units might not see it was irrelevant. Aidan had imposed all the restrictions to bring a pride to the unit itself. Already he had heard some talk that the Falcon Guards should take the name of "Pryde's Pride." Though he did not generally favor nicknames for fighting units, Aidan knew he would not block adoption of this name.

Satisfied, perhaps too satisfied, Aidan pressed his BattleMech forward. Whether it was his own loss of rhythm or some further problem with the *Timber Wolf* itself, the 'Mech misstepped slightly. Not much. An observer would only have seen the right leg jut ever so slightly to the side, but Aidan could have sworn he heard a crackle of sound when the misstep occurred.

"The commander has to stay in line, too," Horse commented. "What happened?"

"I do not know, but I am almost certain it was not due to anything I did."

"Well, stay on your feet. I may not have time to pick you up if you fall."

Aidan was glad Horse's joking only came over their private channel. It would never do for the rest of the Guards to hear such remarks.

Then all this was forgotten when he heard the first reports of an attack on another Jade Falcon unit. Calling up a visual on his primary screen, he scanned the immediate sectors of Prezno Plain. To the far left he saw flashes of fire where some Jade Falcons were involved in a skirmish.

═══ 25 ═══

As MechWarrior Faulk, in his *Gargoyle*, closed ranks with Diana's *Warhawk*, she wondered what was bothering Faulk now. The man was a fine pilot whose courage no one could question, but his habit of irritating his commanding officers was how he had happened to draw the dreaded assignment to the new Falcon Guards. There was nothing belligerent about Faulk, nor did he ever utter an insubordinate word. He was, Diana had decided, just nervous. Yet nervousness was rare among Clan warriors, which made his fidgety ways all the more irksome to his compatriots.

"MechWarrior Diana?"

"Yes, Faulk?"

"I thought I spotted something. Over there. To the left."

Aidan had moved the Falcon Guards to the right flank of the Jade Falcon advance on the Prezno River. Joanna's Star, by her choice, had taken an extreme right-flank position and sent the Elementals back to the main body. Joanna had told Diana that she wanted her own warriors there to counter any ambushes. "We have whipped the other Stars into shape, but I still prefer to cover at least one flank myself."

Diana saw only grid lines of geographical topography in her primary-screen scans. The only movement was among a clump of trees, an orchard near the main road they were now following.

"Might Com Guard units be hiding in that orchard?" Faulk said, his voice so tense that Diana imagined his thin body squirming with apprehension in the command couch. She knew Faulk had accumulated a first-rate codex in his years as a warrior and that his fears would not affect his skill, but the idea of him fidgeting in his seat was not comforting.

"The scan shows only an empty orchard, Faulk. Unless the Com Guards are disguised as some kind of native fruit and are hanging from branches ready to spring at us, I do not think we face any special danger there."

Later she would remember her sarcasm, cursing herself for not taking Faulk more seriously.

As they approached the orchard, Diana turned her attention to the area beyond it, seeking other potential threats.

"Does it not seem strange to you, MechWarrior Diana, that we have been on the march for fully an hour and yet have still had no response from the Com Guards?"

The man's apprehension made his voice tremble on every word of more than one syllable.

"Take it easy, Faulk. And, for the sake of Kerensky, we do not need formal address in the field. MechWarrior is a mouthful of a word, *quiaff*?"

"You have not noticed. I always use formal address, MechWarrior Diana."

"And why in the name of all the Clans do you do that, Faulk?"

"Because—"

Diana never learned Faulk's answer, for the peaceful orchard suddenly erupted into quite another scene. Fruit trees seemed to open up and splay outward, and holes in the ground suddenly disgorged a lance of Com Guard BattleMechs. And when they came out, they came out shooting.

From the Jade Falcon command group Aidan got the news of several minor attacks all around the route of march. The command group derived its information from the surveillance provided by high-flying aerofighters, which spotted 'Mechs emerging from the ground in four areas. In each case the Com Guard units had disguised their hiding place via some manufactured but realistic topographical construction. Besides the lance of 'Mechs coming from the fake orchard, others appeared from an apparent silo, a small hillock that was completely fake, a pile of rocks. With the advantage of surprise, the enemy 'Mechs did considerable damage before retreating just as quickly into the night.

Aidan radioed Joanna for a report on the sneak attack involving her Star. "Any BattleMech damage?"

"A few hits," she said. "One BattleMech severely damaged, needs to be taken back for repair. One pilot down."

Faulk's *Gargoyle* took the first major hit when forty LRMs blazed from a *Bombardier*'s torso and destroyed the *Gargoyle*'s left arm, amputating it messily just as Faulk fired a cluster of SRMs. The missiles landed harmlessly, gouging holes in the ground and exploding in front of the *Bombardier*. Meanwhile, the Com Guard 'Mech rushed onward toward Faulk's 'Mech, burning away large chunks of the *Gargoyle*'s ferro-fibrous armor as it went.

Diana tried to cut off the *Bombardier,* but a *Centurion* blocked her path. Looking like someone wielding a thick pipe in one hand, the *Centurion* fired the pipe, an LB-10X, at her. Much of the fragmented submunitions fell harmlessly around her, the hits only minimal. Diana returned fire with a blast from her extended-range PPC, knocking out the *Centurion*'s center-torso medium laser.

Joanna rushed her *Mad Dog* into the fray, wanting to go after the *Centurion* personally. Firing from a distance were the other two MechWarriors of Alpha Striker, Khastis and Leema. When Khastis' *Hellbringer* hit an *Enforcer* with a cluster of SRMs, the enemy pilot immediately engaged his 'Mech's jump jets and leaped away from the action.

The *Bombardier* was meanwhile raining more damage down on Faulk's *Gargoyle*. With torso bent forward, the Com Guard 'Mech ran swiftly at the *Gargoyle,* its short-range missiles joining the pillars of fire laid by their larger cousins. The *Gargoyle,* disconcerted by the speed of its foe, could not effectively return fire, especially with its left arm gone.

Faulk ejected, but he chose the wrong moment. His trajectory took him through a stream of laser fire not even aimed at him. It sliced away part of the seat and severed Faulk's right leg along with it. Even from where they sat in their cockpits, the other pilots in his Star heard his sudden, earsplitting scream.

The Com Guard 'Mechs, apparently satisfied with the outcome of their ambush, abruptly ceased their attack and withdrew into the darkness. Diana started to pursue, but Joanna ordered her back.

"I want at them," Diana protested angrily.

"It would be a waste of effort," Joanna said. "Those 'Mechs are faster than yours, and none were damaged enough to be picked off as a stray lagging behind. It was one of their hit-and-run operations. The cowards. Filthy freebirth cowards!"

To Diana the freebirth epithet seemed empty when applied to this enemy, who, after all, came from a culture where none of the births were genetically engineered. As she spent more time among the trueborns, Diana had begun to resent their casual rejection of everything freeborn. Freeborn or not, she was a good warrior. Indeed, many of the trueborns in the new Falcon Guards could not claim to have distinguished themselves in past combat.

Horse had told her many horror stories from his life as a freeborn, and she realized she was fortunate. Perhaps because of the invasion or because of her considerable skill as a warrior, Diana was not treated much different than if she were a trueborn.

She could not resolve her feelings about her dual role in this Jade Falcon unit. On one hand, she wanted to show that a freeborn was equal to any trueborn; on the other, she wanted to forget she was a freeborn and just do her job. When she expressed these feelings to Horse, he pondered a moment, then said, "Seems to me you get your armor chipped off either way. Either way you admit shame at being freeborn. Who says trueborn is better just because someone picks out their genes and stirs them up in some vat? Then again, who am I to talk? I'm just one of those lousy freebirths, you know." Diana heard the sarcasm, but the two never found time to finish the conversation.

Dismounting from her 'Mech, Diana searched the nearby field for Faulk. By the time she found him, a medic unit was already ministering to him. His face twisted in grimaces of pain, and she saw that the laser had sheared off his leg neatly just below the hip. This battle was over for Faulk almost before it had begun. He would be fitted for a prosthetic leg, however, and there would be other battles, other wars. Just not Tukayyid.

Joanna came up beside her.

"A clean hit," she said. Faulk, seeing his formidable commanding officer, managed to choke back his moans.

"Yes," Diana said. "I pity him."

"Oh? An odd reaction from a warrior. Are we not supposed to be pitiless?"

"Perhaps you are, Star Captain Joanna. I am freeborn. We are . . . peculiar."

"You certainly are. But I am glad to have you in my Star, Diana."

Joanna walked away before Diana could answer. What a queer bird Joanna was becoming, Diana thought, an even rarer kind of falcon perhaps.

When Faulk was sedated but conscious, Diana knelt down beside him. "Sorry," she said.

"For what? You did nothing, MechWarrior Diana."

"I did not heed your caution, Faulk. You were right about the orchard."

He shook his head. "No, that was coincidence. I feel the same anxiety about every dark patch I pass. Something always seems to be lurking in my mind. This time it was really there. Coincidence, MechWarrior Diana."

"If you say so. Be well, Faulk. I expect to fight beside you again some day."

Faulk seemed confused by what she said, and his lids fluttered until he could no longer hold them open. Soon he was asleep, then loaded into a med hovercraft and taken away.

Aidan felt helpless. Detecting something amiss, Horse asked his old friend what was wrong.

"It is command. They have ordered no retaliation, not even a pursuit of those Com Guard cowards. Worst yet, Khan Chistu has directly ordered the Falcon Guards to maintain its position. He will not yet release us to operate independently."

"Those Com Guards were in swift 'Mechs, and we have not made contact with any major Com Star units. Pursuit would have been useless and the Guards cannot break through an enemy that is not there, *quiaff*?"

"I suppose so. But the implications of it all are what anger me most. They are as cautious in this matter as with the whole campaign. We move ahead slowly, slower than we have to. We use the dead of night for cover.

When has a Clan unit ever hidden in the night? I tell you, Horse, something has changed in the Jade Falcon leadership, perhaps in the entire Clan command structure.''

"What has changed, Aidan?"

"There is a word in the old books we read, Horse. Subtlety. You know what it means. Well, we are being subtle. Imagine, the Clans being subtle in combat or anywhere else. We are a fearless people. Have not Clansmen always preferred the direct, even the brutal, approach? If we did use tricks, we accomplished them in an open field, with no concealment. Now our strategy is more like our enemy's. Eventually, we will be hiding behind disguised topography before springing out.''

"Let us hope not. So you think subtlety—if that is the right word—is the wrong approach?''

"I simply do not know. All I know is how unClanlike it seems.''

Horse laughed quietly, but the sound came distinctly over the commlink.

"What amuses you, Horse?''

"I was thinking back to when first we met. You were not one to worry over whether something was Clanlike or not. UnAidanlike maybe, but not—''

"That is enough, MechWarrior Horse.''

"Yes, sir.''

The march toward the Prezno River slowed even more. Other Com Guard units attacked and did some damage, but no more Jade Falcon BattleMechs went down. However, the Jade Falcon lines were spread thinner, as the Falcon command group ordered several Elemental units to patrol the flanks.

Aidan began to feel uneasy. It made no sense that the Clan forces were not sweeping easily to victory on Tukayyid. How had the previously arrived Clans lost so many encounters? Events were not supposed to turn out like this. The Clans had a cause, a just cause, an almost sacred dream. If the Star League was to be restored, it was only just that the Clans should already have arrived on Terra. Then a strange idea struck him. Perhaps, Aidan thought, it was not justice they were dealing with, but fate.

26

The Falcon command group called a halt to the march ten kilometers from the Prezno River, calling all Cluster commanders to a nearby grove for a war council. The MechWarriors remained in place with their 'Mechs, waiting for rations to be brought them by the field techs.

A thin line of dawn outlined the mountains in the distance as Aidan's VTOL descended to the landing area just outside the grove. He would have liked to take the battle into the mountains, for something about rough terrain appealed to him. The relatively uncomplicated flatland of Prezno Plain seemed favorable only to the defender, especially with the Com Guards' propensity for sneak attacks and ambushes. The enemy had not actually done much damage since the maiming of Faulk, but they had disconcerted the Jade Falcon forces.

What we need now is an all-out assault, Aidan thought. Something that would bind all the Jade Falcon units together. Something that would shock the command group and Khan Chistu out of their ridiculous caution.

The argument was already joined when Aidan entered the war council. Nobody paid him much attention, and being commander of the Falcon Guards would prevent him from having the equal voice in council to which he was entitled. He accepted a bowl of rations from a tech, and began to pick at the meal of mostly vegetables and fruits from Tukayyid as he listened to the discussion.

The issue under debate was whether to give artillery cover to the heavy OmniMechs as they mounted an assault on the two bridges over the Prezno River. Beyond the bridges, which were apparently being held by small units from the Third Com Guard Army and the Eleventh

Com Guards, were the two cities that were the Jade Falcons' assigned objectives. Not only were the Cluster commanders arguing over the issue of artillery cover, they were also bickering about how much ammunition to use.

Bored with listening to the various commanders throwing facts and figures at one another, Aidan glanced around the grove. Like him, most of the Jade Falcon officers were silently watching and listening. Some, however, showed by their body movements and sounds of approval or disapproval which side they endorsed. On the fringes of the grove, a few warriors were moving around nervously, eager to get back to their BattleMechs and the battle.

"Your face shows a sour expression, Aidan Pryde," said a voice from behind him. Recognizing the voice at once, Aidan did not turn around immediately. It was Marthe Pryde speaking. Just hearing her set off vivid flashes of memory, particularly of times in the sibko when she used to speak in just this gentle voice. They had talked of so many things in those long ago days, of falcons in the air, pilots in their BattleMechs, fate in their lives.

He turned to see Marthe standing calmly. In one hand, she was holding a thin branch. With the other hand she was methodically pulling off the few spiky leaves still attached to the bark. But she did it absentmindedly, for her eyes were on him.

"I was not aware I looked—what did you say?—sour?"

"Well, most people cannot read your face as I can, the way I learned back in the sibko."

"I thought you had rejected all memory of the sibko."

"What makes you think that?"

"Something you told me once about leaving sibko days behind."

Marthe nodded. "Perhaps I did say that. I do not always speak well." She tested the stick, which she had stripped of leaves, bending it, letting it go, examining its resilience. "What is your opinion of our Tukayyid campaign so far?"

"It has been too cautious, too slow. We should be on the other side of Prezno River by now, but instead we're sitting in some grove discussing how to get there or how much ammo to use in assaulting the bridges.''

"You do not approve of the strategy debate?"

Aidan felt his hands go involuntarily into fists. "No, I do not *approve*. Not that my approval matters one way or another. They argue like merchants over the price of a bauble. How trivial this is." He inclined his head toward where the heated discussion continued.

"Trivial? I do not think Khan Chistu would like to hear that."

"Someone should tell him."

"Perhaps someone will."

"You have his ear?"

"Sometimes. When I wish it."

"You couple with him?"

"Sometimes. When I want to."

"Not under his orders?"

"I do little under anyone's orders."

"I envy you, Marthe."

"No. I envy you, Aidan Pryde."

She looked away from him, away from the debate. With a whip of one arm, she flung the stick, watched it sail out of the grove, then land near the tail section of one of the VTOLs.

"Marthe, how could *you* envy *me?* You must know of my codex by now. I am one of the tainted ones, in command of a *dezgra* unit, while you, you have ascended to near the top of the Clan Jade Falcon command structure. As you say, the Khan will listen to you."

"But you have become the real Clan warrior, Aidan Pryde. In this campaign, you may choose your own battles, dictate your own fate. And you have more than just the respect of your warriors. They admire you. You know, do you not, that they are calling your unit 'Pryde's Pride'?"

"So I have heard. But the respect of my warriors is no different than what they would grant any commander."

"You are wrong. My Cluster does its duty, to be sure, but no one has named us 'Marthe's Marauders.' But let that go. It is not what I wish to discuss. I am genuinely curious about your opinion of Clan Jade Falcon at present. Tell me as if I were planning an overthrow."

"Are you? Planning an overthrow?"

"Of course not. But tell me. What has prompted that sour look?"

The back of Marthe's left hand rubbed nervously against her trousers. The lines in her forehead were deep, deeper than his. Her mouth had hardened into a thin line, making the triangular shape of her face seem even more geometric. Once they had looked alike. Now the resemblance had diminished. If she resembled anyone, Marthe looked like that young MechWarrior in Joanna's Star, Diana.

"I was thinking back to our cadet days," Aidan said. "Remember when we arrived on Ironhold?"

"Yes. I recall Falconer Joanna giving you a beating, then saying she thought you had a fine chance of testing out and becoming a warrior. I envied you a bit then, too."

"Did you know that Joanna is in my Cluster now?"

"No, I did not. I thought she must be dead."

He told her about how Joanna had drilled the Falcon Guards into a fighting unit.

"You are evading my question, Aidan Pryde. About this meeting and why it seems trivial to you."

"Back when we were cadets, I had so many ideas about what it meant to be a warrior. In my imaginings, a Clan warrior would never be concerned with looking backward."

"I agree. That is how I thought of it, too."

"Then perhaps you also agree that such a Mech-Warrior would not be debating over artillery cover. Such warriors would bid for the right to take those bridges, providing their own artillery cover. For that matter, what BattleMech really needs artillery support?"

"None, really. But there are precedents for considering such tactics in major military campaigns, and for dispensing with bidding after the first *batchall.*"

"Perhaps, but that is more like the Inner Sphere way of thinking. What kind of Star League can the Clans build with Inner Sphere thinking?"

Marthe shrugged. "If it is any consolation, many other Clan officers share your views. Something may be done."

"But is that the Clan way? Is it our way to decide matters through political chicanery? Again, Inner Sphere. The present debate, that is Inner Sphere, too. Is this what a few military losses have done to our natural inclination for warfare?''

"What would you wish then?''

"What do I wish? I do not know. I think I want victory or defeat to depend on the skills of warriors and not on complicated designs made by Clan leaders guessing at the complicated designs of our enemy's leaders.''

"Well, perhaps you are a bit naive about warfare but . . .''

"Naive?''

"Idealistic then.''

"Watch this, Marthe.''

Breaking away from her, he strode toward the center of the grove, where the discussion had degenerated into a series of altercations about how much personnel to commit to the battle for each bridge. Elbowing aside his fellow commanders, Aidan interrupted the debate, shouting, "Dawn is here and there is still argument. Forget artillery cover. Forget how much personnel to assign. I am Star Colonel Aidan Pryde. I bid the Falcon Guard Cluster for the right to take both bridges!''

Khan Vandervahn Chistu held up his left hand for Aidan to hold his tongue. "Star Colonel, I have not authorized bidding for these objectives.''

"Yes, Khan,'' he said, "I understand. Nevertheless the Falcon Guards demand the right to take the Prezno River bridges.''

"Falcon Guards! Hah!'' said an officer standing a few meters away from Aidan. Aidan recognized the scoffing tone that he had heard so often in his life.

He glanced back, saw Marthe scrutinizing him intently. She nodded just perceptibly, a gesture he took as approval. "If there is to be no bidding, then give the assignment to the Falcon Guards, and you can dispense with all this debilitating discussion.''

Screams of protest went up from the other Clan commanders.

"It would bring shame on us to permit the Falcon Guards to lead the Jade Falcons into battle,'' asserted a Star Colonel whom Aidan recognized as a warrior named Senza Oriega. She was said to have one of the most admirable codexes in the entire Jade Falcon Clan.

Others supported her, including Galaxy Commander Mar Helmer. Aidan immediately sensed that he was fighting a losing battle. To them, to the Khan, to Mar Helmer, Aidan's demand was mere bravado. And he did, of course, understand their point of view. It was important who led the Jade Falcons at this point in the campaign. The bridges represented their first major engagement on Tukayyid. Still, there was no need to judge *his* Falcon Guards by the shame brought on the unit by Adler Malthus. Having charged forward with the demand, he could not easily back down.

"If you do not wish to place the Falcon Guards at the head of the bridge attacks, then at least cease this foolish bickering over technicalities. Any Jade Falcon unit may lead the way with proper dignity. We lose time now. Let us end this discussion and go to war!"

Surprisingly, his impassioned rhetoric won approbation from many of the warriors. Some even began to push at one another, on the verge of brawling. Again the Khan raised his hand and demanded quiet.

"Star Colonel Aidan Pryde has spoken well. We must abandon quibbling. It is time to fight!" Turning to Aidan, he said more softly, "I wish to commend you on your leadership of the Falcon Guards, but you can see from the disapprobation of your fellow officers that it is not yet time for the Falcon Guards to lead the charge into battle. That honor goes elsewhere. However, Star Colonel, once contact with the Com Guards is made, your Cluster is authorized to break through at any point possible and head for Olalla. That should be honor enough for your unit even if it does not include being first across the bridges."

Walking back to where Marthe stood, Aidan passed other commanders, some of whom muttered angry taunts at him. He heard the words *dezgra* and *taint* more than once. If the fight for Tukayyid were not so important, Aidan might have demanded several honor duels even before reaching Marthe's side.

"You have not changed so much, I see," said Marthe.

"You refer to my reputation for always overreaching myself?"

"In a way. Perhaps I would say a certain lack of shrewdness. But then, if you had the shrewdness, you might have to adopt some Inner Sphere ways yourself."

Aidan shrugged off any further discussion. Instead, he

said, "Once, Marthe, when we were very young, you claimed to love me. Childish talk, you later told me. You said that we of the Clan did not love. What are your thoughts on the subject now?"

"I have no thoughts on the subject. I can say that what I felt in the sibko is still true. We were close then. We went beyond sibko closeness. We were friends, I think."

"Not exactly a Clan word, either—friends."

"No. But I wish for us to be close always. That is not love perhaps. But it is real."

"I will settle for it, Marthe."

"And perhaps, after the battle, you would spend some time with me in my quarters. Or I could come to yours."

A new surprise. They had not coupled since early in cadet days.

"I would wish that, Marthe.'

"Good. Well-bargained and done."

Dawn had come, and the offensive was now set to begin an hour hence. Watching the council laboriously end its session, the two former sibkin remained silent for awhile, then Marthe spoke.

"War councils and warriors," she said. "The words sound well together, but they do not belong together. Warriors should act, not talk. It is the way of the Clan to avoid waste. We conserve material; we try to conserve lives through bidding the lowest possible force of personnel. But we have no qualms about wasting words, *quiaff*?"

"Aff. Marthe, I fear that the Clans are in danger of losing Tukayyid. And why? Because our numbers and combat abilities came up short? No, I do not believe that. It may be that we had already lost when we agreed to this proxy battle, lost by giving too much respect to the Inner Sphere, to ComStar."

"Respect? I respect no one from the Inner Sphere *or* ComStar."

"And neither do I." He dropped his voice. "But perhaps our leaders do. Perhaps they have been hoodwinked by fancy Inner Sphere *words*. Marthe, we invaded the Inner Sphere. Invaders do battle, take bondsmen, receive *isorla*, leave scars on landscapes. We conquer on our terms. Now, suddenly, we are fighting on *their* terms. It is not right, Marthe. Of that much only am I certain. It is not right. Once the ilKhan agreed to deal with the enemy representative, he compromised the way of the Clan. That is all I know. But I am a loyal Clan warrior and will not fight less fiercely.''

"Would you prefer some kind of revolution? Overthrow?''

"No. Never. That would be Inner Sphere, too, and not Clan.''

"Yes, I agree.''

They were silent for a while. Aidan felt peculiar. He had never expected to find that he and Marthe would be so much alike when they met again. Once he had thought they had grown apart. Though both were plagued with doubts about the conduct of the war, he felt a certain pleasure in their secret alliance.

As the war council began to break up, Marthe and Aidan joined the exodus, stopping when they reached Marthe's hovercraft. She turned toward him, her face partially in shadow.

"What is it, Aidan?'' she asked, seeming puzzled by his expression.

"In this light, you look so much like one of the Falcon Guard warriors—MechWarrior Diana.''

"Perhaps her sibko shared our Mattlov or Pryde gene heritage.''

"She is freeborn.''

"I have never had a child.''

"What a curious thing to say.''

"I know. Clan warriors are rarely parents. Have you ever been?''

"Just the thought of it makes me uneasy. The mere words relating to natural birth make me uncomfortable.''

"If I visit the Falcon Guards, you will show me this MechWarrior, *quiaff*?''

"Aff.''

Marthe began to climb into her hovercraft, then turned back. "I wanted to say that . . . well, I would be proud to enter battle led by the Falcon Guards. By Pryde's Pride.''

Then she was gone, vanished into the darkness of the hovercraft. Aidan walked to his VTOL, along the way hearing further mutterings from Clan commanders. Per-

haps he even heard one of them call the Falcon Guards
"Pryde's Denied."

Diana watched her father leave the VTOL and stride
to the Guard command post. She had accompanied him
during the ride to the Command Group in order to get a
replacement circuit board for her 'Mech. Watching the
exchange between Aidan and Marthe Pryde, she had not
been sure what to think about it.

Although she strove to be a true Clan warrior, it was
still difficult to purge some of her village ways. Coupling
among the lower castes was much less casual than among
Clan warriors, and a taboo existed against sexual contact
between members of the same family. Yet, Clan warriors, members of the same genetic line, the same sibko,
coupled easily and often. She did not begrudge her father
the comfort of sex, but it made her uneasy to think he
might do it with a sibkin.

Then it struck her that she, after all, was the offspring
of Aidan and another member of his sibko, Peri. That
had never seemed significant or ominous. But Peri was
her mother, and Diana had grown up admiring her,
though she was often absent. She recalled Peri once telling her that words for the parent-child relation were
nearly obscene in the sibko, which was why Diana did
not call her "mother." Peri had been raised to believe
the word forbidden, the very concept of parenthood
anathema. Though she had willingly become a parent,
abandoning birth control in order to conceive a child by
Aidan, she had gradually taught her daughter to call her
Peri instead of mother.

"You look somewhat pensive this evening, Mech-
Warrior Diana."

She turned and saw that it was Elemental Star Commander Selima of the First Delta Elemental Star. He was
a tall, dark-skinned man with prominent cheekbones and
a gentle mouth. The tallest of all the Falcon Guard Elementals, he towered over Diana, who was tall for a
MechWarrior. She had always liked him. He was not
gruff or rude like so many Elementals, and seemed capable of serious thought, another contrast to most Elementals. She had never seen him engage in horseplay

with other members of his sub-caste. Generally, he held himself aloof.

"You will not report me for thinking on duty, will you, Star Commander Selima?"

"No. I saw no dereliction. My comment was directed to the expression on your face. You were thinking of something that had meaning for you."

"In a way. But it is a private thought."

"Aahhh. I had not meant to intrude."

"You did not intrude. I am glad you are diverting me from it."

"A pleasure. You are a special MechWarrior, Diana."

"Why do you say that?"

"Because you are complicated. Not many warriors are complicated."

"I am freeborn."

"That may explain it."

"You do not find warriors to be complicated? Do you not think our Star Colonel, for example, complicated?"

"Yes, I do. But like you, he is different. Examine his codex. Not the typical military record."

They talked a while longer. Before Selima left, Diana said to him, "You have not commented on my physical appearance, Selima. Men usually do."

"Elemental men?"

"Well, no, not Elemental men."

"There you have it. We do not even find each other beautiful. We would hate it if we did."

"I hate it, and I am not Elemental."

"You, MechWarrior Diana, are a genetic misfit," he said with a smile that made his words sound complimentary. "And now I bid you good night."

The tall Elemental loped away gracefully, returning to his Star's assembly area.

Diana was suddenly unhappy. This night, which should have been filled with the sound and fury of battle, was filled with words instead. Walking quickly and then breaking into a run, she went toward her BattleMech to prepare for the attack. Well, she thought, at least for now the words will stop.

27

Prezno Plain came to an abrupt end, reminding Aidan of the ancient Terran belief that the world was flat and people would drop off the edge when they reached the end of it. What a piece of strategy that might have been, Aidan thought, staring at the view of the plain's end on his primary screen. What if ComStar had been able to arrange for a flat world so that the Clans would gallop right off its edge? The image was fanciful yet impressive—hordes of Clansmen in their gleaming BattleMechs running off the edge and vanishing into the vacuum of space. He shut his eyes for a moment and saw a vision of hundreds of 'Mechs disappearing into the void.

Horse's voice coming suddenly over their private channel broke Aidan's reverie. "The bridges are in sight, and the forces on Robyn's Crossing have fired on the Twelfth Falcon Cluster. The battle is engaged, sir."

The Twelfth had won the honor of leading the assault on the bridge. Knowing that it had been Mar Helmer's Cluster when he was a Star Colonel, Aidan concluded that politics must have been involved in the choice. That made him angry, for he believed the position should have been open to bidding among all the Jade Falcon contingents, including the Falcon Guards. Another Cluster, the Seventh Falcons, was assigned the other bridge, Plough Bridge. According to Horse, the Seventh had just reached its objective, and no battle had yet begun there.

Until now, both bridges had been out of sight of the oncoming Jade Falcons because they were in a valley. The access to each was down a rocky slope. Recon had established that BattleMechs could not descend without becoming sitting ducks for the bridge forces, so jump-capable 'Mechs had taken the forefront. They leaped into the valley and returned the fusillades of the ComStar 'Mechs.

Aidan monitored some of the fighting at Robyn's Crossing on his primary screen, the visuals rendered pale by the intense light of Tukayyid's sun. For a moment the combat was at a stalemate. At Robyn's Crossing, a fierce defense by the ComStar 'Mechs in front of and on the bridge itself pressed the Twelfth back. Missile fire exploded one Jade Falcon BattleMech, then another was severely damaged, leaving half its right hip detached and hanging. Aidan cursed as he watched the commander of the Twelfth order a retreat back to the foot of the slope to cover the descent of the BattleMechs without jump capacity.

"Bad move, huh?" Horse said. "I agree."

"She has them bunched together so much that she is practically offering the Com Guards target practice."

"We are lucky this is a private channel."

"I would say that to Khan Chistu himself."

Horse sighed. "Yes, you would."

They continued to watch, all the while proceeding toward the battle site. Then Aidan spoke. "Well, it is time."

"What do you mean?"

"Time for us to follow our orders. Once the battle is joined, we are to break through, remember? We are going to help the Twelfth take that bridge."

"You have my enthusiastic approval."

Aidan opened the commline and ordered the Falcon Guards to press forward at the best unit speed. As the unit passed up two other Clusters, they maintained a precision formation that must have been the envy of their fellow Jade Falcons even as many of them were probably cursing every Falcon Guard who had ever existed and the sibkos that spawned them.

As befitted a Clan commander, Aidan Pryde led the way in his *Timber Wolf* to the crest of the slope leading down to Robyn's Crossing. He slowed his BattleMech when he saw the crest, the edge of this particular world, then paced his 'Mech into a graceful, loping walk. Back in the DropShip he had ordered his techs to equip his

Timber Wolf with jump jet modules. That meant sacrificing his machine guns and some lasers normally mounted in his torso, but he was too used to jumping in the *Summoner,* his former 'Mech. He could not give it up now just because jump jets were not a standard feature on a *Timber Wolf.*

The 'Mechs of Horse and Margo, another of his Falcon Guard Command MechWarriors, also had jump ability. They stayed with their commander, a couple of 'Mech paces behind, as he pushed his *Timber Wolf* forward. At the very crest of the hill Aidan engaged his jump jets and glided upward, reaching a quick zenith, then coming down, ahead of the BattleMechs of the Twelfth Falcon Cluster, and closer to Robyn's Crossing than any Jade Falcon BattleMech had yet come.

Descending, Aidan blasted away at the Com Guard 'Mechs defending the head of the bridge. They had not been expecting a BattleMech assault from the sky, which gave Aidan and his pair of cohorts an immediate and significant advantage. An edge at the edge of the world, Aidan thought.

He used his angle to blast away at the head of a heavy BattleMech that his secondary screen identified as a type called a *Thug.* Targeting his large lasers, he made a direct and fatal hit against the head of the *Thug,* no doubt ending the life of its pilot. He did not have time to watch the 'Mech stagger backward against a bridge stanchion, then plunge into the deep waters of the churning Prezno River. The splash it made was impressive, the waters rising up onto the bridge surface leaving puddles along its roadway.

Aidan's attention was on another ComStar 'Mech, a sleek, bigfooted *Sentinel* that was just swinging its autocannon upward to fire at the *Timber Wolf.* Firing over the shoulders of Aidan's 'Mech, MechWarrior Margo, in a light *Mist Lynx,* got a lock onto the center torso of the *Sentinel,* then destroyed it with a set of sleek-arcing missiles. The enemy 'Mech fell to the ground, flames shooting from its chest.

Horse managed to take out a pair of ComStar 'Mechs during his descent, while Aidan gave a ComStar *Rifleman* a limp.

By the time the trio of Clan BattleMechs had landed,

the bridge defense was in disarray. Aidan ordered his group forward, the action prodding the Jade Falcons back at the slope to charge forward.

The ComStar commander apparently decided that the Clan had won this phase, for the surviving enemy 'Mechs began a retreat. They traversed Robyn's Crossing quickly, with only the limping *Rifleman* lagging behind. The bridge was soon clear, an inviting pathway with a few puddles gleaming on its surface, leading to that side of the river where the Jade Falcon Clan objectives awaited.

"There are reports of heavy fighting at Plough Bridge," Horse said. "We are apparently taking the day there."

"Fine. Let us take a little stroll to the other side of Robyn's Crossing, *quiaff*, Horse?"

"Hold it there one minute, Star Colonel Aidan Pryde," said a new voice on the open channel. Aidan recognized the voice immediately from the council in the grove. It was Star Colonel Senza Oriega, the one who had complained that it was inappropriate for the tainted Falcon Guards to lead the entire Jade Falcon army into battle.

She came forward in her savage-looking *Executioner*. Close behind followed a pair of her Command Star 'Mechs, like a pair of thugs backing up a bandit leader.

"You cannot be first onto Robyn's Crossing, Aidan Pryde. That is the right of the Twelfth Falcon Cluster. It is *my* right."

Aidan took a deep breath. In his mind he could see Senza Oriega, with her pale ghostlike complexion, sitting smugly in her pilot seat, throwing her weight around as if it had 'Mech tonnage.

"Your right, you say?"

"Aff. *Our* right, actually."

"Did you down the four ComStar BattleMechs and send the rest into a retreat? Did the Twelfth Falcon Cluster down *any* ComStar BattleMechs? Did Senza Oriega and her Twelfth Falcon Cluster take Robyn's Crossing?"

"None of that, none of your boasting has any effect on the order of march across the bridge. It is an honor the Twelfth Falcon Cluster has earned by its *entire* combat history. It is for us to lead the way across the bridge and into the next phase of battle on the other side of the bridge."

Aidan was seething with anger at Senza Oriega's disparaging tone. "What kind of freebirth stupidity is this?" he screamed into his mike. "Do you dare—"

"Star Colonel, ease up on—" It was Horse cutting in on the transmission.

"I am sorry about the epithet, Horse. I am just so—"

"Forget the epithet. I was not offended. I am counseling calmness here, not lecturing on manners. There is no point in two honorable and courageous commanders—"

"Honorable? Courageous? Horse, she has no right to take away our—"

"My orders are clear," Senza Oriega said coldly. "We have no time for your petty little tantrums. The Khan has decreed that the Twelfth Falcon Cluster shall lead the way across the bridge, and so it shall be. Star Colonel, let me commend you for your combat achievements here. They will receive much praise in my report on the taking of the bridge."

"I am honored," Aidan muttered, but Senza Oriega apparently did not notice the sarcasm. It was not a verbal shading common among Clan warriors, and often they did not perceive it readily.

"Perhaps you will allow me a suggestion," Horse said. "If there is still bad blood between you two after we have won our objectives, a Trial of Grievance might be appropriate. I, for one, will do everything in my power to discourage it, but as often happens, the way of the Clan provides a solution to a problem."

"Your subordinate speaks well, Aidan Pryde. Let us leave matters at that. I will make this one concession. After the Twelfth Falcon Cluster has crossed the bridge, the Falcon Guards may have the honor of coming next."

Aidan held back his anger. "We respectfully decline the honor, Star Colonel Senza Oriega," he said tonelessly.

"As you wish. Please clear the way."

While the Twelfth Falcon Cluster assembled behind Oriega, with those who had been at the crest of the hill coming down the slope with difficulty to join their unit, Aidan, Horse, and Margo cleared the way.

Senza Oriega and her Command Star went first. Aidan was bitterly amused at the delicate way the feet of the Twelfth's 'Mechs had to step over the fallen ComStar

BattleMechs. The movement reminded him of villagers carefully avoiding the deposits left by animals in their streets. He wondered if they would also be shy of the puddles on the bridge. He cursed himself for his un-Clanlike speculations, but he could not help it.

Horse was continuing to monitor reports of the battle for Plough Bridge. "The Com Guard units there have also retreated, with even less damage than what they took here. The Seventh Falcon Cluster is now crossing."

Aidan smiled. "Sounds like they have edged the Twelfth for the honor of getting to the other side of the river. A major achievement, Horse. They—what was that?"

In the distance came the sound of an explosion, then another, then a symphony of overlapping explosions.

"Something has gone wrong at Plough Bridge," Horse shouted. "The Com Guards must have planted—"

As though completing Horse's transmission, the demolition charges the Com Guards had concealed on Robyn's Crossing began to explode. The first explosion came just as Senza Oriega's BattleMech crossed what was approximately the halfway mark of the bridge roadbed.

The Twelfth 'Mechs waiting to pass onto the bridge were rocked backward, the force of the continuing blasts knocking some of them into each other, and a few fell like dominoes.

Although Aidan and the two other Falcon Guards were far to the side, they too felt the impact of the explosion. The trio managed to keep their 'Mechs upright, but Margo's *Mist Lynx* took a load of metal debris right in the upper torso. The 'Mech kept its legs in spite of its lightness, but the torso rotated on its hips. Medics who later checked out the battlefield discovered Margo, still seated and with her hands on her controls. She had been killed when a metal piece smashed into the cockpit and hit her sharply in one temple.

When Aidan heard the news much later, he regretted her death. Margo had been one of the best light 'Mech pilots he had ever met.

28

Just as the Com Guards had appeared mysteriously from out of the ground during their hit-and-run raid, they now emerged from the cloud of smoke and debris created by the bridge explosions. The long, gradually sloping hillside on the other side of Prezno River suddenly teemed with Com Guard BattleMechs, attack vehicles, and ground forces.

A squadron of aerofighters appeared beyond the far hillside, first soaring upward, then down toward the 'Mechs near the riverbanks.

The first air wave swept toward the bridge itself, passing low over the smoldering, smoky structure, zeroing in on the remaining Twelfth Falcon Cluster, wreaking havoc with short-range missiles and medium lasers. Several 'Mechs, pinned against the cliff wall, became easy targets. One exploded, others merely fell.

Downriver from the bridge, neither Aidan nor Horse yet realized that MechWarrior Margo had been killed, only that she did not respond to them over the commline.

Because of the high slopes, the aerofighters could not come in close to the Jade Falcon BattleMechs. Instead they had to veer away to avoid crashing. With their undersides exposed, the fighters became the targets, and a *Dire Wolf* pilot disemboweled an *Ironsides* with a missile cluster. The aerofighter fell into the already-steaming river, creating more heat waves as it rapidly sank.

In the distance another wave of aerofighters had arrived, their short- and long-range missiles striking dangerously close to the 'Mechs of Aidan and Horse.

"I do not think we can do much good here," Horse said. "We should get out while we can."

"But whether we stay or go, we have problems. If we stay here, we are up against terrible odds. If we retreat, our own forces block the way while they are trying to leap over or climb up the hillside. If we jump, we become sitting ducks for the next aerofighter attack."

"What do you suggest, Aidan?"

"The river may be the safest place. I am looking at it on my secondary screen. The waters are immediately deep off the bank."

"I hate operating a 'Mech underwater."

"I will take complaints later. Into the water then. Did you get that, MechWarrior Margo? Margo?"

"Something is wrong, Aidan. Should I get her out?"

"No time. We have to leave her."

After a slight hesitation, Horse said quietly, "Yes, sir."

"We will progress downstream two and a half kilometers, then come out and take our chances, *quiaff*?"

"Aff."

Jumping together, they hit the water just as the next wave of aerofighters flew over. One of the fighters reacted quickly to the pair of jumping 'Mechs, letting loose a cluster of short-range missiles. The attempt came too late, and the missiles merely flung up a lot of dirt. The two 'Mechs were already in the water, with only ripples showing where they had entered.

For Joanna and Diana the sudden battle created almost overwhelming chaos. Surviving 'Mechs of the Twelfth Falcon Cluster rushed past them in a disorganized retreat from the fierce artillery barrage now being launched by the ComStar forces. Leaderless, the Twelfth was not able to form up and make a stand.

For a while the Falcon Guards tried to counter the barrage and hold the line. They were able to hang on for awhile, but Joanna, now in command because Aidan Pryde's whereabouts were unknown, saw that the Guards' ammunition was dangerously low and that they were taking too many hits. She ordered the Falcon Guards to join the general retreat, which was now endorsed by the Galaxy Commander, Mar Helmer, himself.

The battle went on for most of the day. While the Com Guards blasted away relentlessly with long-range missile fusillades, their aerospace wing continued to rain heavy damage on the fleeing army. Eventually, however, the Jade Falcons were out of effective range of the Com Guard weapons. The Jade Falcon lines were also spread thin, by order of Mar Helmer. The ComStar commander ordered a cease-fire, and the aerofighters, their ammo exhausted, returned to their DropShips.

When the Jade Falcon forces came to a rest, Joanna noted that they were only about twenty kilometers from where they had originally landed. Making a quick check of the terrain maps, she saw that, after coming within twenty kilometers of their objectives, they were now fifty kilometers away. Joanna did not want to be the one who would have to take the blame for the failure of the march toward glory.

Fortunately, miraculously, the Falcon Guards had not suffered serious casualties. Some 'Mech armor had been chipped and gouged away, some weapons had overheated and required immediate repair, and most of the 'Mechs needed some internal tinkering, but the Falcon Guards had come through the ComStar counterattack better than most of the other Jade Falcon units.

Aside from MechWarrior Faulk, the warrior injured earlier, three Falcon Guards were listed as missing in action. Lamentably, this trio included the Cluster commander and namesake of "Pryde's Pride." No matter that Joanna had despised Aidan Pryde for so many years, she sincerely hoped that it was not the cowardly ComStar strategy that had done him in.

The laborious movement of an underwater 'Mech was agonizing, stultifying even, made more so by the swirling, rushing waters of the Prezno River. Yet no BattleMech could move efficiently under even the calmest of waters. Rather, the 'Mech became as clumsy and slow as someone sadly out of shape trying to relearn an old physical exercise.

The river worked in their favor, however, speeding their progress. Even at these depths the rapid currents of Prezno River buffeted the two 'Mechs along with a force that Aidan felt even in his cockpit. With the turmoil of the waters keeping the riverbed stirred up, he could see little of it. He would not have been sure they were getting anywhere, no matter what his sensors revealed, were it not for the light projecting from Horse's cockpit. It poured steadily forth, illuminating the riverbank to their left. The blobs that swam in and out of the murky luminescence were, Aidan assumed, various types of underwater creatures. In the distorted light, none of them looked anything like fish.

Soon enough the two and a half kilometers had been covered. Looking toward the bank of the river, Aidan saw that it had just enough slope to permit a 'Mech to gain footing and push upward. His first try failed, however, and the *Timber Wolf* settled back into the water. How he wished he could use the jump jets underwater, but water entering the intakes would make the 'Mech explode. Patiently, laboriously, he tried once more. This time he broke surface, gained a foothold on the slope, and pulled himself and his 'Mech out of the river. Horse followed soon after.

Everything seemed quiet at this part of the river. Looking back upstream, they could see the smoke and river-steam completely obscuring the battle.

"Things look bad," Aidan commented.

"I take it that we are not returning to *that*."

"No, we want to be brave, but not suicidal. We will run along the flank, see what we can do, and try to rejoin the Falcon Guards."

"I hope the Guards have come out of this better than the Twelfth did."

"Senza Oriega was a great warrior, but she was a fool."

"Fool? Arrogant, perhaps, even rude, but a fool?"

"She led her command into total disaster."

Horse paused for a moment, giving Aidan a hard stare. "Do not forget that it was you agitating for the right to be first over the bridge. Instead of calling Senza Oriega a fool, you might say that she took the bullet that was meant for you."

Diana could not explain the inner emptiness she felt. When night fell and Aidan Pryde was still listed as missing, she began to fear that he was a definite casualty of the battle of Robyn's Crossing. Had she been wrong to withhold her identity from him? It had seemed the best course while he was still alive, but now she wished for a chance to reconsider.

So many had been lost at Robyn's Crossing that her father and the others were only a fraction of the casualties. Yet his deeds had been memorable, and many warriors spoke of them all through the encampment. If he had died, his death was one worthy of a warrior.

Then Joanna came to her with the news that Aidan Pryde had survived, that he had just now rejoined the Falcon Guards.

Diana stayed her distance, disturbed by how relieved she was to see this stranger who was her father alive. She watched him move here and there through the camp, speaking with many of the warriors, reviving their spirits and in turn receiving their respect.

Diana was sure that after this night the nickname "Pryde's Pride" would stick, at least among the Falcon Guards themselves. She wondered whether she, too, might become Pryde's pride if she were to reveal to him their blood tie. Probably not, she told herself. Anyway, she had already lost the urge to tell him.

29

As Aidan had told Horse, the way of the Clan was not particularly subtle, but he had to admit that the shape of the events following the destruction of Robyn's Crossing and Plough Bridge were taking on a subtle shading. Prezno River became a powerful symbol for the officers of the Falcon command group. In the war councils, he could hear in his fellow warriors' words that the river was no longer a mere body of water. It had begun to represent the fight for Tukayyid itself. The river's roiling surface and strong current were like the ComStar artillery barrages that lay ahead, with their apparently endless supply of ammunition. Its murky depths reflected all the tricks and deceptions of ComStar strategy. A jutting branch could pierce a warrior's back like a ComStar ambush, river debris swim in and around him like darting ComStar light 'Mechs. Moving slowly, a warrior became an even better target for the enemy.

Aidan wanted to berate his fellow warriors for their attributing human motives to the river. It is just a river, he wanted to say, just water and the ordinary elements found in water. There was no reason to invest the river with mystery. Symbolism was an Inner Sphere style of thinking. He should know, having read enough of their books in his time.

And yet the river did seem to have turned against them. Ever since the destruction of the bridges, several units had tried to discover places where it was possible to ford the river. Each attempt had ended in failure and, frequently, disaster. The few BattleMechs that made it partway into the river at relatively shallow points were almost immediately swept up by the swift currents and knocked downstream. Some of them came out of the river in a battered condition, some were never heard from again. There were already rumors that recon planes had spotted pieces of 'Mechs, seat cushions, interior paneling, myomer bundles, and the like crowded into river inlets, looking like sewer debris.

The only aspect of the battle going well for Clan Jade Falcon were the assaults of their aerofighters, many of which had successfully strafed Com Guard 'Mechs and vehicles. The ComStar air arm had become surprisingly quiescent, and the only aerofighters that had been spotted were staying away from the obviously superior Jade Falcon aircraft. Most of the successful air activity took place beyond the river. Near the riverbanks the Com Guard forces delivered fierce attacks and counterattacks.

With the ComStar barrage temporarily halted and its aerofighters out of action, the calm night hid the ravages suffered by the countryside of Prezno Plain. Only the smells of scorched armor, cordite, and the faint metallic odors of overheated BattleMechs suggested the scale and scope of the battle that had so recently taken place there.

When Aidan could not bear to listen to any more folderol, he asked to address the council. Though he sensed the disapproval of the other Clan commanding officers, he strode forward.

"Star Colonel Aidan Pryde, we commend your courage at the Battle of Robyn's Crossing," Galaxy Commander Mar Helmer said. The Khan, sitting next to him, nodded agreement. "What have you to say to us here?"

"I believe this talk of our engineers building a bridge across the river is a waste of time," Aidan said. Some murmured objection buzzed among the assembled warriors, but no one stood to contradict Aidan. "We need to get personnel onto the other side of Prezno River, warriors who can defend the other end of any bridge we attempt to construct. Otherwise the Com Guards will pick off our engineers at their leisure."

Star Colonel Gran Newclay of the Third Falcon Cluster stood up suddenly. He spoke in the nasty voice he always used to convey derision with some simple words. "And without the bridge, how does the noble hero of Robyn's Crossing intend to get units across the Prezno River?"

"Those of us equipped with jump jets can jump across."

Gran Newclay made a sound in the back of his throat that must have been some distorted version of a laugh. He was a tall, thick man with skin that looked like cracked and over-oiled leather.

"And is the noble hero of Robyn's Crossing aware that the river is too wide for the longest jump-jet leap a Jade Falcon BattleMech can manage? The Prezno is some two hundred-fifty meters wide at its narrowest crossing. The Star Colonel must have been asleep when we discussed the terrain at the last council. We decided then that no jumps were possible and that the bridges—"

It was a breach of decorum during a Clan council to interrupt an officer who was senior in grade, even when the gathering was an improvised war meeting such as this one. Aidan did so anyway, "I know all the proper data, Star Colonel Gran Newclay. I know it as well as you. But let me say this: My Falcon Guards have all been ordered to mount jump jet modules, and we can find a place to use them, and we will use them."

"Respectfully," Gran Newclay said, "I submit that the noble hero's plan is too audacious, and the Clan must not adopt it. We must set into motion the engineer units, assign BattleMechs to protect them—a duty I am sure the Falcon Guards could fulfill very well—and get them to the river for—"

Aidan committed another breach of council etiquette, interrupting Newclay a second time. "ComStar will pick them off even as they are constructing the bridge, *unless* my Falcon Guards can get to the other side, along with any other jump-equipped 'Mechs that can be detached to join us. Then, as I stated, we can defend that side so that the engineers can build their structure under proper protection. With 'Mechs to provide long-range support and our Elementals to proceed further into the countryside, we can provide just that."

"I submit again," Gran Newclay said, his voice louder now, "that the Clan leaders cannot approve such a short-sighted strategy. The Prezno River is too treacherous at all points. Its current will merely sweep our BattleMechs away instead of—"

And Aidan interrupted Gran Newclay a third time,

which would have been grounds for an honor duel in noncombat conditions. "Yes, we may lose some of our 'Mechs, but that is war, *quiaff*? Whatever sacrifice is made, we must do this or wind up taking potshots at the Com Guards from across the river, while the rest of the Clans garner the glory elsewhere on Tukayyid."

Aidan's appeal to the competition between Clans was calculated. If anything could rouse Clan warriors to action, it was the suggestion that the success of rival Clans might bring shame to them.

"The way is difficult," said Gran Newclay, now clearly ruffled, "but approved combat procedures are the only way we can hope to—"

Could Aidan Pryde interrupt Gran Newclay a fourth time? No doubt about it. "Gran Newclay, you take your approved combat procedures and drop them in the Prezno River with the sharded remnants of the two bridges."

"I approve of Star Colonel Aidan Pryde's alacrity to enter battle," Galaxy Commander Mar Helmer said, "but I believe that such a drastic proposal would only serve to—"

Mar Helmer, his face as pale and his manners as calm as ever, was a warrior whom Aidan would not dare interrupt. But someone else could.

"I would remind the Galaxy Commander that Aidan Pryde has been given free reign in all his actions during this campaign by rule of Khan Chistu." From out of the shadows came Kael Pershaw, his half-mask catching the light and then casting it out again strangely to the assembly. He limped slowly forward, nodding to Mar Helmer and Khan Chistu. Pershaw was as much a legend to the leaders as to the ordinary warriors. "I endorse Aidan Pryde's plan. It will not only give us a military position worth holding, it will gain us the time necessary to build our bridges. I would remind those among us who believe that the bridges are the only solution that the waters of the Prezno are so active, presenting so many obstacles, that constructing a bridge would be difficult even under the best of circumstances."

The crowd became utterly silent, while Kael Pershaw's very breaths became stentorian in the stillness. He limped over to Aidan Pryde and touched him on the shoulder with his good hand. He glanced over at the still-silent

Khan, who responded with a quick nod. "I think you are free to go. Assemble the Falcon Guards and find your way across the river. You go with the blessings of your Khan, your Clan, and the immortal Kerenskys."

A few warriors whispered, "Seyla."

"May I address the assembly?" asked Star Colonel Marthe Pryde, stepping forward from the milling crowd of Clan commanders. Mar Helmer granted the request. Marthe stood up, feet spread apart, arms akimbo. "I command the Second Falcon Cluster," she said. "Many of our 'Mechs are equipped with jump jets. I wish to volunteer those 'Mechs, mine included, to join Star Colonel Aidan Pryde in this mission. I believe that the more personnel we can commit to the campaign to take the other side of the river, the better the chances of our success. I at this time formalize the request."

Neither the Khan nor the Galaxy Commander spoke for a long moment, then the Khan nodded toward Mar Helmer. "Permission granted," Helmer said.

Aidan could not have said why, but he felt an odd surge of elation at Marthe's act. As her former sibkin, he was glad to have her on his side. As a commander, he welcomed the cooperation and assistance of one of the finest warriors in Clan Jade Falcon.

30

MechWarrior Diana had never seen river rapids before. Standing on the edge of the embankment, looking down several meters of steep cliff at this stretch of Prezno River, she was amazed by the rush of the frenzied, white-capped waters of the river. Waves splashed off pitted rocks, sometimes rising high, then dissipating into misty vapor. The water twisted and turned, as if refusing to follow the river course downstream. A large whirlpool had formed in an inlet. It spiraled downward relentlessly, seeming to beckon any observer into its darkness, its watery black hole. Spray from the rapids left little droplets on her *Warhawk*'s viewport, distorting the exterior images into a wavery, impressionistic scene. Only on her primary screen was the view of the river sharply detailed.

Over the commline, she heard Joanna make a sound of disgust.

"What was the point of sending us here, do you think?" Joanna said.

"Recon thought they spotted a possible jumping place two kilometers further downstream," Diana told her.

"No. The commander has surveyed that area, and he says there are no other possibilities. He is on his way here now."

Enemy resistance to the Jade Falcon search of the river had been meager. Diana thought that the Com Guards might be playing a child's game with the Clan warriors, the kind where the dominant side holds back to one side of a line and then, with taunts and dares, tries to lure the disrupted side across the line. Come and get me, might be the Com Guard's present taunt. They had only launched some air attacks, their aerofighters going after any units or individual BattleMechs separated from the main body. The fighters were like pesty insects, zooming in to do some damage but slipping away again before any counterattack could be effective. Occasionally, the sound of artillery fire echoed from upstream, but Joanna had received no information on whether any of it had hurt Jade Falcon 'Mechs.

The other side of the rapids was undefended. Diana thought that was probably because it seemed so unlikely that a unit would ever attempt a cross here. No engineer with any sense would suggest building a bridge across this steep chasm, above these treacherous waters.

"Any news, Star Captain Joanna?" MechWarrior Leema asked. She had brought her *Stormcrow* right to the cliff's edge and was conducting a depth scan of the waters below. The figures changed quickly as she watched them, for the depth was highly unstable.

"Just the same information. The engineer battalion has been pinned down by artillery several kilometers from the river. They are trying to reach both the Robyn's Crossing and Plough Bridge sites."

"A tough mission for those techs," MechWarrior Khastis cut in, "since the enemy is keeping at least one regiment at both sites."

"And that will be our destination," said Star Colonel Aidan Pryde as he hove into sight from behind a riverside grove. "The other side of Robyn's Crossing. We will take out the ComStar forces there, and we will build the bridge across the river at that point."

"A simple task," Joanna said dryly. "The only hitch is figuring out how to cross the river."

"A problem, I will admit, but I have solved it."

"Oh? What place are we using for the exercise, Star Colonel?"

"Why, right here, of course."

Though Joanna and Diana could not see each other, neither would have been surprised to find the other examining the turbulent, rocky rapids incredulously before hearing Aidan's explanation of how the exercise would work. Even then they were leery of the Star Colonel's plan.

"Assemble the Falcon Guards and the BattleMechs

from the Second Falcon Cluster at this point," he ordered. Whatever her option, Joanna sent out the call.

When Aidan asked for volunteers for the first phase of Operation Skipping Stone, the names of every Clan warrior from both units appeared on his primary screen. Even all the Elementals, none of whom could be used in this phase, volunteered. He was not surprised by the number of volunteers, but the ritual had to be accomplished. Setting his computer for random selection, five MechWarriors were chosen, with a pair of alternates. He eliminated any 'Mechs from Trinaries Delta and Echo so that they would be free to carry their Elementals to the opposite side of the river. Joanna suggested that other Elemental units be carried on BattleMechs of various Stars. Aidan vetoed the suggestion, saying he wanted no extra weight on BattleMechs that did not normally carry Elementals. "The weight of one Elemental could throw off a pilot's control, and we cannot risk even a fraction of error." Instead, he announced a different plan.

Falcon Guard MechWarriors Ta-Ken from Trinary Bravo and Peel from Trinary Charlie were the first to jump into the middle of the Prezno River. The spot chosen for their landing was a relative shallows. Nearby rocks had slowed the current somewhat, though it still rushed violently past the 'Mechs' legs at a breakneck rate. Ta-ken's 'Mech swayed and immediately fell sideways into the water. As instructed by Aidan, Ta-ken guided the 'Mech's fall, first going down on one knee, then sliding its leg backward. He then let the 'Mech slide into the water while rotating its torso to the left so that the cockpit was still above the surface when the machine had settled into the water. Most of the 'Mech was now underwater, with only a leg, the front of the torso, and an arm above water. While Ta-ken's 'Mech went down, Peel was executing similar maneuvers so that his 'Mech came down next to Ta-ken's, with the bottom third of its legs slightly behind the upper section of the other 'Mech's torso.

In the second group of jumping BattleMechs were one from Marthe's unit, piloted by Star Commander Todik, and two more Falcon Guard MechWarriors, Fenn from Trinary Alpha and Shank from Trinary Charlie. These three made their leaps, one jumping a second after the other. Todik's 'Mech came down next to Peel's, Fenn's beside Todik's, and Shank's beside Fenn's. Then they maneuvered their machines so that each slightly over-lapped the other in a line. The five 'Mechs now formed a breakwater, diverting turbulent water around each end and creating a tranquil pool in the center of the river.

But the forming of the breakwater was not without a cost. Fenn's 'Mech crashed into the river with its cockpit submerged, and when Shank landed, the fall into the river breeched his 'Mech's torso, flooding the engine com-partment and killing power to the 'Mech. Trapped in their cockpits, both Shank and Fenn suffocated within fifteen minutes.

As Aidan oversaw the creation of the makeshift break-water, Joanna lined up the other BattleMechs in groups of four. Some Jade Falcon officers, detached by the Khan to observe the operation, watched as she set several even lines of quartet groupings going back from the edge of the river, each line at about the same distance from the one in front of it.

When the last 'Mech had settled into the river and the current was obviously diverted, Aidan took stock of his creation and, in a godlike way, felt pleased. There was a kind of austere beauty to the way the visible parts of the five 'Mechs formed a thin metal island in the middle of the river. Some water sprayed over them and left droplets on their surfaces. The light on the droplets sparkled with activity. The water of the tranquil pool was clear and the underwater sections of the 'Mechs were distorted into shimmering patterns.

"Star Colonel?" Joanna said. "The first line is ready to jump at your order."

"The first one will jump after me," Aidan said, set-ting his *Timber Wolf* by the edge of the embankment.

"You intend to be the first?"

"Who better? It is my plan. If it is poor, I should be the one to pay the consequences."

"But—"

Without waiting to hear her objection, Aidan engaged his jump jets for the leap. He had already prepared the coordinates for landing.

His stomach did its own little leap as the *Timber Wolf*

rose into the air at a slight forward angle. It went up to the height Aidan had calculated, then came down. He could use only his primary screen to guide his fall into the chasm. Directing an external camera downward, he watched the surface of the river come toward his 'Mech's feet. It was shooting up at him faster than he wanted. At first the tranquil pool seemed like a tiny puddle that the BattleMech could not possibly hit on target, but then it enlarged in the viewport until he saw he was zeroing in correctly. His calculations had been accurate.

His hands securely on the controls, Aidan felt the *Timber Wolf* hit the water, then come to a rough stop as its feet made contact with the riverbed. His secondary screen showed that, as originally estimated, the depth of the tranquil pool measured two meters.

He immediately set the jump jets for the second leap and soared upward toward the far shore. The second stage of the leap was easier, if only because he knew he would come down onto solid ground. His heart leaped, though, when the 'Mech's feet landed only centimeters from the edge of the embankment.

He moved the *Timber Wolf* forward a few meters to clear the way for the next 'Mech landings, then turned to observe the operation. Moving to his left, he found a slight rise that gave him a good view of the other side and the chasm, where the makeshift breakwater looked as solid as a series of rocks.

Joanna, in her usual efficient way, had started the first 'Mech of the front line forward. It soared upward—Aidan thought a bit shakily—but, with a clear shift of arc by its pilot, came down into the tranquil pool, splashing water all around its legs. Its jump to the ComStar side of the river was smoother, and it landed a few meters away from Aidan's observation point.

After several 'Mechs in a row jumped successfully, Aidan was feeling new confidence in his plan. That was when a *Summoner*'s jump jets malfunctioned at the top of its arc, and the 'Mech crashed heavily into the basin. It missed the breakwater but landed behind it. The rough current sent it crashing into the breakwater, where it hit with an impact that reverberated through the chasm and beyond. Aidan leaned forward to study the breakwater.

Was he mistaken, or did the middle BattleMech look damaged and ready to slip away from the others?

Joanna kept the next 'Mech from jumping until it was certain that the breakwater had held. After half a minute, a body bobbed to the surface, floating head-down. The pilot had evidently drowned. No doubt his cockpit canopy broke with the impact and water had flooded in. Checking his screen, Aidan saw that the dead man was MechWarrior Obdoff from Trinary Charlie. About all he could recall about the man was that he was one of the old ones.

When Joanna thought the maneuver was safe, she sent the next line of 'Mechs successfully over the river. As they landed on Aidan's side of the river, Star Captain Jula Huddock of Alpha Heavy assigned them defensive positions. What arrogance the ComStar forces were showing, he thought. Or stupidity. Did not their intelligence detect the Jade Falcons crossing the river, or were the rapids such an unexpected place for the move that the enemy was not maintaining vigilance on this sector of the river?

On the other side of the river, he saw the two observers coming down the hill toward the point where Joanna was giving the jumping drill to a line of BattleMechs. When they were within meters of Joanna's 'Mech, the third 'Mech of the current line made a sputtering noise at the height of its arc and began to sway from side to side as it came down. It landed just outside the target area and was immediately swept up by the current. Before Aidan could focus well on the 'Mech, it was several meters downstream being shattered against a cliff wall. Its pilot managed to eject, but could not get control of the ejection seat. The man bounced off the cliff wall, then plunged down into the waters, disappearing quickly. As Aidan scanned the surface of the river, looking for a sign of the pilot, the 'Mech itself slid down into the water. Like the pilot, it vanished without a trace—except for some twisted metal that still clung to the cliff wall.

Aidan checked his secondary screen. The lost MechWarrior was named Xavier and was a member of Marthe's Cluster.

The remaining BattleMechs of the line all made successful jumps while Aidan was still searching for the lost pilot, but no movement came from Joanna's side of the river now. She opened the commline. ''Star Colonel, the observers want us to scrub the mission at this point and go forward with the BattleMechs that have already jumped. What are your orders?''

Aidan had agreed to listen to recommendations from the observers, as long as all their messages could be conveyed to him through Joanna. ''We are losing this battle because of a new mood of caution among Clan warriors. That has never been our way. We have lost only two 'Mechs, with the ones forming the breakwater at least out of commission for the immediate future. I would say the exercise is going well. Continue.''

Joanna gave the order to the next line. Aidan saw that the first to jump was the *Warhawk* of MechWarrior Diana. He held his breath as it came off the opposite cliff. He did not know why the fate of this particular warrior would matter so much to him. Perhaps it was because of the way she had fought beside him at Vreeport. Or perhaps her freeborn feistiness reminded him of the days when he had lived as one of that caste. Or perhaps it was because she was so like Marthe. Whatever it was, her fate was of deep concern to him, even if the feeling was a mystery.

Diana took her BattleMech higher than any other pilot had, an impressive feat for such a heavy 'Mech, then she came down with her 'Mech's feet straight, right on target. Aidan let his breath out. Then the *Warhawk*'s legs seemed to buckle and it looked like its feet were going to slip out from under, and into the current. Instead, Diana engaged the jump jets at the last possible moment and the machine rose shakily upward.

For a moment it looked as if the *Warhawk* would not clear the edge of the cliff, but in midair she somehow eased her 'Mech's legs forward so that its feet came down heel first on the embankment's edge. Then she shoved her joystick forward and managed to get the BattleMech upright before it could fall. Aidan shouted into his microphone for her to clear the way fast before the next 'Mech came in for a landing.

The rest of the operation did not go smoothly, though most of the BattleMechs succeeded in crossing the Prezno to the other side. Four more were lost in various accidents. One, MechWarrior Elaine, was from Marthe's

Cluster. The pilot survived, but her 'Mech missed its second leap and did not manage to reach the far shore. The other three, all Falcon Guards, were killed and their 'Mechs destroyed by the fierce Prezno River currents. All MechWarriors, they were Mondav of Bravo Heavy, Dhrima from Trinary Charlie, and Smit from Delta Nova. The crash of Smit was particularly costly, because his Elementals were also lost, dropping away from the 'Mech as it plunged downward. Only Elemental Point Commander Danton survived by shedding his armor, swimming to the tranquil pool, and then pulling himself onto the breakwater.

Joanna and Marthe were the last to jump. Both did so with an ease and grace that could have served for a training holotape, if there was ever a need for a tape on the most bizarre way to get across a wide, active river.

As Joanna joined him, he said briskly, "Report, Star Captain."

"Six BattleMechs lost in the river, while the five forming the breakwater cannot be immediately salvaged."

"And the pilots."

"Among the five breakwater pilots, two are dead and the rest are alive and awaiting pickup. One of the Elemental Stars still on the other side of the shore is mounting a rescue operation. Elemental Star Commander Torvald assures me that they have already cast a rope out onto the breakwater. It has been secured with magnetic pitons at both ends and the three pilots will be rescued before the Elementals cross."

"And the other 'Mech pilots?"

"MechWarrior Smit and the Elementals he carried are missing in action, except for Point Commander Danton. You saw him get to the breakwater. The bodies of MechWarrior Obdoff and Monday have been recovered. Of the other four, three are missing and probably dead. Mech Warrior Elaine has been rescued. I am told she is in shock, but will live."

"All in all, a successful operation, *quiaff*?"

"Aff. Though eleven 'Mechs are no small loss."

Down below, the three pilots had been brought to shore. Still on the BattleMech breakwater was Point Commander Danton, who, with two other Elementals, had cast the line to the ComStar side of the river, where it had been secured. At a signal from Danton, who had released the pitons on the breakwater 'Mechs, the line, with Danton and the other two Elementals clutching it with short attached ropes, was raised and made relatively taut. Now it stretched from shore to shore. Elementals immediately clamped their short ropes onto the line and began to slide across the chasm. When Danton stepped off onto the other side of the river, the line was filled with crossing Elementals, spaced at precise distances from one another.

Aidan did not have time to watch the entire Elemental crossing. "Jade Falcons, proceed to Robyn's Crossing," he said into his headset mike.

He led the march, with Joanna's 'Mech on one side of him, Marthe's on the other.

"I had a strange thought," Marthe said suddenly over their private channel. "A very strange thought."

"What?"

"It is as if the three of us, you, Joanna, and me, were back on Ironhold—cadets and training officer proceeding down a Crash Camp road."

"A very strange thought, Marthe. Best to forget it."

"I agree."

Now that Marthe had planted the seed, it was Aidan who could not shake the image from his mind. Fortunately, Robyn's Crossing was not far away.

=====31=====

As Aidan had suggested to the Falcon Command Group, aerofighters were now strafing the positions still held by ComStar units at the wrecked bridges. From what Aidan's sensors could tell him, they were doing considerable damage. That was good. With that support Aidan was confident enough to detach the 'Mechs of the Second Falcon Cluster to Plough Bridge to assist the Jade Falcon assault there. Marthe led her troops off toward their objective at a dust-churning run.

But the Falcon Guards were still several kilometers from Robyn's Crossing. Overhead, a Star of aerofighters had joined them, providing some cover against ambush on the way to the bridge. Aidan thought he and his men must be an impressive sight, more than a Cluster of BattleMechs and Elementals charging along the riverside, battle-ready and formidable.

To Diana, in the midst of the 'Mech throng, the Falcon Guards looked like chaos on legs. It was all she could do to keep her *Hellbringer* from bumping into other 'Mechs or avoid stepping on the swift-running Elementals. And it was all she could do to keep from being nudged toward the fearful Prezno River. This was not being a warrior, she thought, but more like being a techno-athlete. It took skill, yes, but it was manipulation not battle. And it was for battle that she longed. Except for the skirmish on Prezno Plain and some combat during the retreat, this campaign had not yet really given her a taste of what it was to be a warrior.

Tukayyid was her first real war, and she thought it should be the kind of thrill she had imagined so often since the days when the other village youngsters had laughed and teased her for saying she would be a warrior when she grew up. So far her military career had consisted of minor skirmishes on backwater planets, mop-up operations, and the little war experience she had received as a Falcon Guard. She was eager to get to Robyn's crossing and some close combat.

Perhaps it was these thoughts distracting her that made Diana's 'Mech nearly stumble. Though she quickly recovered her balance, she saw in her peripheral vision a particularly violent stretch of Prezno River that might have been her watery grave. No, she told herself firmly. It would not happen that way. She had already survived one near-plunge into the river. If she was going to die in this battle, it would not be by drowning, but among the flames and explosions of the field, a Clan warrior fighting alongside others of her kind.

To Marthe, the expedition along the riverside had a kind of military beauty to it, something equivalent to the pleasure a warrior might take in the study of a good war map or a passage from *The Remembrance*. There was an aesthetic to a legion of Clan warriors going forward toward their destiny. Here were OmniMechs, the most fearsome BattleMechs ever created, piloted by genetically engineered warriors whose whole lives were devoted to the way of war. Running speedily and gracefully alongside them were the two-and-a-half-meter-tall Elementals, also the products of genetic engineering, their bodies in armored suits that made them awesome compared to footsoldiers anywhere else in the known universe. Overhead were magnificent aerofighters, also manned by pilots who had been genetically bred for such tasks. The image, as she imagined it would appear to enemy warriors who must counter the Clan attack, was pleasing, artistic.

Keeping her BattleMech abreast of Aidan's and Joanna's, Marthe thought the three of them made a fine vanguard against their ComStar foes.

To Joanna, the advance had neither strategic, aesthetic, nor emotional significance. Like an old-time footsoldier, she was most concerned with the performance of duty. Were all the units in their proper places? Had the techs loaded all the ammo before leaving the camp on Prezno Plain? Had she forgotten something vital in the short training time she'd had to whip this misbegotten crew into shape?

She wondered why she could never lose this habit of thinking like a training officer. There were times when she felt that training was, finally, her specialty. The Bloodname she had never won, the minor battles she had fought, the hatred inspired in her by almost all other humans—none of it mattered when she was satisfied with her performance of duty.

Star Captain Joanna, who had never won her Bloodname, who now was among the aging warriors, could not know that among so many soldiers, she was the ideal Clan warrior. Clan military theorists as far back as Nicholas Kerensky himself would have admired her total dedication. On a battlefield she carried in no weight that could not in some way be used in the combat. Even her hatred, deep as it ran, was useful to the objectives of warfare. And in the entire Jade Falcon Clan few warriors could build up a killing growl like Joanna.

Riding along on the side of a *Gargoyle*, just behind the vanguard BattleMechs, Star Commander Selima saw the upcoming battle from an Elemental's point of view. Elemental training emphasized the transitoriness of life. No Elemental truly feared death because he or she knew that death was an honorable fate for a warrior. Not that an Elemental would seek a suicidal end in combat. No, an Elemental fought to the last moment, never letting up, never letting a fatal wound stop him from firing one more time or making one more thrust. If they embraced death, it was only because Elementals knew that, whether it came abruptly or slowly, sooner or later, it was *only* death. Even Clan MechWarriors did not quite understand the Elementals' ways. Needing to survive to fight again another day, a Clan warrior did not quite share the same easy acceptance of death.

Selima, a man more serene than most Elementals, had become an officer because he inspired loyalty, even among the crude and quarrelsome Elementals. Looking about him now, at the towering 'Mechs, at the other Elementals clinging to their own BattleMech rides, he saw the upcoming battle as merely another moment in his life. Like all Clanspeople, Elementals were taught that it was the great mission of the Clans to return to the Inner Sphere, where they would conquer its worlds, and restore the glory of the Star League. Yet the idea of the Star League, with its history and significance, had little meaning to an Elemental. As Clan infantrymen, Elementals simply did as they were told. They had been bred that way.

The first sign of the enemy came when an aerofighter detected a force of ComStar BattleMechs, now detached from the bridge defense, advancing toward the Jade Falcons. Aidan ordered some of the 'Mechs behind him to spread out, away from the river, so that they could present a wide front.

The maneuver worked, for the Com Guards, the surfaces of their 'Mechs gleaming even whiter in the bright light of the hot Tukayyid sun, advanced in a narrow column. It was now almost midday, the weather hot even for Tukayyid. Heat shimmers rose from the whole line of the 'Mechs, creating an aura around the oncoming force.

The ComStar 'Mechs began to slow their advance, preparing for battle. Their officers knew it was the Clan custom to fight 'Mech-on-'Mech, with each Clan warrior selecting his opponent and initiating his own combat tactics.

Knowing what ComStar would expect, Aidan had ordered a change of usual tactics. The Galaxy Commander had cautioned against it, but Aidan had the endorsement of Kael Pershaw to proceed entirely on his own. As was his wont, Star Colonel Aidan Pryde ignored caution and went forward.

"Joanna," he said over the commline, "initiate battle plan."

Joanna responded immediately over the open channel, giving the BattleMechs the first of Aidan's orders. "Slow to half-speed."

When the Jade Falcon advance visibly slackened, it was a ploy to make the enemy conclude that the Clan force was preparing for its usual stand-and-deliver style of combat.

Then, at a precisely calculated interval, Joanna gave the second command of the sequence. "Those who are to speed up, advance at double rate. Those who are to jump, jump in ten seconds."

Aidan led the way for the accelerating 'Mechs, all now running at peak speed, while Marthe held back and launched her 'Mech simultaneously with those selected for the jump-tactic.

Exhilarated by the rush to war, Aidan barely noticed the uneven pacing of the *Timber Wolf*'s lope. Nor did he pay attention to the erratic, shifting numbers for his ammo levels and weapon-readiness that his secondary screen was displaying. As his first target, he had selected a *Goliath*, a heavy 'Mech that looked more like a tank on legs than the often-humanoid BattleMechs of the Inner Sphere.

The *Goliath* was firing ineffectively with its long-range missiles, trying to mow down some of the Elementals running ahead of the Jade Falcon 'Mechs. Its PPC was lowered and pointed at the *Timber Wolf*.

Because running speed would reduce his accuracy, Aidan merely shot steadily with the lasers in both arms of the *Timber Wolf*. He did some damage to the *Goliath*'s legs, slowing it down.

But he did not care about downing the enemy 'Mech at this stage. Instead, he ran straight at the ComStar 'Mech, then continued on past it. Before he slid by, Aidan got off a good shot at the enemy 'Mech's large cockpit. The *Goliath* halted completely as Aidan's 'Mech continued on, firing at the BattleMechs in the next rank.

Aidan had no time to view the scene behind him, so he did not see Joanna finish off the *Goliath* as she too passed it by. The ComStar 'Mech's legs buckled. Nudged by another Jade Falcon 'Mech, it crashed sideways and slid into the Prezno River.

The Jade Falcon BattleMechs were attacking either on the run or by jumping down into the right flank of the ComStar 'Mechs. As the Falcons began to land in the open spaces between 'Mechs, the ComStar pilots at first did not react at all or else showed extreme confusion. The Jade Falcon BattleMechs were using ComStar's own hit-and-run tactics with a vengeance. The jumping 'Mechs peppered the enemy with varied shots and well-placed missiles, then jumped again, farther along the bank, closer to Robyn's Crossing. Seeing the ComStar forces in disarray at the unorthodox Clan assault, Aidan ordered his marauding 'Mechs to pour straight through their lines, shooting steadily as they ran. He could see they were doing plenty of damage.

The element of surprise could not last forever, however. Finally responding to the charge, a few Com Guard MechWarriors mowed down a pair of rear Falcon Guard 'Mechs. Aidan saw on his secondary screen that the MechWarriors lost were Keye and Gist. Joanna told him they had lost some Elementals, too, but it was not possible to get exact information on them until later.

Though Clan warriors always attempted to prevent or reduce losses, in war such losses were unavoidable. Yet Aidan knew his tactic had been a success. The Falcon Guard charge had destroyed many ComStar BattleMechs and severely damaged others. They had rendered at least three machines temporarily inoperable. The rest were turning and trying to pursue. Aidan ordered Delta Nova to delay the pursuit for as long as possible before jumping back to rejoin the Jade Falcon forces.

The plan had worked even better than he had hoped. The main goal had been to get past any bridge defenders sent out to confront the Jade Falcon advance. Their original aim had not been to destroy the enemy 'Mechs, merely to get by them. They had done that and had come to within a few kilometers of Robyn's Crossing. The rest of the ComStar forces defending the bridge would now be forced to divide their strength as the 'Mechs of the Seventh Falcon Cluster advanced on Robyn's Crossing and fired across the river.

Ahead of him, Aidan saw some debris being bounced along the swift currents of the Prezno. Some bits were obviously BattleMech sections, some were unidentifiable pieces of metal, but Aidan saw at least one strut that he was certain was part of the Robyn's Crossing bridge. Soon Clan warriors would be fighting to reclaim Robyn's Crossing. He could almost smell the heated odors, taste the burning metal being carried on the air, feel the rough tremors of weapons fire and explosions.

32

"How unClanlike," came a voice that seemed to fill Aidan's cockpit and which he recognized immediately as Kael Pershaw's. The man in the half-mask had patched into the Falcon Guard commline.

"What is that?" Aidan said, hoping that Kael Pershaw's voice was not now coming from the spirit world, even if it sounded like it did.

"Why, your maneuver, of course. What nonsense to go charging past your enemy, taking potshots and dividing your attention among BattleMechs." An odd reverberating noise seemed to fill the cockpit, and it was a moment before Aidan realized it was not some *Timber Wolf* malfunction, but merely the amplified sound of Kael Pershaw clucking his tongue. "Dreadfully unClanlike. Too bad it worked so well, Star Colonel. You are now being praised among those who would have preferred to speak of you in smug castigation."

"Where *are* you, Kael Pershaw?"

"In a scout aircraft, a *Specter*, high above you. Right now we are flying as high as the atmosphere of a planet permits, but the craft's sensors can study the terrain below down to the smallest speck of dust. I exaggerate, perhaps, but I was able to watch your charge in great detail. I enjoyed it. It reminded me of an Inner Sphere entertainment holotape I once viewed."

"I am pleased that you have a new toy. Are you going to interrupt me frequently with immediate reports on my actions?"

"I do not plan to. But I may, Star Colonel Aidan Pryde."

Now that the Jade Falcons were only three kilometers

from Robyn's Crossing, Aidan could see wreckage strewn from one bank of the wide Prezno River to the other. Com Guard 'Mechs were moving out to meet them, this time with more caution than the first detachment had shown. The latter, though still in disarray, was currently attempting a clumsy pursuit.

"You intend to be my conscience, *quiaff*?"

"Neg. More like your overseer. I am sincere in saying that I wish you to do well, Aidan Pryde. I wish to be present when they accept the contribution of your genes into the gene pool."

"You may live forever then, which I can believe. Perhaps you have not examined my codex lately."

As if to emphasize his point for Kael Pershaw, Aidan raised his right arm, where the codex was worn. He knew Pershaw could not see the gesture; then again, in his splendiferous *Specter*, perhaps he could.

"On the contrary, Aidan Pryde. I *have* looked at your codex. I am a student of it."

"Then you know it is a long record of tainted achievements. Not the codex of a warrior whose genes would be deemed worthy of the gene pool."

"But what you do now can expunge the past. You have inspired the Falcon Guards to confidence and success. The unit is no longer shamed by *dezgra*. What they achieve now will also bring you new honor. What *you* do will gain you the gene pool, I am certain."

"That matters little now, Kael Pershaw. My personal wishes are irrelevant. I am a Clan warrior and my responsibility is clear. My task is not to win the honor of the gene pool, but to fight for the Clan."

"Admirable sentiments. But no warrior ever quite forgets his blood legacy. Go forward, Aidan Pryde. Robyn's Crossing is near, and it is nearly yours."

There seemed a sudden change in the atmosphere of the cockpit, and Aidan knew that Kael Pershaw had ended the transmission from the *Specter*. Or from some spectral world.

Aidan considered the possibility of the gene pool for about five seconds, which was all the time the sudden onslaught of the ComStar forces would allow.

* * *

MechWarrior Diana felt her *Warhawk* rock from side to side as a broad and massive 'Mech that her screen identified as a *Victor* made a solid hit near the cockpit. The enemy Mech looked so human that she directed a cluster of short-range missiles right at its head. She was lucky, she knew, when two of the missiles hit, destroying the cockpit shield and incinerating the pilot inside. The relatively undamaged *Victor* ground to a halt, balanced precariously on its legs, becoming a faceless but silent witness to the fierce battle for Robyn's Crossing.

Diana had no time to study her kill. Rotating her 'Mech's torso to the left, she took on a tough-jawed *Vindicator* that was presently aiming its right-arm PPC directly at her. Had she not suddenly rotated the torso, the crackling bolts of energy from the PPC might have torn into her *Warhawk*, wreaking heavy damage. As it was, the hits just grazed her 'Mech's chest and back. Facing her opponent now, Diana saw that the *Vindicator*'s own chest had been damaged in an earlier encounter. Just above the LRM rack in its left torso was gouged out a huge hole. If the apparently damaged missile rack still contained missiles, she knew a PPC hit into the hole would explode the *Vindicator* without need to use up valuable ammunition trying to wear it down.

Firing her PPC, she watched as the bolt of unbound lighting hit paydirt. The *Vindicator* rocked backward, then went up in an explosion so massive it almost took out a pair of lighter 'Mechs.

Looking around Diana saw that the Jade Falcons had pushed the ComStar force back toward Robyn's Crossing, where their backs were practically up against the 'Mech's of those trying to defend against the now-heavy firepower coming at them from across the river.

She could not tell why the ComStar 'Mechs had not pulled away from the bridge, especially now that the Clan Elementals were among them and picking away at them. Then she saw her father and his *Timber Wolf*, with Star Captain Joanna beside him in her *Mad Dog*, ferociously taking on three ComStar 'Mechs at once and advancing toward Robyn's Crossing. Recognizing him, she felt a twinge of joy.

* * *

Star Commander Selima had waved the surviving eighteen Elementals of his Star into the midst of the fray. Even with their heightened skills, the Elementals had to move fast to avoid being crushed under the giant feet of the BattleMechs and falling debris. More than once Selima had thought Elementals in battle were like the maddening presence of insects, but with a bit more potential for doing damage. Selima, with some help from his Point, had destroyed one ComStar 'Mech and was now looking to do the same for another.

He had fired off his short-range missiles and detached the mount, leaving it on the shore a kilometer or two downriver. Now all he had left was the small laser that was the left arm of his suit and the claw that served as the hand for his right. For an Elemental that was all that he needed.

A *Rifleman* hove into view out of the smoke of the battle. Though it was weaving a bit, having taken several hits to both its leg and chest armor, it was firing effectively at the *Timber Wolf* of the Falcon Guard Commander.

Selima admired Star Colonel Aidan Pryde, as much as an Elemental could respect a BattleMech officer. He also knew it would be wasteful to lose a commander in the battle for Robyn's Crossing.

He gestured to four of his Elementals, and then the five of them jumped onto the back of the *Rifleman*. Working with crisp efficiency, the Elementals tore away at the armor covering the ComStar 'Mech's back, then they jammed their small lasers into the breeches and fired. Megajoules of energy flowed into the 'Mech, myomer bubbles burned, support struts melted, and then, finally, the ammunition exploded.

The explosives went off in a rhythmic sequence, as the shells lit off one another. The structural support of the 'Mech failed and the *Rifleman* collapsed clumsily, its legs seeming to bend unnaturally, twisting on themselves, sending the machine crashing face-down onto the debris strewn ground. Halfway down, the pilot ejected. The Elementals on its back were tossed into the air and slammed into the ground. The explosion crushed some of them in their suits, but Selima survived, rising to his feet in time to see the enemy pilot's ejection seat deploy its parachute.

Bringing his laser to bear on the ejection seat, Selima easily picked off the pilot. With her blood spraying in several directions, she fell directly into the wreckage of her *Rifleman*.

Selima scanned the smoky terrain for his next attack. He immediately saw that MechWarrior Diana's *Warhawk* was in jeopardy, pinned between two ComStar 'Mechs. It was easy to recognize the *Warhawk* by the crude falcon insignia that had been painted onto its center torso.

At a signal from him, the Elementals nearest Selima joined him in wading forward, lasers blazing with blue fire. They shot off an arm from one of the ComStar 'Mechs, giving MechWarrior Diana a chance to fire with all her medium lasers straight into the cockpit of the other 'Mech. For this one, there was no need for Selima to kill its pilot.

"They are retreating!" Star Captain Joanna shouted with enthusiasm, combat being the only time she ever expressed that emotion.

Aidan and his Falcon Guards had taken the position by the wrecked bridge, pushing the ComStar forces inland. After some weak counterfire, the Com Guards had finally turned and walked away from the action.

Robyn's Crossing was now the Clan's. Aidan signaled the engineers on the other side of the bridge to come forward so they might immediately start work on constructing a bridge. There was no telling when the next ComStar attack might come.

In the next few moments, he received two radio messages, each welcome in its own way.

The first was from Marthe. "We have taken Plough Bridge," she said. "Congratulations, Star Colonel Aidan Pryde, on the conquest of Robyn's Crossing."

Aidan said he would see Marthe tonight in her quarters and signaled off.

The second call was from Kael Pershaw, in his *Specter*. "I second Star Colonel Marthe Pryde's congratulations. Indeed, you are both to be praised for your victories. From what I can see of the area around Robyn's Crossing, those parts not obscured by the smoke and dust of battle, your ragtag Falcon Guards have laid low a good number of ComStar 'Mechs. I commend you again, Aidan Pryde. Supply vehicles are now heading toward your position. A supply depot will be set up on your side while the bridge is being built. You have done well, Star Colonel. I now envision the scientists accepting the contribution of your genes.''

"For winning one skirmish?"

"More than a skirmish, Aidan Pryde. More than a skirmish. But you are not done yet. Soon you will attack Olalla. The Jade Falcons have a wonderful opportunity here. The other Clans, those that landed before the Jade Falcons, have not done well. Thus does it fall to us to recapture honor for all the Clans. Perhaps we can even become the ilClan.''

"I would like to contribute to the Jade Falcons winning the honor of ilClan on Terra."

"You will, Aidan Pryde, you will. Continue to follow your own instincts. Listen to none other. Do not even listen to me."

"Hard to achieve that, since you invade my cockpit with your ruminations."

"I will attempt to stay silent. And I like that word, ruminations. You have gained something from all those books you hide away, Aidan Pryde."

"How do you know about the books, Kael Pershaw?"

But there was finally silence in the cockpit.

33

The engineers worked furiously. The discovery of myomer several centuries before had considerably simplified the task of throwing up an emergency tactical bridge that was also easy to deconstruct and move to a different location. The light and flexible bridge pontoons could be carried easily to a location in sections, and then connected with slack myomer cables. Applying a simple electrical charge drew the cables taut and by varying the charge, it was possible to change the tension of the cables to suit the conditions.

The pontoons were assembled on the Clan side, in forty-meter sections. Each section was maneuvered out and linked to the end of the bridge as it stretched its way across the river.

The difficulty the engineers encountered was in keeping the linked pontoons in place in the turbulent river. Cables of every size and shape were strung to anchor the bridge and its sections. More cables were used to steady and maneuver the new sections to the end bridge. The shattered buttments of the old bridge, trees, Battle-Mechs, Elementals, and even simple techs were used to steady the floating sections.

Watching edgily from the Falcon Guard side of the river, Diana thought the sight somewhat comical, but also irritating because she was so anxious for it to be done so they could resume real combat. The fighting so far had intoxicated her. As in all addictions, she wanted more of it. Not later, not even soon, but now. She realized she was like a child at some village game, but did not care. All her dreams and expectations of the warrior life were being fulfilled in this Tukayyid campaign, and she was impatient with such unexceptional tasks as providing cover for bridge-building.

Diana's fingers tapped nervously on her joystick. Intelligence reports detected no ComStar activity anywhere near Robyn's Crossing, though the enemy had carried out some hit-and-run attacks at Plough Bridge. Marthe Pryde's BattleMechs and Elementals had easily beaten them back. Intelligence suggested that the Com Guards had pulled back into Olalla and Humptulips, ready to defend the objective cities against an expected onslaught. Well, of course, Diana thought. What else but an onslaught? After getting this far, the Jade Falcons were not about to cease being their usual fierce, merciless, and brutal selves.

When the fourth section of the bridge had been completed, all its pieces interlocked, all its sections tested by the fastidious engineer commander, the pontoons were hauled out into river. One pontoon slipped off its cable and went roaring down the river, bouncing on its surface like a child's balloon on a rush of air.

The cables were now attached to hooks on the bottom of a VTOL, which dragged them across the river to the other side. Several engineers were dropped from the vehicle to the bank, where, using battlesuited Elementals and a *Viper* to clutch the cables, the pontoons were positioned at this end while the opposite end of the bridge began to reach across the river toward the section on which assembly was continuing.

As the newest piece of the bridge was being maneuvered into place, a sudden shift in the river currents made one pontoon surge up, and the new section of the bridge buckled. The engineer in charge slipped to the edge of the bridge piece and nearly fell into the river. Grabbing a cable, he held on for dear life as the bridge piece teetered and seemed about to drop into the river.

Watching all this on her primary screen, which squeezed together the details of the scene to give a wider survey of it, Diana saw an Elemental break away from the pontoon cable that was his assignment. Shucking off his body armor with remarkable quickness, the now-naked Elemental ran toward the river bank. She saw that it was the Elemental she knew, Star Commander Selima.

* * *

Selima had studied the bridge-building with a scholar's detachment. It was just this curiosity about how anybody did anything that had helped him rise rapidly through the Elemental ranks to officer status.

When the disaster on the bridge occurred, Selima did not take time to think. That was not in his nature. A Clansman needed help. Warrior or tech, it did not matter. He let go the cable.

He ran toward the riverbank, the slight breeze off the river acting like a cooling vest on his skin. When almost there, he saw the engineer's grasp on the cable slip as the bridge piece shifted. The man slipped further down the cable and nearly fell off. The fall slid him away from the outstretched hands of would-be rescuers on the bridge itself.

It was just as Selima reached the riverbank that the man lost his grip on the bridge cable for the final time. Screaming, he fell into the chasm, landing first on the side of a pontoon, then falling away into the frenzied waters.

Selima dived into the river, his long body arched into a perfect swan dive. He entered the water with the smoothness of an athlete. Remaining underwater, he swam easily for several meters before surfacing near the pontoons. The people on the bridge gestured and pointed toward the spot where the engineer was last seen, his head emerging above water for the third time.

With quick strokes, Selima swam to that area, then dove underwater again. Using his keen eyesight, he scanned the area all around, up and down. He immediately spotted the drowning man, sinking downward, his body slack. The breath Selima had been holding all this time began to press painfully against his lungs, begging for release. As he let out just a bit, the bubbles tickled the skin of his face as they danced upward.

Fighting the underwater current with his tremendous strength, Selima reached the drowning man with swift, even strokes. Irrational resistance from the victim would be no problem for he was now unconscious. Grabbing him under the shoulders and holding one hand over the man's nose and mouth to reduce the swallowing of water, Selima used his powerful right arm to stroke upward toward the surface. Letting out his own breath shallowly, he felt the river try to push him back. But he overcame its resistance as easily as he might overcome an enemy infantryman.

When Selima finally broke surface and pushed the victim into the air, other Elementals on the shore cast a cable out to him. He grabbed it and let his comrades pull them to shore. The engineer did not seem to be breathing. Reaching the shore, Selima yelled to the others to bring him his battle suit.

As he pulled the engineer onto the bank, he saw the man's face turning blue while his body remained limp. Once they were both out of the water and up the bank, Selima told one of the Elementals from his Star to hold wide the opening of the suit. Lifting the body from the bank, he virtually dunked the engineer into the Elemental armor. Immediately the battle suit's medical diagnostic system began to operate, diagnosing the problem and pumping stimulants into the engineer. It was only moments before the man's body jerked suddenly and he began to breathe. Selima glanced up at an engineer officer who had just arrived at the scene.

"Works a bit quicker than mouth to mouth, *quiaff*?" Selima said.

"An attractive rescue," said Kael Pershaw unexpectedly.

Aidan was beginning to hate the way the voice erupted out of nowhere, just when he was concentrating on something else. Clan warriors were trained to react to sudden events, but nothing in any training or any manual prepared a warrior for a disembodied voice in the cockpit of his 'Mech.

"Are you sure? What if the Elemental had drowned? Was the life of a mere engineer worth the risk? The bridge will be built no matter how many engineers are sacrificed to its construction. But the life of that Elemental could mean the difference between victory or defeat in battle."

Kael Pershaw made a sound that might have been laughter, might have been scorn. From what he knew of Pershaw, Aidan opted for scorn. "I merely said the rescue was attractive," Pershaw said evenly. "I did not say it was necessary. Still, it shows the courage you have instilled in your Falcon Guards, and that is worth something to your codex. I checked the codex of this Elemental, by the way. His name is Selima. He can always be counted on to risk his life, even in such trivial situations as this. He is not like other Elementals, except in his wonderful fighting skills. In all other ways—his gentleness, his foolish risks—he is unlike most of his kind. In the same way a certain Clan warrior I know is not like other Clan warriors.''

''All right, Kael Pershaw, you have made your clever point. Is that why we are speaking again?''

''Neg. My purpose at present is to give you new orders. Cancel that. Certainly I cannot *give* you orders. I may only suggest possible modes of action that might conceivably assist the Clan cause, then implore you to accept them.''

''You are getting doddering in your old age, Kael Pershaw.'' The reference to Pershaw's age was a calculated insult, and the gruff sound that filled the cockpit told Aidan the barb had hit its mark. ''Tell me now what you expect from us. The Falcon Guards will serve the Clan.''

''Those are the words that send shudders up a warrior's spine. An *old* warrior's spine. Aidan Pryde, you and the Falcon Guards will be joined by Marthe Pryde's unit at a point four kilometers from where you now stand. The engineers at Plough Bridge have had too many disasters, and we are abandoning that bridge. The combined unit, under your command, will proceed to Olalla. Your mission is to take the city for Clan Jade Falcon by any means possible. We are concentrating our efforts on that city only. Once it is ours, we will mount an assault on Humptulips. Any questions, Aidan Pryde?''

''How does the battle for Tukayyid proceed elsewhere?''

''Better for you not to know. Clan Wolf will be dropping down soon, if that is any indication.'' It was. The other Clans had hoped to be victorious on Tukayyid before the despised Clan Wolf could enter the fray.

''When are the Falcon Guards to leave Robyn's Crossing for Olalla?''

''Immediately. Robyn's Crossing is not under imminent threat. Soon the end of the bridge will be close enough to the other shore for the 'Mechs equipped with jump jets to use it as a way over, much like your Operation Skipping Stone. The supply depot is already one-third built, and the bridge will soon be completed. It will not be long before the bridge and supply depot are well-defended by the Fifth and Ninth Falcon Clusters. Your troops will attempt to lay siege at Olalla. Reinforcements will arrive within hours. I suggest you organize your Falcon Guards, re-arm yourselves with the first supplies brought in for the new depot, and get on the move.''

Again the voice went away abruptly. Aidan first scanned the area to test whether Kael Pershaw's evaluation was accurate, and not just misty words from a *Specter*. Then he informed Star Captains Joanna and Jula Huddock that the Falcon Guards would be moving out immediately.

MechWarrior Diana nearly shouted with glee at the new orders. Visions of glory at Olalla invaded her mind. She tried to shake them, but she was a Clan warrior, and a Jade Falcon one at that—a proud member of Pryde's Pride. How could she *not* dream of glory?

=======**34**=======

If Olalla had not been one of the two predetermined Jade
Falcon objectives, according to the agreement between
ComStar and the ilKhan, no self-respecting military outfit would have wanted it as a target. Surrounded by hills
and laid out in an ugly, patternless sprawl across a pallid
stretch of Prezno Plain, it displayed no purpose. According to intelligence reports, Olalla was a marketplace for
harvested crops. Indeed, it possessed a number of areas
that no doubt served as large open-air markets when the
planet was not under invasion. But the buildings around
these areas were gray and dull-looking, their windows
dirty, the roof shingles hanging at odd angles. Few streets
were paved, and Olalla looked old and somehow unfin-
ished.

Like me as a warrior, thought Star Commander Jula
Huddock, gazing down from a hill onto Olalla. She would
never speak such a thought aloud, however. Jula Huddock rarely talked at all. If addressed by a superior officer, she responded in crisp military style. When she
needed to communicate with subordinate warriors or
techs, she did so efficiently, wasting no words, in a series
of short sentences.

Other warriors said that Jula Huddock spoke best with
her weapons. She rarely wasted a shot or used a missile
ineffectively. Even age had not diminished her abilities.
Upon taking command of the Falcon Guards, Aidan had
been impressed by her codex, enough to wonder briefly
if the Clans were wise to relegate old warriors to lesser
roles. In a way, Jula Huddock's assignment to the Guards
had prolonged her career as a warrior. On the verge of
reassignment to a training unit on Ironhold, she had been

reclaimed for real combat when older warriors had been recruited to fill out the slots in the Falcon Guards.

As always, she was ready to do her best in the coming battle.

But where was the battle? In front of the Falcon Guards was an unsightly little city that seemed abandoned and unimportant. No ComStar 'Mechs were about, no evidence of any firepower in service to Olalla. Scanners detected no BattleMech activity in the surrounding area.

Jula Huddock tensed, awaiting the moment when the order would come to fire, launch, jump, or die.

"Do you think they are ceding Olalla to us?" Aidan asked Horse.

"Why? Because we demolished their forces at the bridge? Not likely."

"Remember," Joanna said, "the Com Guards are in the habit of attacking from ambush. Maybe they are concealed down there."

"I see no building big enough to hide a 'Mech," Marthe said. "And the buildings look too old to be recent camouflage."

"I agree," Aidan said. "What is your view, Jula Huddock?"

"I sense danger, but do not know why."

"MechWarrior Diana?"

There was a delay as Diana reacted with surprise at being addressed at all. Her being a new warrior and a freeborn, why would anyone want her opinion?

"Perhaps we should go in and take a look around," she said.

"That may be just what they want us to do," Horse commented. "Especially if Star Captain Joanna is right about the possibility of ambush."

"I am surprised to hear you agree with me, MechWarrior Horse. We were such enemies once."

"In a situation like this, the past is prologue."

"An interesting phrase. A freeborn phrase?"

"In a way."

Only Aidan would know that Horse was quoting from one of the books in their secret library.

"I believe it would be a mistake for the entire unit to

enter Olalla. One Star will go on ahead, while the rest of us cover their advance. Volunteers?''

The commline was in commotion as all the Star commanders volunteered.

''Sir?'' It was the soft voice of Jula Huddock after the voices of the rest had died down.

''Yes, Star Captain?''

''I recommend my Star be chosen. We are the only intact Star in all the Falcon Guard Trinaries. All others lost BattleMechs to combat, the breakwater, the jump across the Prezno. We are the only Star that still has five BattleMechs functional.''

This might have been the most anyone had ever heard Jula Huddock speak at one time. Aidan realized for the first time that the woman had a beautiful voice, deep and with an earthy sound to it. It went so well with the worldly knowledge in her eyes.

''Well-bargained and done, Star Commander Jula Huddock. Proceed.''

''Gladly. Alpha Heavy, forward echelon right, twenty meters apart.''

Jula Huddock's *Executioner* led the way toward the city. She was followed, in order, by the 'Mechs of MechWarriors Alyn, Lan, Eleny, and Crocco. They made a pretty picture, Aidan thought, as each 'Mech in the diagonal line kept an even distance from the others. Joanna had trained all the Falcon Guards well in all aspects of Clan warrior discipline, and her skill showed continually in everything the Guards did.

All around them the landscape was darkening. The sun had just about disappeared behind the distant mountains, and lengthening shadows slowly erased the finer details of the landscape. The dull-colored city of Olalla lost even more definition and became an odd blend of grays and browns.

Where had the ComStar forces gone?

As Jula Huddock and her Star crossed into the city, she was more certain than ever that Olalla had never been meant for a defense. It was designed all wrong. It did not even possess city walls. It was an open city, accessible from all directions.

Up close the buildings of Olalla were no better-looking

than from a distance. If anything, they looked worse. Even through the *Executioner*'s small viewport, one could see the architectural decay of the place. Buildings were chipped, peeled, or full of jagged holes. Broken glass, rubble, and other debris littered the streets. Had anybody ever lived in Olalla?

"Something is wrong down there," Kael Pershaw announced abruptly.

"We realize that, Kael Pershaw," Aidan said.

"No. I mean something *specific*. I have just checked some old records of Olalla with the conformations down there. They do not jibe."

"What are you saying? That this is *not* Olalla? It is at the exact coordinates provided by—"

"The coordinates are fine. But ComStar is up to something. The pre-invasion holos that I have of Olalla show a well-kept, architecturally sound village. The buildings should be pristine, and some of them with more storeys than those you see below. The city's streets are organized in a grid pattern, not the haphazard pathways you see. The marketplace areas were landscaped in green grass, with many colorful booths permanently set up. That is what I mean when I say this is not Olalla. Olalla is gone."

"How can that be?"

"I am not certain, but I suspect that before our arrival insystem, the old city was razed or somehow moved, evacuated with its citizenry. This motley collection of buildings was substituted for the original. The marketplaces were altered. Aidan Pryde, this Olalla is a false city. It is designed to lure you in. Do not, I repeat, do not commit your entire force to Olalla. Wait."

Kael Pershaw's last word was clipped, as if he had flipped his sign-off toggle while still speaking. Aidan went on the general commline and passed on Pershaw's information to the other Jade Falcons. "Does it make sense to any of you?" he asked.

"Yes," Diana said. "Remember the first ambush, when MechWarrior Faulk lost his leg? The Com Guards came out of the orchard, from under the ground."

"But why do we not detect their presence? At this

range Alpha Heavy's sensors should have picked up something," Horse said.

"Perhaps ComStar has been able to mask their presence so that sensors cannot pick them up," Marthe suggested. "Something that rejects scan waves or sends false information back with them. There are technological precedents for—"

"We must get Alpha Heavy out of there!" Joanna said, just as the ComStar assault began in Olalla.

Jula Huddock had sensed anomalies even before Aidan and the others began to discuss them. The buildings looked thrown-together and never lived in. There were traces of old foundations peeking out from the fake constructions. When viewed up close, everything about Olalla seemed fraudulent, jerrybuilt.

Later, Aidan would realize that Alpha Heavy's early presence may have saved the rest of the Cluster. The ComStar forces had certainly intended to ambush all of them. They would have waited until the Guards were comfortably in Olalla or close enough to it, and then sprung their trap. But in monitoring communications between the Jade Falcon warriors, the ComStar commander saw that the opportunity for an ambush had passed, so he ordered an all-out attack instead.

"Jula Huddock!" Joanna yelled over the commline. "Withdraw your Star at once!"

But the warning came too late for Alpha Heavy. Large metal portals hidden underneath a hastily laid, thin layer of soil suddenly sprang open in each market area. The dirt went flying in all directions, creating a dark cloud from which emerged the first ComStar BattleMechs, leaping out of the underground vaults with their jump jets aglow. Close on their heels were the heavier 'Mechs, clomping out of the vault with their weapons firing and missiles launching. As the sudden strike engulfed Alpha Heavy, Jula Huddock realized how wrong she had been to think Olalla offered no form of camouflage. The barrenness of the marketplace had deceived her, even though she knew that the last area that should look barren was a marketplace originally designed for the sale of fresh crops.

Just then, a cluster of SRMs exploded against Mech-

Warrior Lan's *Mad Dog*, followed by intense laser fire that sent the 'Mech reeling backward before it fell. Lan ejected but was picked off by autocannon fire.

The rest of Alpha Heavy was soon surrounded by attacking ComStar 'Mechs, with no retreat route. They fought fiercely and well. Three ComStar BattleMechs fell almost simultaneously, then another pair, as Jula Huddock and the others fired rapidly. But one by one the Falcon Guard 'Mechs were destroyed. First MechWarrior Eleny's *Hellbringer*, then the *Summoner*s of MechWarriors Crocco and Alyn.

Finally it was just Jula Huddock's *Executioner*. She stood her ground, firing sharply, efficiently, and calmly at the mass of ComStar BattleMechs coming at her. Then she became aware that the Jade Falcons outside the town were launching LRMs, which exploded distantly and sent bits of ComStar 'Mechs into the air.

Jula Huddock merely kept on firing, with no let-up. First one ComStar machine went down, then another. When the end came, Jula Huddock knew it was all over. But first she had the satisfaction of seeing the enemy 'Mech begin to explode just as its last missile salvo made its fatal strike against her *Executioner*.

=== 35 ===

Even before Jula Huddock had fallen, Aidan began to shout orders into his commline. Joanna turned his words into action, deploying BattleMechs across the field between the Jade Falcons and Olalla.

Jula Huddock's destroyed *Executioner* was just toppling over when Aidan launched his first LRMs at the first rank of ComStar 'Mechs, now pouring out of Olalla toward the Jade Falcon lines. The air outside the village was filled with missiles and the streak of laser fire.

Jula Huddock's BattleMech was falling toward the ground when Aidan struck a *Kintaro* with blasts from his large lasers. Flames shot from the twin holes he had opened in the right torso.

Jula Huddock's BattleMech hit the ground as the *Kintaro* exploded, disintegrating into an impressive fireball. Without hesitation, Aidan turned to face his next foe.

Joanna meanwhile had waded into a group of ComStar 'Mechs, firing left and right, hitting with a precision born of more than two decades of training and experience. Seeing a trio of enemy 'Mechs standing especially close together, she launched swarm missiles at them. Two of the enemy 'Mechs staggered under the impact of high torso strikes; the third, hit low, suddenly shifted sideways as its leg collapsed. A follow-up barrage from Joanna annihilated all three.

But there were so many. For every ComStar 'Mech that fell, another seemed to materialized immediately to take its place.

Diana, standing her ground and firing at any ComStar BattleMech that came near, was thrilled to discover that she was a born warrior. All her target practice paid off as she took care of one ComStar machine, then rotated her 'Mech's torso to the left and got another with a swift shot to the head. Almost gleefully, she watched the enemy's cockpit canopy crack, then open. A fire had started somewhere inside the cockpit and the flames leaped outward. But she had no more time to watch the pretty sight as yet another powerful ComStar BattleMech came into her line of vision. Diana whirled her 'Mech's torso to defend against it.

Aidan was surprised at how fragile these ComStar BattleMechs seemed. Hits that would have done no more than stall a Clan OmniMech were ruinous to them. Although outnumbered, the Falcon Guards and the 'Mechs from Marthe's Cluster were more than holding their own. In mere moments they had stopped the ComStar advance, held them in a toe-to-toe for a short while, then driven them back toward Olalla. Night had come, and victory would soon be theirs.

The battle was fierce, to be sure, but for every Clan 'Mech damaged or lost, the Falcons had knocked down, destroyed, or blown up at least three ComStar 'Mechs. At Aidan's order, the Jade Falcons began to move methodically toward Olalla.

When Aidan nearly cut a *Crab* in half, Kael Pershaw's voice again intruded. "A fine effort, Aidan Pryde. A fine effort. Again you prove your worth and the restoration of the Falcon Guards."

"We have them, Kael Pershaw. They are on the run."

"That is true. But, unfortunately, you have not won."

"Why not?"

"Look to the skies beyond Olalla."

Aidan saw nothing at first, then a dot became a ball and the ball became a DropShip. It was not the only DropShip headed toward Olalla. There were six. They were like unwelcome insects, announcing their arrival before delivering their poison.

"Another unit?" Aidan asked.

"Reinforcements from the Humptulips garrison. With no one to fight there, ComStar has sent some of those warriors here."

"All right. We will take care of them too while Jade

Falcon command sends a Cluster to claim Humptulips without a fight. Both objectives will be gained.''

"If that were only possible . . .''

Aidan was as irritated as he was puzzled. Pershaw always had some bit of information he was deliberately holding back. He recalled Kael Pershaw's penchant for unusual punishment when Pershaw was the Glory Station Commander and Aidan just one of his Star Commanders.

"Tell me all, Kael Pershaw. All. Now.''

"We have no Clusters to send to Humptulips. We cannot even send in a single Elemental to plant a banner and claim it. All are engaged in the new battle for Robyn's Crossing.''

"The new battle?''

"It came swift and fierce, something like the Prezno River itself. What you see coming at you is about a third of the Humptulips warriors. The rest swept down onto Robyn's Crossing not long after the bridge was finished and the supply depot set up. The Jade Falcon warriors have fought well, but casualties are high on both sides. But the ComStar 'Mechs used infernos, and the flaming gel of those missiles turned the supply depot into a raging inferno in less than a minute. The ammo and missile explosions are lighting up the skies behind you. If you had looked, you would have seen it. Had you not been under attack yourself, you would have heard it, felt it.''

Aidan was suddenly aware that the night skies were considerably lighter than when the battle had begun. Turning to look back, he saw a yellow aura arcing over the flatland.

Turning his attention forward again, he said, "Then we must take Olalla for the Jade Falcons. If one objective is gained, then—''

"Have you checked the ammunition status for your 'Mechs? And how many tons of armor and repair parts are necessary to bring your unit up to full strength? With the supply depot gone, how will you rearm, reload, and repair your 'Mechs? And with the fight so intense at Robyn's Crossing, you cannot hope for reinforcements.''

"We will do the job ourselves.''

"No. You cannot. The Humptulips warriors are arriving fresh, fully armed, fully supplied. No matter how great your skill, they will wear you down. I suspect the maneuver was calculated, part of ComStar strategy. Once they saw we would concentrate on Olalla, they must have plotted to make us use up our firepower there before they brought in reinforcements.''

"Your words are too full of caution, Kael Pershaw. What has happened to the Clans?"

"We are being defeated on Tukayyid, that is what has happened. Supplies are insufficient and casualties are mounting. Other Clans did not even get this close, Aidan Pryde. Only Clan Wolf seems to stand between the Clans and total defeat.''

"Then we will fight these ComStar forces to the death. We will at least die honorably.''

"You will not even do that. The Falcon Guards are needed back at the bridge. Our warriors are pinned down. We are to retreat to the DropShips, and I must ask—no, order—the Falcon Guards to provide cover for the withdrawal.''

"But Olalla—we have come so far and have almost captured the objective.''

"Yes, *almost*. I have the best computer setup possible here in the *Specter*, and have run all information through it from every angle that I know. And, as you are aware, my ability as a strategist is the only reason I am still active in a Jade Falcon uniform. I see no way for the Falcon Guards to take and hold Olalla, Aidan Pryde. You must retreat.''

"I wish to fight.''

"If you wish useless heroics, then fight. If you wish to do your duty by the Clan, begin the retreat. The ComStar DropShips are landing on the other side of Olalla. You are about seven kilometers from death. The choice is yours. If the Falcon Guards are annihilated at Olalla, it will be an echo of the unit's shameful defeat in the Great Gash. If you choose to withdraw, you can save Falcon Guard lives and assist the evacuation of all the Jade Falcons off Tukayyid. As I say, your choice.''

"You do not present a balanced case, do you?''

"I did not intend to, Aidan Pryde.''

Aidan looked around the cockpit of the *Timber Wolf*, fully expecting to see a transparent, phantasmal version of Kael Pershaw standing behind him. But there was no ghost. Aidan was alone in the cockpit, alone with his decision.

"The retreat then,'' he said sullenly, all the while every nerve, every muscle in his body, urged him forward.

36

Aidan Pryde's warriors did not need their 'Mechs' inertial guidance systems to find their way back to Robyn's Crossing. They needed merely follow the glow in the night sky. Every time it flickered, threatening to vanish below the horizon, there would follow a new explosion that turned the sky momentarily into daylight just as it had been settling back into the beckoning glow.

MechWarrior Diana did not know what to think. It galled her that they were beating the ComStar forces back and were about to enter the city of Olalla, when the order had come to turn back the way they had come instead. She understood that the enemy reinforcements would be fresher, that they would have the fighting edge, that they would even probably wear the Falcon Guards down. But she had wanted to see the Clan force take the city, even for moments, and would have been willing to die for the victory. That was what it meant to be a Clan warrior, she supposed. The way of the Clans and all that. Because the concept was so deeply ingrained, she felt a deep frustration, perhaps even despair, that they must turn tail and run.

It did not help to see the DropShips containing Hump tulips warriors pass high overhead, their aerofighter escort blasting away any Jade Falcon fighter that attempted to intervene. They were evidently on their way to join in the annihilation of the Jade Falcons at Robyn's Crossing. And where were they going, the vaunted Falcon Guards? To the same place. What had been the real choice? she wondered. To die at Olalla or at Robyn's Crossing? Did it matter where?

* * *

Aidan ordered his units to veer toward the Prezno River to meet it downriver from the bridge. "We are coming in along the river bank," he told his warriors. "They may not be looking for us there."

"I have news," Marthe said. "Plough Bridge is completely lost. The Jade Falcons there have either crossed over or been pushed down toward Robyn's Crossing. They are fleeing, in disarray. I have an idea, though. While you are taking the Falcon Guards along the river, I will try a pincer attack, coming in straight at them."

Aidan, for once in his life, felt a pang of fear in his chest. The battle was turning into a rout. The Jade Falcons could be wiped out. It would be worse than Twycross, where at least the destruction had been limited to the Falcon Guards Cluster.

Part of their route to Robyn's Crossing was littered with the debris of their earlier charge. The Falcon Guard 'Mechs had to step over downed BattleMechs and clumps of twisted metal, but nothing could impede their progress. Ahead of them the lights of battle were beacons that drew them on.

Aidan's strategy worked. No one on the ComStar side was looking for a riverside offensive. The Falcon Guards waded into the battle, firing freely at the heavily massed ComStar BattleMechs, transforming a few of them into wreckage. Simultaneously with the Falcon Guards' entrance into the battle, Marthe brought her Cluster's 'Mechs through the rear lines, creating a similar trashheap of ruined ComStar 'Mechs. So concentrated had the ComStar forces been on the ever-smaller group of Jade Falcons defending the bridge that they were not fully prepared for sneak attacks from units they had smugly expected to be wiped out back at Olalla.

The units of both Aidan and Marthe were at the bridge itself within two minutes of their first shots.

"Who is in command here?" Aidan yelled into the general commline.

"Star Colonel Gran Newclay," came the familiar voice of the Clan officer who had opposed Aidan in council.

"Gran Newclay, retreat your units across the bridge. The Falcon Guards will cover the retreat."

"You cannot order—"

"I will settle anything you wish in the Circle of Equals,

Gran Newclay, but I speak with the authorization of Kae
Pershaw and Jade Falcon Khan Chistu.''

Gran Newclay grumbled a bit, but the order for retrea
went out, and the Jade Falcon BattleMechs began to cros
the bridge. Because the makeshift bridge was so narrow
they could only go two by two, and could not move a
top speed. Gradually the Falcon Guards and the
BattleMechs from Marthe's Cluster closed the gap in fron
of the bridge, creating their own bridge of laser fire aimee
at the attacking ComStar 'Mechs.

The maneuver stopped any advance by the ComStar
forces, but created havoc on both sides as 'Mechs were
stripped and gouged of armor, as weaponry jammed, and
as some 'Mechs fell where they stood, more ComStar
than Jade Falcon.

The Jade Falcon Elementals did serious damage. Sta
Commander Selima alone, with little infantry resistance
was ferocious in his attacks against the ComStar
BattleMechs, peeling armor off the unsuspecting 'Mech
and firing accurately at leg joints. Other Elementals kep
up a steady series of hit-and-run attacks on 'Mechs too
occupied to notice the damage done by the human gnat
until one of their machine's legs collapsed or a fusion
engine blew out.

Selima suddenly found himself on the other side of the
ComStar lines. Looking around, he searched for an opportunity to do some fatal mischief. The idea came t
him immediately, literally dropping out of the skies.

Ahead of him, far enough away to be protected from
Jade Falcon 'Mech attack, a ComStar DropShip was descending onto a landing area that had been prepared, no
doubt hastily, for it. Running at his best speed, Selima
headed toward it, oblivious to danger.

Selima guessed that once the ship landed, its crew
would immediately begin to unload reinforcemen
BattleMechs. Those fresh 'Mechs would probably finis
the Jade Falcons at the bridge. Using his jump pack to
leap onto the side of the ship, he landed just above the
unloading door, where he waited.

As a ComStar *Highlander* began to lead his fellow
'Mechs down the ramp, Selima dropped from his perc
on the DropShip to land on the head of the 'Mech. He

stared through the canopy viewport at the startled ComStar MechWarrior. Drawing back his arm, Selima rammed the armored claw through the canopy. One, two, three times, he drove his fist, pistonlike, through the transparent armored glass. When the glass finally broke on the third blow, Selima reached in with his mechanical claw and seized the throat of the disbelieving Mech-Warrior. A twitch of his fingers and the pilot was dead.

Selima jetted off the *Highlander* as it toppled back against its fellows in the DropShip. A muffled explosion inside the ship gave testimony to the instability of a BattleMech's ammunition supply. He did not use up much time gloating, however, but ran straight back into the fray, continuing to do any damage possible to the enemy as he raced back to the Robyn's Crossing bridge.

When the last of Gran Newclay's 'Mechs had stepped onto the bridge, Aidan ordered his Elementals to weave their way across with these last 'Mechs.

When Newclay's 'Mechs were over, Aidan told Marthe to move hers across. "ComStar 'Mechs are sweeping across Plough Bridge, according to most recent reports. They are attacking the retreat on the right flank. Proceed there, and cover that part of the retreat."

The survivors of Marthe's Cluster made their jumps quickly and efficiently.

Now only the remnants of the Falcon Guards were left on the enemy side of Robyn's Crossing.

"Joanna!" Aidan screamed into his headphone. "Move us out!"

37

After jumping to the crest of the slope on the Jade Falcon side of Prezno River, Marthe took a moment to glance back at Robyn's Crossing. Down below, with the river churning and swirling under the bridge, the Falcon Guards had begun their evacuation. In precise groupings, the kind of drill for which Star Captain Joanna was famous, the Falcon Guard 'Mechs jumped to the center of the bridge, then to the other side. One 'Mech would have just touched and initiated its second jump when another came down immediately, as if deliberately fitting its 'Mech foot into the footsteps of its predecessor. The pontoons swayed and bucked with each landing Mech, but by some miracle the bridge stayed together.

As Joanna paced the BattleMechs in their escape across the bridge, Aidan, Horse, Diana, and the other 'Mechs kept up a steady barrage at the confused and disorganized ComStar forces.

Marthe wished she could remain to be sure Aidan got across, but she knew he would wait till last, deliberately and gladly putting himself in the greatest jeopardy. She did not disapprove. Such bravado was exactly what she had come to expect from Aidan Pryde.

When about half the Falcon Guards were across the river and sending fusillades back to assist the remaining defenders, she realized how much she wanted Aidan to survive this battle. They had often talked about love, but that was not what she felt for him. It was a concern for his life, something just as alien to a Clan warrior as the sentiment of love. The way of the Clan placed so little value on individual human life that Marthe was both surprised and pleased to care, if only for a moment, about the fate of one of her kind.

But now it was time to act again. She headed for the right flank, where she and her reunited Cluster would go on to successfully delay and, in fact, significantly blunt the ComStar attacks there. Marthe would not only survive the Tukayyid conflict, she would emerge from it as a Jade Falcon covered in glory.

Horse was reluctant to make the jump. He wanted to stay at the bridge and go down in flames. He knew that if the Clans lost at Tukayyid and had to honor a fifteen-year truce, this might be his last chance to die as a Clan warrior. Not many freeborns had the chance to do so well, certainly not so well as he. Freeborns rarely had the chance to go down at the front. It had taken the reborn Falcon Guards to give Horse his opportunity, and he would regret losing it.

But he was still alive when Joanna called his name, and he had no choice but to engage his jump jets and make the leap toward the center of the makeshift Robyn's Crossing bridge. It seemed to sway beneath him as he came down just behind MechWarrior Diana's *Warhawk*. They almost collided when Diana's 'Mech nearly toppled, but then she managed the second jump. Horse came in behind her, then went aloft again, cruising after Diana to the other side. Once there, Horse joined the Falcon Guards in their covering barrage.

Later, after he had survived the battle of Prezno Plain, Horse would find that his exploits were so confused in his memory that he did not remember what he had done when. Whatever these exploits were, they earned him commendations and a mention in the Jade Falcons' *Remembrance*. Two lines that extolled a freeborn who knew his place.

In the back of her mind Joanna wondered if Aidan Pryde would even make the jump. She thought he might send everyone else back, then buy some milliseconds for the others by staying behind. As the number of Falcon Guards lessened one by one, the remaining warriors had to keep closing ranks. This went on until only Joanna and Aidan were left.

It was time for Joanna to jump, but, uncharacteristically, she hesitated, the drillmaster disobeying the drill, to check on Aidan. He was blasting away with his medium lasers while at least a dozen ComStar warriors were shooting back without much success. The shots that did hit sent armor flying off from all over Aidan's *Timber Wolf*.

Then Joanna engaged her jump jets and began her leap, calling over the commline for Aidan to follow her. Glancing at her primary screen, she was almost surprised to see that he had jumped and was, according to the drill, right behind her.

On the other side, the Falcon Guards were already dispersing and making the jumps up the cliffside to gain a better position to defend the general withdrawal. Joanna requested permission to stay at the bridge with any volunteers to pick off ComStar BattleMechs as they crossed.

"Not this time," Aidan said. "We have to cover the retreat, and the retreat is retreating from us."

The Falcon Guard stand at Robyn's Crossing had allowed the Jade Falcons to make significant progress toward the waiting DropShips, but the Com Guards were not done with the Jade Falcons. When the Clan lines had retreated sufficiently from the Prezno River, the enemy brought in DropShips full of warriors and their 'Mechs.

"What are they up to now?" Joanna said. "Are we not retreating? Do they want to wipe us out completely?"

"That must be their intention," Aidan said. "We have damaged them sorely. They need their honor satisfied."

"What has honor to do with it now? The battle is over."

"It could turn, Joanna. It could turn."

"We have absorbed losses, our supplies are depleted, our—"

"But we are Jade Falcons, and we are the best of the Jade Falcons—the Falcon Guards. Marthe once said of me that I was a jade phoenix, a bird that dies only to rise again."

"I have heard of the phoenix legend, though this is the first time I have heard of it as the *jade* phoenix."

"That was Marthe's idea, her fanciful thought that even if I fell into the mire, I would always rise out of it on bright flames." Aidan smiled at the exaggeration, but it touched him that Marthe thought of him so. "Perhaps it is really the Jade Falcons who fit the legend best. We are a fierce Clan, and no adversity ever stops us. Perhaps *we* are the jade phoenix.''

"I think you should volunteer for a *solahma* unit. You are obviously old and doddering. Phoenix? Sounds like freebirth nonsense to me."

They had no time to continue the discussion, for the newly arrived ComStar 'Mechs were now heading toward the Falcon Guards. The two sides met in a ferocious and brutal struggle. The Falcon Guards, weary and low on ammunition, their 'Mechs pitted and scarred, nevertheless held off numerous attacks and managed to keep the Com Guards from breaking through their lines until most of the Jade Falcons had been lifted off Tukayyid. Joanna was among the fiercest of the Falcon Guards, topped perhaps only by her commander, Star Colonel Aidan Pryde.

With the retreat nearly complete, it was time for the Falcon Guards to make a dash for their own DropShip, the *Raptor*, which had just landed in the pickup zone. Aidan, Joanna, Horse, and MechWarrior Diana stood their ground, while the others raced toward the ship. No matter how many ComStar 'Mechs littered the field, there always seemed to be more, as though they had developed some kind of amoeba 'Mech that could split in two, then again, and again, and again. Intelligence had by this time broken down (nor had Aidan heard from Kael Pershaw for some time), so no one knew where the new 'Mechs came from. Aidan supposed that DropShips were landing new ones behind the lines.

"Everyone has reached the *Raptor*," Joanna informed Aidan.

"So quickly?"

"There are not so many of us left, Star Colonel."

"Yes, I suppose so. All right then, all remaining BattleMechs, evacuate!"

Joanna turned her *Mad Dog* toward the *Raptor*, Diana in her *Warhawk* right beside her. She almost did not hear the whining sound of the missile coming at them, but her 'Mech was rocked with its explosion. A second passed before she realized that the missile had hit the *Warhawk*, which was now toppling over. Joanna rotated her 'Mech and started to fire at the closest ComStar 'Mechs, without any idea which was responsible for the hit against Diana's *Warhawk*.

"MechWarrior Diana?" Joanna shouted. "Are you all right?"

The voice came back weak, faint. "I am—no, I am not all right. Something crashed through my cockpit. I am trapped in my seat. I cannot work the eject mechanism."

"What is wrong, Star Captain?" It was Aidan, who now stood alongside the fallen BattleMech.

"It is MechWarrior Diana, sir. She is trapped. Somehow the ejection—"

"I heard that, Star Captain. It is unfortunate, but there is nothing we can do. Our orders are to get to the *Raptor* immediately. Die bravely, MechWarrior."

"If I die," Diana said, her voice trembling, "I plan to die bravely."

"We leave her behind them?" Joanna asked.

"All techs have left the planet, medic or otherwise. There is no one to extricate her."

"I will extricate her," Joanna said.

"There is no time. You must not sacrifice your BattleMech for a single warrior, Star Captain Joanna. What has gotten into you? Into the *Raptor*!"

Joanna did not understand, never understood, what she did next. Or why she did it.

"I must tell you, Aidan Pryde, that MechWarrior Diana is the daughter of a scientist named Peri. You are her father."

"Father?" Aidan said in an odd voice.

"You were not to tell," Diana accused, but her voice seemed to fade out on the last word.

Aidan could never have explained to anyone the thoughts that went through his mind at Joanna's words. He remembered a time when he had sat by a lake considering the concept of father for a very long time. He had never really been able to understand what the word meant, or what the hated words mother or son or daughter or *parent* could mean to those people who assumed such roles in one another's lives.

Right now, he could imagine MechWarrior Diana in her cockpit, but what did it mean that she was his daughter? She might be a product of the liaison between him and Peri, but that was as far as he could proceed with the idea. Even all the books of his secret library, with their frequent tales of families, could not prove the meaning of what he had just been told by Joanna. He had been Aidan of the Mattlov/Pryde sibko, then Cadet Aidan; he had posed as the freeborn MechWarrior and Star Commander Jorge; he had reassumed his identity as Aidan, then won the Bloodname Pryde; had been a Clan warrior for almost two decades, had become Star Colonel Aidan Pryde of the Falcon Guards. Those were enough identities for anyone's life. How could he be *anything* to this MechWarrior Diana?

"Get to the DropShip, Star Captain Joanna!"

"And you?"

"You do not run a drill on my life, Joanna. Go!"

Joanna did not look back as she ran to the *Raptor*, nor did she think again of MechWarrior Diana for some time. She was astonished when she and her *Mad Dog* were taken into the *Raptor* and away from the now-despised planet of Tukayyid. Later, when she was honored for her role in the retreat, she scoffed, especially as the honors did not carry with them a permanent promotion back to Star Captain. But she accepted the commendations and the medals that went with them.

Elemental Star Commander Selima stood outside the *Raptor*, guiding the survivors from the Elemental Stars into it. The last ones had entered, with Selima taking one last look around when he saw Diana's 'Mech take the hit and crash with an impact whose tremors reached all the way to the DropShip. Characteristically, Selima did not stop for even a moment to think. He instantly began to sprint toward the fallen 'Mech, the loping sides of his battlesuit bringing him to it quickly.

Climbing onto the machine, he saw the crack in the cockpit. It was a fairly narrow crack, but an Elemental battle suit could rip through it, given enough time. Stepping up to the breech, he grasped one edge with his hand and braced his foot on the other. The servos on his suit's exoskeleton began to whine and strain. The heads-up-display flashed with warnings of stress tolerances exceeded and overload conditions. Selima continued to pull. Then with a sharp crack the twisted armor gave way, and he was looking into the cockpit.

MechWarrior Diana was in her command couch, large

pieces of twisted metal holding her down. One piece seemed wrapped around the ejection lever.

"MechWarrior Diana?" Selima said. There was no response. A passing light illuminated her face for a moment, and he saw her eyes were closed. Then the light went away, and he could not see her face any more.

Selima never stopped to speculate on possibilities. He just went to work, using his great strength to pull away pieces of metal that might be removed without further injuring the pilot.

As he reached for the neurohelmet, the BattleMech was rocked by another hit, apparently in the lower torso. Selima noticed an odd odor. Not being a MechWarrior, he could not know what it was, but he was able to sense danger in many ways, including through the sense of smell.

"Who is that in there?" boomed an amplified voice outside the *Warhawk*. Selima immediately recognized the voice of Star Colonel Aidan Pryde coming through his external speakers.

Quickly, Selima followed Aidan's instructions and identified himself.

"Star Commander Selima, report the situation inside the cockpit as simply as you can."

"The pilot is trapped in her seat. I have removed some of the constraints. I can remove the others, I believe."

"Is MechWarrior Diana still alive then?"

"Yes, sir."

"Continue, Star Commander—"

Aidan could not finish the sentence because suddenly he was fending off an attack from a trio of ComStar BattleMechs. Selima could hear him firing, and he caught his breath when he heard a missile explode against some part of the *Timber Wolf*'s surface.

Delicately, he lifted the neurohelmet off Diana's head. Her black hair spilled out as her head dropped back. He lifted her head and examined the rest of the cockpit seat. Keeping hold of her head with his right hand, he worked at the twisted metal with his left. For a moment, it looked as though the metal was too interlocked to come loose, then suddenly the whole mass of it freed up enough for Selima to slide Diana's body slowly upward and out of the cockpit seat.

It felt as if she were all right, with no major bones

broken. Holding her against his side with his right arm, her feet dangling down to his knees, he used his left hand to widen the canopy crack sufficiently to get both of them out.

As he was squeezing them through, Diana said suddenly, "Selima?"

"Be quiet," he told her.

"My . . . father . . . I mean . . ."

"Quiet. Do not try to speak now."

When they came out of the cockpit, Selima looked up and saw that Star Colonel Aidan Pryde was taking on several ComStar BattleMechs at once. Some of them had come around to block his path to the *Raptor,* while all were firing on him at will. He was rotating his 'Mech's torso back and forth, getting off shots every which way at the enemy.

"Take her to the *Raptor,* Star Commander Selima," Aidan's voice roared out of the external speakers.

Selima responded immediately, activating his jump pack and sailing for the DropShip with MechWarrior Diana cradled in his arms.

Selima was praised among Elementals for his rescue of the Clan warrior, but received no commendations or medals. Even those MechWarriors who knew of his name and his deed soon forgot all about him. Except for one MechWarrior. Diana never forgot him.

As soon as her 'Mech took the missile hit, Diana blanked out, coming to only long enough to hear the exchange between Joanna and Aidan. She tried to protest, but could not focus her speech coherently. What had possessed Joanna to tell Aidan Pryde who she was? The next moment she was dreaming that Aidan was in her village, living with Peri. Diana was a small child, so small she did not seem capable of speech. She wanted to talk to her father, but she could not speak. She could not even make a coherent noise. He spoke to her. She saw his mouth move, but she could not hear what he was saying. She was sitting on a rug. He reached toward her to pick her up, and suddenly she was looking at the visored face of Elemental Star Commander Selima. He was in her cockpit. What was an Elemental doing in her cockpit? They were not allowed there, were they? She could not move. In the darkness Selima's high cheekbones seemed more pronounced. He did not see her looking at him. Her eyes closed again.

In the new dream, Selima was talking with Aidan. Selima said that he wished to be Diana's father and asked Aidan to declare him her father. Aidan refused. Aidan said she was not his daughter, but he would not allow anyone else to have her for a daughter either. She screamed that she had to have a father somewhere, did she not? He said no. He said she was a trueborn, like him. Trueborns did not have parents. They were trueborns and they were warriors, he said. For some reason, his words made her feel good.

She woke up again and saw that Selima had carried her out of the cockpit. She heard her father's voice ordering Selima to take her to the DropShip. She tried to talk, to shout to her father that he need not accept her as his daughter. But her voice was gone and she was drifting back into sleep.

Later, after her citations, she thought back to that moment and wished that her voice had not, like her BattleMech, been disabled.

Star Colonel Aidan Pryde noticed with some amusement that neither his primary screen nor his secondary one showed any information. The effect, in this dark Tukayyid-dan night, was something like pillow-fighting in the dark. He was shooting off clusters, launching missiles, firing pulsing beams at targets that were only shadows in his viewport. Perhaps Horse had been right about this *Timber Wolf.* Perhaps it was jinxed. Something in it always seemed to be going off track or not functioning at all.

"You cannot get back to the *Raptor,* Aidan Pryde," Kael Pershaw said. "Why in the name of the Kerenskys did you delay? Just to allow time for one Elemental to rescue one MechWarrior? It makes no sense to me."

"Remain puzzled, Kael Pershaw."

Aidan wondered if he were really hearing Kael Pershaw or whether the voice was in his mind. It must be the real thing. No one would want to imagine Kael Pershaw.

What would Pershaw say if he knew that the rescued MechWarrior was Aidan's daughter? Kael Pershaw, after all, was one of the most virulent haters of freeborns.

Aidan had learned that back on Glory Station when he had endured Pershaw's trenchant and devastating insults against all freeborns.

The two of them might even have a long argument about how the rescue was not the way of the Clan. Aidan might have to explain about the jade phoenix. He might have to say that the rescue was another incarnation of the rise from the flames, this time with Diana being given the chance.

All Aidan Pryde knew was that he was satisfied about the MechWarrior's rescue. That was enough. There was no time now to consider anything else.

When a cluster of missiles exploded against the *Timber Wolf*'s right leg, he felt it shift a bit. When he tried to make the leg move, it did not respond. What did it matter? There was nowhere he could go.

He wondered how much ammunition he had left.

"To your right, Aidan Pryde, fifteen degrees," Kael Pershaw said. Aidan fired.

"Good. A head hit. That one is down. It was a *Rifleman*. Now, twenty-five degrees the opposite direction. Launch a missile salvo. Good. Direct hit. You hit one in the torso, the other near the cockpit. I think it is going down."

A blast of heat rushed over him like wave. The targeting system for his right-arm weapons shorted out, then the one for his left. He was out of missiles. Another hit on his legs made the surface of his *Timber Wolf* seem to shudder. But it did not fall.

Kael Pershaw's voice had stopped. Aidan discovered that the small laser in his left torso still worked. He kept firing it. Outside the viewport there was a huge flash. He had hit something.

There was no way he could come out of this battle alive. The flames would envelop him again. For one of the few times in his life, he laughed. Firing blindly, he laughed again when he felt the reverberations of a nearby ComStar BattleMech exploding. Another blast, and another 'Mech went down.

His death could not be fearful, he thought. Was he not, as Marthe had said, the jade phoenix?

Epilogue

"Joanna, when you told my father the truth about me—why did you do it?"

"I am not sure. I could not let the moment pass. Perhaps I have grown so old that my judgment is impaired."

"I would not say that. I mean, look at the way you whipped the Falcon Guards into shape, then ran the unit with so much precision during the Tukayyid battles."

"I did my duty, Diana."

"More than that. What of all the commendations you won?"

"Meaningless. We lost the battle, did we not? We must now accept a disgusting fifteen-year truce period, playing the part of mere occupation troops on the worlds we conquered instead of advancing victoriously toward Terra."

"All true, but the Falcon Guards distinguished themselves on Tukayyid."

"And most died, too."

"Yes, but no one can say the Jade Falcons did not fight well. Except for Clans Wolf and Ghost Bear, all the others lost their fights. Our campaign was at least judged a draw."

"A draw is a loss for the Clans, especially since Clan Wolf was victorious. And I am no better off now than before. They have demoted me back to Star Commander."

"And what about the honors awarded my father?"

Star Commander Joanna paused for a moment. "Yes," she said, "They were impressive. Very impressive indeed."

* * *

Diana, Joanna, Horse, and the remnants of the Falcon Guards were called back to the Jade Falcon planet of Ironhold. Not having been informed of the reason for the summoning, they were astounded by the respect with which they were addressed and the honors showered on them once they arrived. During the course of the ceremonies, they heard words that the Falcon Guards, led by courageous Star Colonel Aidan Pryde, had so distinguished themselves in the Tukayyid campaign that they had earned a prominent place in the history of the Clans, even some lines in *The Remembrance*. Although the name of Twycross was never mentioned officially, it was clear that the shame of the Great Gash had been washed clean.

But the best ceremony was saved for last. The Falcon Guards were summoned to a large building that stood alone on the shore of a beach whose sands shone even whiter in the bright sun. The light glittered and danced over the sands almost as much as it did on the waters.

The broad two-storey building stretched from one end of the beach to the other, built just in front of a landscaped, almost sculpted, woodland preserve. The trees were heavy with leaves and their bark looked scrubbed. As the group flew in over the building, Diana caught sight of a colorful garden nestled deep among the trees.

"What is this place?" she asked Horse, as they stood in front of the building's thick gray metal doors. Diana was enthralled by the door's many engraved symbols, none of which she could interpret.

"It is a gene storage center. Genes of Jade Falcon warriors are kept in large underground vaults, where they are tended by the scientist caste."

"Horse, you have been speaking without contractions for a long while. You are impressed, I can see that. Why?"

Horse only shrugged at first, then seemed to reflect briefly. "I am not sure, but I think it has something to do with forbidden territories."

Diana frowned. "Forbidden territories? What does that mean?"

"Diana, we are freeborns, and no one wants us ever to forget it. Trues walk among us like gods, dispensing favors and granting privileges. Their way may be wrong, but it is the life we live and to which we adapt, especially those of us who are warriors. I would change it if I could.''

"I would not. I am happy enough as a warrior.''

"Happy, a strange word. But yes, you are meant for exactly the life you lead. As am I. But we will never be the gods. That is the way of the Clans.''

"I should not want to be a god. All this genetic stuff and the honor that goes with it, it is too much responsibility. I prefer to mount the cockpit of a BattleMech and do my job. That is all the life I need.''

Horse's eyebrows raised quizzically. "You are young. And lucky. You have yet to experience some of what I have as a freeborn or what your father did when he pretended to be one of us.''

"Horse! You knew he was my father. How? Did Joanna tell you?''

The bearded warrior made a face. "Hardly. Joanna is not likely to impart any important secrets to me. No, I saw his face in yours the first time I laid eyes on you.''

"And you said nothing to him?''

"No. I knew that if he wanted to find out, he would.''

"Thank you, I think. But what about this place, Horse? Why does our being born differently make you hold the gene center in such awe?''

"This is where the trueborns come from. That makes it magical. Whether or not the scientists do create such perfect warriors as they think through stirring up the genes, the magic of it starts here. The essences of two warriors are mixed together with a wand, dropped into the magic hat, and the future trueborns of the sibko fly out of it.

"As a freeborn, I may think my lot sometimes unfair, but I am not immune to magic. If it is awe that I feel for this place, then that must be the reason why. It is like a church, but not just any church—perhaps a church from medieval times on Terra, with high spires, crouching gargoyles, saints grasping mitres and orbs, clerestories with birds flying in and out. The medieval church had its awesome mysteries, and the gene center has its own. Am I confusing you enough, MechWarrior Diana?''

"Definitely. You do often speak strangely, Horse. As if your words come from another place.''

"And, in truth, they do.''

"Now what are you saying?"

"I will show you after the ceremony," he said, smiling mysteriously.

Horse kept his word. He showed Diana the secret library of print-on-paper books that Aidan Pryde had carried with him everywhere. He told her about how he and Aidan had snatched time to read them, of how they had discussed them quietly—away from the other warriors—usually in the dark of night. He told her of how they had to be so careful in their conversations with others not to reveal what they had learned in the books.

"These volumes are also full of awesome mysteries, Diana. Your father often admitted that he did not completely understand them, especially anything connected with bizarre social customs like parenthood."

Diana flipped through the pages of several books, picking up first one, then another, then another, eventually filling her arms with them.

"I cannot understand some of the words, and some of the names are mouthfuls. But you are right, Horse. They are impressive. Would you let me read some?"

"They belonged to your father. Now they are yours, Diana. You can take over the tedious work of transporting them from place to place. I am happy to be quit of that particular duty."

Not knowing what to say, Diana said nothing. Instead she immediately sat down and began trying to make sense out of one of the books. When she became aware of her surroundings again, several minutes later, Horse was gone.

At the gene center Joanna, resplendent in ceremonial robes decorated with an array of colorful feathers, joined Diana and Horse, who were also in formal dress.

Joanna peered at the insignia on the uniform partially revealed beneath Horse's robe.

"You have been promoted, I see," she said to Horse. He merely nodded in response. "Star Commander Horse. That is a real tongue-twister. And uncomfortable in the bargain. Considering our past, I will find it hard to get used to."

"Perhaps I will be transferred."

"Let us hope so. Years ago, I would never have expected that we would one day share the same rank."

"For what it is worth, Joanna, I think that it was wrong of them to reject your field promotion because of age, after your valorous—"

"Shut up, Star Commander. I still am senior enough to berate you."

The ushers had opened the magnificent doors of the gene center, and the group was waved inside. They were led through long, barely lit halls whose undecorated walls seemed curious to Diana. After the ornate entrance, she had expected a similar magnificence inside.

A large platform took the group downward, into the depths of the building. The platform stopped and three of its walls seemed to drop away, revealing a sight that made even a veteran warrior like Joanna draw in a quick, astonished breath.

They were standing in a large hall, so enormous that its wall seemed kilometers apart. But the Falcon Guards were not concerned with the walls or their whereabouts. What dazzled them was the crowd of people seated in tiered benches all around the hall.

Scanning the multitude, Diana realized that almost all the Bloodnamed warriors of the entire Jade Falcon Clan were present. The audience, if that was what it was, maintained a dignified silence as the ushers led the Falcon Guards from the platform to a massive center table whose legs were sculpted to duplicate the legs of a BattleMech. Some people were already seated at the table. Diana saw her mother, Peri, standing behind the table among a group of scientists. Like the others, she wore the long, flowing white robe with black piping that was formal dress for members of the scientist caste. Although not surprised to see her mother in the gene center, Diana did wonder why she was present for this ceremony and dressed so ceremonially.

Joanna strode up to the table and peered into the eyes of a bald man whose face was heavily lined, its wrinkles crisscrossed with a series of deep scars. He wore crisp fatigues.

"Nomad," she said, "is that you?"

"I see you still have good vision, Joanna. For an old person, I mean."

"Rudeness and sarcasm. It could only be Nomad. They told me you were killed."

"I nearly was. You see the proof of it on my face. I was trapped under some girders for several days. But I will tell you about all that later. They are about to begin the ceremony."

The Falcon Guards took seats around the table, but only those who had fought on Tukayyid had been invited. The new replacements, none of them misfits, none of them too old, had been left behind.

In the welcoming rituals the Falcon Guards were again praised for their many acts of courage and honor at Robyn's Crossing, their near-victory at Olalla, and their dogged defense during the Prezno Plain retreat. Many warriors stood up and delivered heartfelt encomiums. If doubt remained in anyone's mind about the vindication of the Falcon Guards, it faded away during these speeches.

Then Marthe Pryde stepped forward.

"It is my honor to serve as Loremaster for House Pryde and I am especially honored to guide the officers of Clan Jade Falcon in the ritual we perform this day. Ferocious bravery is the hallmark of all Clan warriors, but at times there are those who transcend even that. These warriors deserve particular praise and a special place in the history of the Clan."

"Seyla," whispered several warriors seated among the tiers. Some others immediately echoed them, the word "Seyla" spoken slightly louder. Then it was the assembled multitude who joined in. "Seyla!" they shouted, the chorus of voices deep and strong.

"Such a warrior was Star Colonel Aidan Pryde."

Diana looked at Joanna, whose face remained expressionless. As far as the young warrior knew, Joanna, Peri, and now Horse were the only people in this room who knew that she was Aidan Pryde's daughter. What fantastic luck, she thought, to be included in this ceremony so accidentally, as just a member of the Falcon Guards.

While Marthe was ceremoniously naming the exploits of Aidan Pryde (only the heroic ones, none of the tainted episodes), Diana felt many mixed emotions. She rued not having had more chance to get to know her father, especially regretting falling into unconsciousness just at the moment he finally learned of her identity. He had fought to protect her, to save her, but he was dead by the time she regained full consciousness.

He had dispatched so many Com Guard BattleMechs that the exact number could not even be recorded on his codex. Yet, pleased as she secretly was to see him elevated to such high status, Diana wished she could have seen his face when he had learned who she was, wished she might have talked to him about how she had imagined him throughout her childhood and even decided to become a warrior because of him. It was not Clanlike to be sentimental, and Diana was not sentimental. She had never expected that Aidan would accept her as his offspring in any way. That would not have been the way of the Clan, after all. It was just that she wished simply that they might have spoken together once.

"And finally," Loremaster Marthe Pryde was saying, "it was the leadership of Aidan Pryde that kept the retreating Jade Falcons from being destroyed by the enemy. He and his Falcon Guards courageously held the line against the Com Guards. Because Aidan Pryde and the Falcon Guards destroyed so many ComStar BattleMechs, Clan Jade Falcon did not lose the battle, but earned a draw. For that act alone, he deserves all the honors we can bestow upon him."

"Seyla," called out the assembled warriors.

"With the approval of Khan Chistu and by a unanimous vote of the Clan Jade Falcon Council, the *giftake* of Aidan Pryde will give life to the next generation of Jade Falcon warriors."

Diana was astonished at these words. Even the normally impassive face of Joanna showed a flicker of surprise. More often than not, the *giftake*, a gene sample taken from a dead warrior, would be stored for years before transfer to the active gene pool—if ever.

"Do you realize the honor?" Joanna whispered to Diana, leaning in toward her.

"I am not sure."

"The genes of Aidan Pryde will enter the active gene pool immediately, without the customary interval between acceptance of the genes and judgment that they may be used to form sibkos. Diana, it is among the highest honors.''

Marthe Pryde raised her right hand and gestured toward a control panel raised on a dais next to the black wall to her right. A tech came forward and manipulated several buttons and switches of the panel. With a tremulous groan, the wall began to come open, gradually revealing an honor guard standing on either side of a rather short woman wearing the uniform of the scientist caste. The woman was quite old, a shock to Diana, who had seen old people so rarely since her village days. In the warrior caste, those considered old were about half the age of this woman.

The woman was holding a small wooden box of black wood set on a black cloth. Engraved on the top of the box was a delicately rendered picture of a swooping jade falcon. Falcons were also stitched into the edges of the black cloth.

Slowly, in precisely measured steps, the woman walked forward, the honor guard forming up behind her. With the honor guard's change in formation was revealed another figure, a man wearing the plain uniform of the active warrior instead of ceremonial dress. The uniform was crisply starched and decorated with many medals and honor patches. This was a warrior with long service, Diana thought.

''Who is he?'' she whispered to Joanna.

As the man limped into the dim light, which revealed his half-mask, she knew that she had heard of this particular warrior many times.

''His name is Kael Pershaw. He must be here to represent the Khan. Notice what he is carrying.''

In his good hand Kael Pershaw was holding a black leather folder that, Diana realized immediately, must carry the official papers relating to the ceremony.

''He looks like a ghost,'' she observed.

''Some think he *is* a ghost.''

The procession stopped in front of the table. Led by Peri, the entourage of scientists that had been standing behind the table came around to meet the woman carrying the box.

''Do you carry the spawn of the honorable warrior, Aidan Pryde?'' Peri asked the woman.

"This box contains the spawn of Aidan Pryde," the woman replied.

"I am empowered to accept the spawn of Aidan Pryde. I do so, conscious of the honor it confers upon me."

Peri accepted the box from the woman, who bowed slightly and moved to the side. As Peri turned, the honor guard formed around her and the other scientists. Marthe Pryde gestured toward the opposite wall, where a tech operated the controls to open it.

As the two sections of the wall parted, they revealed a black cabinet about two meters high. Above the cabinet was a series of holograms picturing the jade falcon in various stages of flight.

Peri walked slowly to the cabinet, with the cadre of scientists and the honor guard keeping deliberate pace with her. Kael Pershaw, in spite of his poor leg, also managed to keep an even, ceremonial distance from the others. For years afterward the transfer of the spawn of Aidan Pryde was vividly remembered because of the phantasmal presence of Kael Pershaw.

At the cabinet Peri stopped. Another scientist activated a mechanism on the side of the cabinet and its top slid open. From inside a small shelf rose up. Peri held the box toward the cabinet and said, "I offer the genetic legacy of Aidan Pryde for the Clan Jade Falcon gene pool. The legacy of this noble warrior is of fine heritage, with outstanding skill and splendid courage. Clan Jade Falcon benefits greatly by the acceptance of this genetic legacy."

Then she placed the box on the shelf and stepped back. The people behind her separated so that Kael Pershaw could come forward. Holding up the leather folder, he spoke in a solemn but oratorical voice. "This folder contains the official documents of honor for Aidan Pryde, whose codex shows him to be among those Jade Falcon warriors who have particularly distinguished themselves in virtuous combat." He placed the folder beside the genetic legacy container on the shelf. The shelf descended into the cabinet, whose top then closed.

The entourage turned and walked away from the cabinet. The walls closed behind them.

"All hail the genetic legacy of Aidan Pryde," Marthe shouted.

"Seyla!" sang out the assembled warriors.

"All hail his deeds in battle."

"Seyla!"

"All hail his life as a Jade Falcon warrior."

"Seyla!"

As Marthe continued to lead the ritual, Diana glanced at Joanna, wondering what she was thinking, especially the part about Aidan's life as a noble Clan warrior. Was she thinking of the taint that had clung to him, now officially removed by this ceremony?

As the ritual ended, a hush fell over the assembled crowd, broken suddenly when a warrior several rows behind Diana stood up abruptly.

"I am Star Colonel Caro Pryde of Trinary Bravo of the Twelfth Jade Falcon Cluster, and I herewith nominate my finest warrior, MechWarrior Isak, to compete in the Trial of Bloodright for the most honorable Bloodname bequeathed to the Jade Falcons by the warrior Aidan Pryde."

Before Marthe could even respond, two other Jade Falcon warriors from House Pryde had stood up.

"I am Star Commander Darya Pryde of Trinary Charlie of the Second Jade Falcon Cluster, and I herewith nominate the brave and distinguished MechWarrior Novalis to compete in the Trial of Bloodright for the most honorable and eternally admirable Bloodname bequeathed to the Jade Falcons by the warrior Aidan Pryde."

"I am Star Captain Mansoor Pryde of Trinary Echo of the Fifteenth Jade Falcon Cluster, and I herewith nominate the gallant and superbly resourceful Star Commander Velyn to compete in the Trial of Bloodright for the most deserving and honored Bloodname bequeathed to the Jade Falcon lineage by the warrior Aidan Pryde."

At first Diana marveled at the subtlety with which the various warriors of House Pryde embellished their nominations, as each one rose to offer his or her candidate for the valorous lineage of Aidan Pryde's Bloodname. However, as the ceremony continued, she could not hold back tears. This was her father and, though it was not the way of the Clan, Diana was happy at the unprecedented renown that had come to him and his name on this day, a day she would remember forever.

Finally she was at peace with Aidan Pryde. They had known each other only in her mind, and that indeed was enough.

After the ceremony, when all had returned to the upper levels of the gene center, Peri stepped out from a doorway to confront Diana.

"So," she said, "It seems you found your father."

"He never knew who I was, except perhaps at the very end of his life, and I am not sure about that."

"You look well. Being a warrior has made you even more beautiful."

"I do not care about that."

"I know you do not. But at this moment I wonder what you must be feeling toward me."

"I do not understand the question. You are my mother."

"And what does such a concept mean to you, as one who comes from a union that has muddled both the trueborn and freeborn concepts of parenthood? I am asking you as a scientist whose lifework has been the study of genetic heritages in and out of the sibko."

Diana shuddered involuntarily. "You are like him, you know, like Aidan Pryde, distant."

"Do not forget that I, too, was once a warrior cadet," Peri said. "I am trueborn. If I seem distant, it may be only because of that. But tell me how you interpret parenthood."

"Well . . . I do not know what to say. During this ceremony I felt confused. I am too trueborn to be a freeborn, too freeborn to be a trueborn. I am some kind of misfit and maybe that is what he meant!"

"What who meant?"

"Aidan Pryde. I asked him why I was a Falcon Guard, and he merely said because he wanted me there. Maybe he sensed that I belonged with the Guards because I was as much a misfit as the rest, caught between two worlds."

Peri nodded and began to walk away. "Is that all?" Diana called after her.

Peri turned and smiled in a way that was neither trueborn or freeborn. "You have given me my answer."

"May I come to see you in a few days, and you can explain it to me?"

"No."

Peri turned around and strode away, leaving Diana still saying, "Mother?"

The ceremony over, Marthe Pryde was alone in the large hall. She stared at the wall behind which Aidan's genetic legacy had taken its place as part of the gene pool.

She remembered that she and Aidan were to meet after the battle in the quarters of one or the other. It was too bad, she thought, that the meeting had never taken place. In some way, it would have rounded out both their lives, from the sibko to their brief reunion.

Well, she thought, it did not happen. Tears had sprung to her eyes during the *giftake* ritual, but she would forget Aidan Pryde now. There was too much to do.

A shuffling sound in the darkness made her rise quickly, ready to fend off any attack.

Looking more spectral than ever, Kael Pershaw came into the dim light.

"You did well, Marthe Pryde," he said. "The ceremony was stirring; the nominations for Bloodright were positively inspiring."

"What will happen now? What of the Clans? Must we be content to merely administer the conquered worlds while this fifteen-year truce drags on?"

"Oh, I am sure we will find reasons to fight someone. If not the Inner Sphere, some other enemy. We are of the Clans, after all. We are warriors. We fight. That is the way—"

"I know. The way of the Clan. But is that all, Kael Pershaw? Honor and combat and Bloodnames and Bloodrights?"

"Is that not enough for you, Marthe Pryde?"

"For me, Kael Pershaw? Yes, enough for me."

"Then it is enough."

"Seyla," Marthe whispered, then swept by Kael Pershaw out of the hall.

"I had not expected the ceremony to be quite so impressive," Joanna told Diana. "I stopped Kael Pershaw when it was over and asked him if he had influenced the decision to transfer the genetic legacy so soon."

"And?"

"He acted like Kael Pershaw. He refused to speak with me. He just reached up his hand, made some tiny adjustment to that foul mask of his, and walked away. I hated that man when I served under him at Glory Station, and I hate him even more now."

"But you say you hate everyone, even me."

"Well, perhaps not you, Diana. You are no prize, but I do not feel a trace of hatred for you. As for everyone else, well, yes, I suppose I hate most of them."

"What about my father? What about Aidan Pryde?"

Joanna seemed to ponder the question. "He was a different sort of warrior, that is certain. When he first arrived on Ironhold with his sibko I predicted that he would test out all the way. And so he did."

"Did you like him then?"

"No, I did not like him. Sometimes I hated him *more* than anyone else."

Seeing the disappointment Diana could not hide, Joanna was amazed at the contradictions in this superb warrior. Why did she care about a father whom she had merely observed from afar?

"But I think I hated him less than most," Joanna went on. "Definitely. I hated him less than most."

Diana smiled, then frowned.

"He tested out all the way," Joanna said.

Glossary

Clan military unit designations are used throughout this book. The structure of each unit is as follows:

Point	1 'Mechs or 5 infantry
Star	5 'Mechs or 25 infantry
Binary	2 Stars
Trinary	3 Stars
Cluster	4–5 Binaries/Trinaries
Galaxy	3–5 Clusters
Nova	1 'Mech Star and 1 infantry Star
Supernova	1 'Mech Binary and 2 infantry Stars

ABTAKHA

An *abtakha* is a captured warrior who is adopted into his new Clan as a warrior.

AUTOCANNON

This is a rapid-firing, auto-loading weapon. Light autocannon range from 30 to 90mm caliber, and heavy autocannon may be 80 to 120mm or more. The weapon fires high-speed streams of high-explosive, armor-piercing shells.

BATCHALL

The *batchall* is the ritual by which Clan warriors issue combat challenges. Though the type of challenge varies, most begin with the challenger identifying himself, stating the prize of the contest, and requesting that the defender identify the forces at his disposal. The defender also has the right to name the location of the trial. The two sides then bid for what forces will participate in the contest. The subcommander who bids to fight with the *least* number of forces wins the right and responsibility to make the attack. The defender may increase the stakes by demanding a prize of equal or lesser value if he wins.

BATTLEMECHS

BattleMechs are the most powerful war machines ever built. First developed by Terran scientists and engineers, these huge, man-shaped vehicles are faster, more mobile, better-armored, and more heavily armed than any twentieth-century tank. Ten to twelve meters tall and equipped with particle projection cannons, lasers, rapid-fire autocannon, and missiles, they pack enough firepower to flatten anything but another BattleMech. A small fusion reactor provides virtually unlimited power, and Battle-Mechs can be adapted to fight in environments ranging from sun-baked deserts to subzero arctic icefields.

BLOODHERITAGE

The history of the Bloodnamed warriors of a particular Bloodright is called the Bloodheritage.

BLOODING

Blooding is another name for the Trial of Position that determines if a warrior cadet will qualify as a Clan warrior. The candidate must first demonstrate physical prowess in personal combat by defeating at least one of three successive opponents. If he defeats two, or all three, he is immediately ranked as an officer in his Clan. If he fails to defeat any of his opponents, he is relegated to a lower caste. If the candidate is successful in the trial, a complex ceremony takes place. He or she must be ritually defended by several Clan warriors when challenged by other representatives of the Clan, or else face those representatives in mortal combat.

BLOODNAME

Bloodname refers to the surname of each of the 800 Warriors who stood with Nicholas Kerensky during the

Exodus Civil War. These 800 are the foundation of the Clans' elaborate breeding program. The right to use one of these surnames has been the ambition of every Clan warrior since the system was established. Only 25 warriors, which corresponds to 25 Bloodrights, are allowed to use any one surname at one time. When one of the 25 Bloodnamed warriors dies, a trial is held to determine who will assume that Bloodname. A contender must prove his Bloodname lineage, then win a series of duels against other competitors. Only Bloodnamed warriors may sit on the Clan Councils or are eligible to become a Khan or ilKhan. Most Bloodnames have gradually become confined to one or two warrior classes, but certain prestigious names, such as Kerensky, have shown their genetic value by producing excellent warriors in all three classes (MechWarrior, fighter pilot, and Elemental).

Bloodnames are determined matrillineally, at least after the original generation. Because a warrior can only inherit from his or her female parent, he or she has a claim to only one Bloodname.

BLOODRIGHT

A specific Bloodname lineage is called a Bloodright. Twenty-five Bloodrights are attached to each Bloodname. A Bloodright is not a lineage as we define the term because the warriors who successively hold a Bloodright might be related only through their original ancestor. As with Bloodnames, certain Bloodrights are considered more prestigious than others, depending largely on the Bloodright's history.

BONDSMAN

Clans can keep prisoners taken during combat. These are called bondsmen, and are considered members of the laborer caste unless and until the capturing Clan releases them or promotes them back to warrior status. A bondsman is bound by honor, not by shackles. Custom dictates that even Bloodnamed warriors captured in combat be held for a time as bondsmen. All bondsmen wear a woven bracelet called a bondcord. The base color of the bondcord indicates to which Clan the individual is now bound, and the striping indicates which unit captured him.

CANISTER

Clan slang for the eugenics program of the warrior caste. It can also refer specifically to the artificial wombs.

CASTE

Clan society is rigidly divided into five castes: warrior, scientist, merchant, technician, and laborer. Each caste has many subcastes, which are based on specialties within a professional field. The warrior caste is based on a systematic eugenics program that uses the genes of prestigious, successful current and past warriors to produce new members of the caste (see **Sibko**). These products of genetic engineering are known as trueborns. Other castes maintain a quality gene pool by strategic marriages within each caste.

CHALCAS

Anything or anyone who challenges the Clan caste system is considered a *chalcas*.

CLANS

During the fall of the Star League, General Aleksandr Kerensky, commander of the Regular Star League Army, led his forces out of the Inner Sphere in what is known as the first Exodus. After settling beyond the Periphery, more than 1,300 light years away from Terra, Kerensky and his followers settled in a cluster of marginally habitable star systems near a large globular cluster that hid them from the Inner Sphere. Within fifteen years, civil war erupted among these exiles, threatening to destroy everything they had worked so hard to build.

In a second Exodus, Nicholas Kerensky, son of Aleksandr, led his followers to one of the worlds of the globular cluster to escape the new war. It was there on Strana Mechty that Kerensky first conceived and organized what would one day be known as the Clans.

CODEX

The codex is each warrior's personal record. It includes the names of the original Bloodnamed warriors from which a warrior is descended. It also records background information such as the warrior's generation number, Blood House, and codex ID, an alphanumeric code noting the unique aspects of that person's DNA. The codex also contains a record of the warrior's military career. See also **Master Codex.**

COMSTAR

ComStar, the interstellar communications network, was the brainchild of Jerome Blake, formerly Minister of Communications during the latter years of the Star League. After the League's fall, Blake seized Terra and reorganized what was left of the communications network into a private organization that sold its services to the five Successor Houses for a profit. Since that time, ComStar has also developed into a powerful secret society steeped in mysticism and ritual. Initiates to the quasi-religious ComStar Order commit themselves to lifelong service.

CONTRACT

A contract is an agreement between the commanders of two units that allows the commander of one to include the units of the other in his bidding for rights to a battle or trial. During the invasion of the Inner Sphere, Cluster commanders within Galaxies frequently made contracts to allow greater, and often more extravagant, bidding, while still maintaining a good mix of BattleMech, Elemental, and fighter combat units.

CUTDOWN

The minimum force necessary to win any trial for which there has been bidding. Bidders who can push their opponent into making a bid below the cutdown are considered clever. Commanders who win with a force smaller than the cutdown are greatly honored.

DEZGRA

A fighting unit that disgraces itself is known as a *dezgra* unit. The name also refers to the ritual whereby that unit is marked and punished. Any unit that refuses orders, panics in the face of the enemy, or takes dishonorable action is disgraced.

DROPSHIPS

Because interstellar JumpShips must avoid entering the heart of a solar system, they must "dock" in space at a considerable distance from a system's inhabited worlds. DropShips were developed for interplanetary travel. As the name implies, a DropShip is attached to hardpoints on the JumpShip's drive core, later to be dropped from the parent vessel after in-system entry. Though incapable of FTL travel, DropShips are highly maneuverable, well-armed, and sufficiently aerodynamic to take off from and land on a planetary surface. The journey from the jump point to the inhabited worlds of a system usually requires a normal-space journey of several days or weeks, depending on the type of star.

ELEMENTALS

Elementals are the elite, battle-suited infantry of the Clans. These men and women are giants, bred specifically to handle Clan-developed battle armor.

FREEBIRTH

Freebirth is an epithet used by trueborn members of the warrior caste, generally expressing disgust or frustration. If a trueborn warrior refers to another trueborn as a freebirth, it is is a mortal insult.

FREEBORN

An individual conceived and born by natural means is freeborn. Because the Clans value their eugenics program so highly, a freeborn is automatically assumed to have little potential.

GIFTAKE

This is the sample of DNA taken from a warrior who died with great glory in combat. The *giftake* is considered the warrior's best DNA sample and the one most likely to produce improved warriors.

HEGIRA

Victorious Clan warriors sometimes extend the courtesy of *hegira* to defeated opponents. *Hegira* allows the opponent to withdraw honorably from the field without further combat or cost.

INNER SPHERE

The Inner Sphere was the term originally applied to the star empires of human-occupied space that joined together to form the Star League. The states, kingdoms, and pirate domains just beyond the Inner Sphere are known as The Periphery. When Aleksandr Kerensky led his exiles out from the Inner Space, they traveled even beyond The Periphery, to regions yet unknown.

ISORLA

The spoils of battle that warriors can claim as their right, including bondsmen, are known as *isorla*.

KHAN

Each Clan elects two leaders, or Khans. One serves as the Clan's senior military commander and bureaucratic administrator. The second Khan's position is less well-defined. He or she is second-in-command, carrying out duties assigned by the first Khan. In times of great internal or external threat, or when a coordinated effort is required of all Clans, an ilKhan is chosen to serve as the supreme ruler of the Clans.

KURULTAI

A *kurultai* is a Clan war council. A *Grand Kurultai* is a war council of all Khans of the Clans. Only the ilKhan can convene a *Grand Kurultai* at any time or place. A normal Grand Council, on the other hand, may only be convened by petition of three or more Clans, and must be held in the Hall of Khans on Strana Mechty.

JUMPSHIPS

Interstellar travel is accomplished via JumpShips, first developed in the twenty-second century. These somewhat ungainly vessels consist of a long, thin drive core and a sail resembling an enormous parasol, which can extend up to a kilometer in width. The ship is named for its ability to "jump" instantaneously across vast distances of space. After making its jump, the ship cannot travel until it has recharged by gathering up more solar energy.

The JumpShip's enormous sail is constructed from a special metal that absorbs vast quantities of electromagnetic energy from the nearest star. When it has soaked up enough energy, the sail transfers it to the drive core, which converts it into a space-twisting field. An instant later, the ship arrives at the next jump point, a distance of up to thirty light years. This field is known as hyperspace, and its discovery opened to mankind the gateway to the stars.

JumpShips never land on planets. Interplanetary travel is carried out by DropShips, vessels that are attached to the JumpShip until arrival at the jump point.

LASER

An acronym for "Light Amplification through Stimulated Emission of Radiation." When used as a weapon, the laser damages the target by concentrating extreme heat on a small area. Battlemech lasers are designated as small, medium, and large. Lasers are also available as shoulder-fired weapons operating from a portable backpack power unit. Certain range-finders and targeting equipment also employ low-level lasers.

LOREMASTER

The Loremaster is the keeper of Clan laws and history. The position is honorable and politically powerful. The Loremaster plays a key role in inquiries and trials, where he is often assigned the role of Advocate or Interrogator.

LRM

This is an abbreviation for Long-Range Missile, an indirect-fire missile with a high-explosive warhead.

OATHMASTER

The Oathmaster is the honor guard for any official Clan ceremony. The position is similar to that of an Inner Sphere sergeant-at-arms, but it carries a greater degree of respect. The Oathmaster administers all oaths, and the Loremaster records them. The position of Oathmaster is usually held by the oldest Bloodnamed warrior in a Clan (if he or she desires the honor), and is one of the few positions not decided by combat.

OVKHAN

This is a term of respect reserved for someone of higher rank.

PERIPHERY

Beyond the borders of the Inner Sphere lies the Periphery, the vast domain of known and unknown worlds stretching endlessly into interstellar night. Once populated by colonies from Terra, these were devastated technologically, politically, and economically by the fall of the Star League. At present, the Periphery is the refuge of piratical Bandit Kings, privateers, and outcasts from the Inner Sphere.

POWLESS

Powless is the vulnerability that a warrior, particularly an Elemental, feels when forced to fight without his accustomed weapons. The word is probably derived from "powerless."

PPC

This abbreviation stands for Particle Projection Cannon, a magnetic accelerator firing high-energy proton or ion bolts, causing damage through both impact and high temperature. PPCs are among the most effective weapons available to BattleMechs.

QUIAFF/QUINEG

This Clan expression is placed at the end of rhetorical questions. If an affirmative answer is expected, *quiaff* is used. If the answer is expected to be negative, *quineg* is the proper closure.

RANSOM

Clan custom dictates that a warrior who has been successful at his Trial of Bloodright may be rewarded with a gift by the Clan. Depending upon the warrior's success during the Trial, the ransom might range from the right to choose what type of weapon he will use as a warrior to the right to command a special unit. At the time Khan Natasha Kerensky returned from the Inner Sphere and then underwent her second Trial of Bloodright, ilKhan Ulric Kerensky awarded her a ransom of the right to form the Thirteenth Wolf Guards.

REDE

One of the many forms honor takes in the Clans, a *rede* is an honor-bound promise. Breaking a *rede* may be punished by death.

REMEMBRANCE, THE

The Remembrance is an ongoing heroic saga detailing Clan history from the time of the Exodus from the Inner Sphere to the present day. *The Remembrance* is continually expanded to include contemporary events. Each Clan has a slightly different version reflecting their own opinions and experiences. All Clan warriors can quote whole verses of this marvelous epic from memory, and it is common to see passages from the book lovingly painted on the sides of OmniMechs, fighters, and even battle armor.

RISTAR

This term refers to a particularly gifted warrior on his or her way to high position. It is probably derived from the expression ''rising star.''

SATARRA

A Clan council may cast a veto, or *satarra*, to settle or postpone disputes between castes within their jurisdiction. *Satarra* is invoked only when negotiations seem at an impasse and/or threaten to disrupt the work order of the Clan. It seems to be more a ritual than an act of legislation.

SAVASHRI

A Clan epithet.

SEYLA

This word is the ritual response voiced in unison by those witnessing solemn Clan ceremonies, rituals, and other important gatherings. No one is sure of the origin or exact meaning of the word, but it is uttered only with the greatest reverence and awe.

SIBKO

A sibko consists of a group of children produced from the same male and female geneparents in the warrior caste eugenics program. The members of the sibko are raised together, then begin to undergo constant testing. As various members of the sibko fail at each test, they are transferred to the lower castes. A sibko consists of approximately 20 members, but usually only four or five remain at the time of the final test to become warriors, the Trial of Position. These tests and other adversities may bind the surviving "sibkin" together.

SRM

This is the abbreviation for Short-Range Missiles, direct-trajectory missiles with high-explosive or armor-piercing explosive warheads. They have a range of less than one kilometer, and are accurate only at ranges of less than 300 meters. They are more powerful, however, than LRMs.

STAR LEAGUE

The Star League was formed in 2571 in an attempt to peacefully ally the major star empires of human-occupied space, or the Inner Sphere. The League prospered for almost 200 years, until civil war broke out in 2751. The

League was eventually destroyed when the ruling body, known as the High Council, disbanded in the midst of a struggle for power. Each of the Great House leaders then declared him or herself First Lord of the Star League, and within months, war had engulfed the Inner Sphere. This conflict continues to the present day, almost three centuries later. This era of continuous war is now known simply as the Succession Wars.

STRAVAG

A Clan epithet, probably a combination of the Clan words *stran,* meaning independent, and *vagon,* meaning birthing.

SUCCESSOR LORDS

After the fall of the Star League, the remaining members of the High Council each asserted his or her right to become First Lord of the Star League. Their star empires became known as the Successor States and the rulers as the Successor Lords. The Clan invasion has temporarily interrupted the centuries of war, the Succession Wars, that first began in 2786. The battleground of these wars is the vast Inner Sphere, which is composed of all the star systems once occupied by Star League's member-states. The Successor Lords temporarily put aside their differences in order to meet the threat of a common foe, the Clans.

SURKAI

The *surkai* is the Right of Forgiveness. The Clans honor uniformity in thought and belief above all else in their society. When warriors disagree, when a Clan disagrees with the Clan Council, or when a member of one caste offends a member of another caste, *surkai* is expected. It is a matter of pride that the offending party freely admit his wrongdoing and request punishment. Those who show great *surkai* are held up as examples to others for their willingness to accept the consequences of their independent thoughts. Those who do not show *surkai* when it is expected of them are viewed with suspicion.

SURKAIREDE

The Rede of Forgiveness, or *surkairede* is the honorbound agreement between the majority and any dissenters. According to the *surkairede*, once a dissenter accepts punishment for having disagreed with the majority, he should be allowed to resume his role in society without suffering any further disgrace for having spoken out.

TOUMAN

The term given to the fighting arm of a Clan.

TRIAL OF BLOODRIGHT

A series of one-on-one, single-elimination contests determines who wins the right to use a Bloodname. Each current Bloodnamed warrior in that Bloodname's House nominates one candidate. The head of the House nominates additional candidates to fill thirty-one slots. The thirty-second slot is fought for by those who qualify for the Bloodname but who were not nominated. The nature of the combat is determined by "coining." Each combatant places his personal medallion, a *dogids*, into the "Well of Decision." An Oathmaster or Loremaster releases the coins simultaneously, so that only chance determines which coin falls first to the bottom of the well. The warrior whose coin lands on top chooses the manner of the combat ("Mech versus 'Mech, barehanded, 'Mech versus Elemental, and so forth). The other warrior chooses the venue of the contest. Though these Bloodname duels need not be to the death, the fierce combat and the intensity of the combatants often leave the losing candidate mortally wounded or dead.

TRIAL OF POSITION

The Trial of Position determines whether a candidate will qualify as a warrior in the Clans. To qualify, he must defeat at least one of three successive opponents. If he defeats two, or all three, he is immediately ranked as an officer in his Clan. If he fails to defeat any of his opponents, he is relegated to a lower caste.

TRIAL OF POSSESSION

This trial resolves conflicts in which two or more Clans claim the right to the same thing, be it territory, a warrior's genes, or even supremacy in a difference of opinion. This trial uses the formal challenge of the attacker and the response of defending forces, and favors those commanders from the attacking Clan skillful enough to bid minimal forces.

TRIAL OF REFUSAL

The Clan councils and the Grand Council vote on issues and laws that affect the community. Unlike Inner Sphere legislation, however, any decision can be challenged and reversed by a Trial of Refusal. This trial allows the losing side to demand the issue to be settled by combat.

The forces used in the Trial of Refusal are determined on a pro-rated basis. The faction rejecting the decision declares what forces they will use. The side defending the decision (the attacker) can field a force equal to the ratio of winning to losing votes. For example, if the contested vote carried by a three-to-one margin, the attacking forces can field a force three times the size of the force challenging the decision. Bidding usually results in a smaller attacking force, however.

TROTHKIN

Used formally, this term refers to members of an extended sibko. Less formally, a warrior will use the term trothkin when referring to someone he considers his peer.

TRUEBORN/TRUEBIRTH

A trueborn is a product of the warrior caste's eugenics program.

ZELLBRIGEN

This is the Clan word describing the body of rules used to regulate and ritualize duels. *Zellbrigen* means that combatants engage in one-on-one duels, even if both sides have many warriors. Those not immediately challenged are honor-bound to stay out of the battle until an opponent is free (meaning he has defeated his enemy). To attack an enemy already engaged with an opponent is a major breach of Clan code, usually resulting in at least loss of rank.

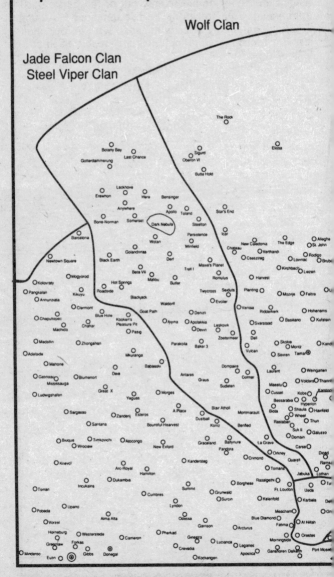

Map of the Inner Sphere Coreward Sector

Wolf Clan

Jade Falcon Clan
Steel Viper Clan

The Rock

Elassa

Botany Bay

Last Chance

Gotterdammerung

Sigurd

Oberon VI

Butte Hold

Lackhove

Erewhon

Hera

Bensinger

Anywhere

Apollo

Toland

Star's End

Bone-Norman

Somerset

Dark Nebula

Stealton

Barcelona

Wotan

Persistence

Icar

Golandrinas

Winfield

Chateau

New Caledonia

The Edge

Alleghe

St. John

Varthandi

Newtown Square

Black Earth

Derf

Maxie's Planet

Csesztreg

Lovmac

Rodigo

Kirchbach

Brubie

Liezen

Kokovraty

Mogyorod

Beta VII

Malibu

Butler

Tret I

Romulus

Harvest

Hot Springs

Mozyrje

Feltre

Ull

Pangkalan

Annunziata

Kikuyu

Roadside

Blackjack

Waldorff

Twycross

Sedulis

Planting

Varisaa

Ridderkerk

Hohenams

Clermont

Goat Path

Denzil

Evciler

Basiliano

Kufstein

Chapultepec

Blue Hole

Kookan's
Pleasure Pit

Ayyina

Apotakkia

Leskovik

Svarstaad

Skokie

Moritz

Kandi

Chahar

Pasig

Devin

Zoetermeer

Dell

Sevren

Tamar

Machida

Zhongshan

Parakoila

Baker 3

Vulcan

Madellin

Mahone

Miuranga

Dompaire

Laurent

Weingarten

Adelade

Babaski

Antares

Graus

Colmar

Cusset

Volders

Thannil

Karkson

Gatriaayu

Blumenort

Deva

Sudeten

Masstu

Kobe

Mississauga

Great X

Morges

Bessaraba

Hyperion

Ludwigshafen

Yeguas

Biota

Shaula

Hanfeld

Sargasso

Zanderij

Esteros

A Placa

Blair Atholl

Montmarault

Rastaban

Wheel

Thun

Santana

Dustball

Benfled

Suk II

Galuzzo

Buque

Timkovichi

Abscongo

Bountiful Harvest

Koniz

Graceland

La Grave

Domain

Carse

Wroclaw

New Exford

Ballynure

Orkney

Quarel

Dodd

Ramse

Knevci

Arc-Royal

Hamilton

Kandersteg

Pandora

Crimond

Tomans

Jabuka

Lothan

Tsinan

Incukalns

Dukamba

Summit

Borghese

Rasalgethi

Ft. Loudon

Ueda

Tur

Pobeda

Upano

Cumbres

Grunwald

Suron

Kelenfold

Karbala

Deli

Vorzel

Lyndon

Meacham

Al Hillah

Horneburg

Westerstede

Cameron

Pharkad

Blue Diamond

Fatima

Orestes

Greyslane

Forkas

Aima Alta

Garrison

Arcturus

Morningside

Port Moseb

Minderoo

Euln

Gibbs

Donegal

Ginestra

Lucanca

Leganes

Gananoren

Dalkeith

Crevada

Aposica

Kochangen

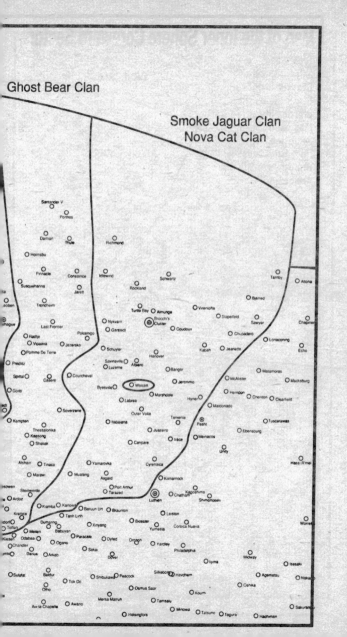

Type: Adder
Mass: 35 tons
Chassis: Endo Steel
Power Plant: 210 XL
Cruising Speed: 64.8 kph
Maximum Speed: 97.2 kph
Jump Jets: None
    Jump Capacity: None
Armor: Ferro-Fibrous
Armament:
    1 Flamer
    16.25 tons of pod space available

ADDER

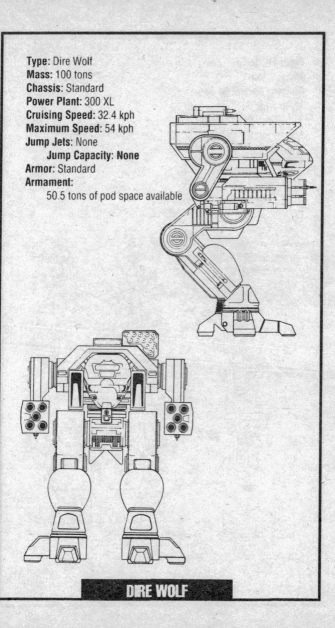

Type: Dire Wolf
Mass: 100 tons
Chassis: Standard
Power Plant: 300 XL
Cruising Speed: 32.4 kph
Maximum Speed: 54 kph
Jump Jets: None
    Jump Capacity: None
Armor: Standard
Armament:
    50.5 tons of pod space available

DIRE WOLF

Type: Elemental
Mass: 1 ton
Cruising Speed: 32 kph
Jump Jets: 3
    Jump Capacity: 90 meters
Armor: Ferro-Fibrous
Armament:
    1 SRM 2
    1 Small Laser

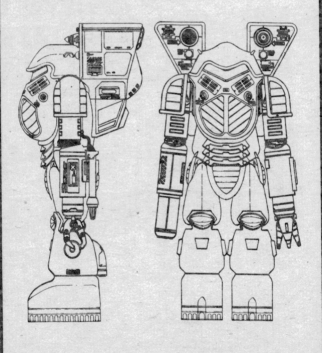

ELEMENTAL

Type: Executioner
Mass: 95 tons
Chassis: Standard
Power Plant: 380 XL
Cruising Speed: 43.2 kph
Maximum Speed: 64.8 kph
Jump Jets: 6
　　Jump Capacity: 120 meters
Armor: Ferro-Fibrous
Armament:
　　26.25 tons of pod space available

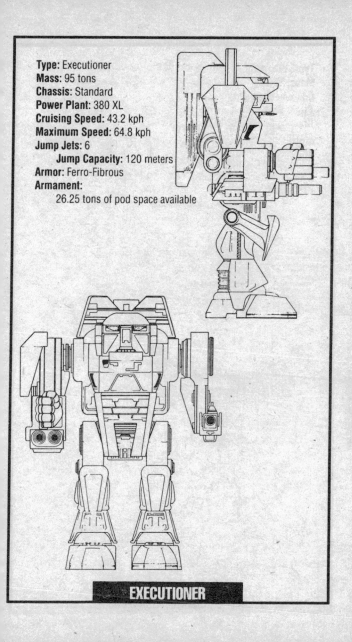

EXECUTIONER

Type: Fire Moth
Mass: 20 tons
Chassis: Endo Steel
Power Plant: 200 XL
Cruising Speed: 108 kph
Maximum Speed: 162 kph
Jump Jets: None
  Jump Capacity: None
Armor: Ferro-Fibrous
Armament:
   6.75 tons of pod space available

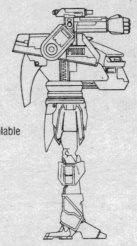

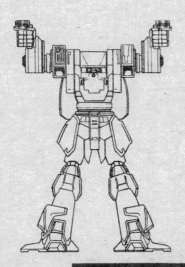

FIRE MOTH

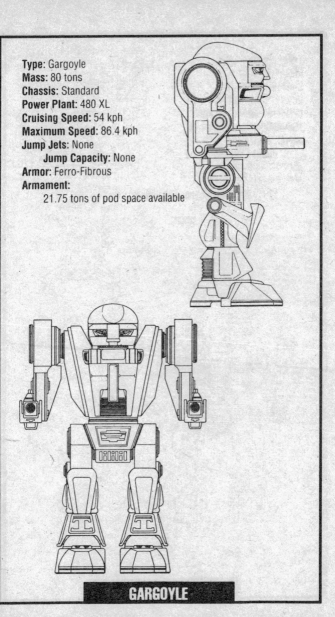

Type: Gargoyle
Mass: 80 tons
Chassis: Standard
Power Plant: 480 XL
Cruising Speed: 54 kph
Maximum Speed: 86.4 kph
Jump Jets: None
    Jump Capacity: None
Armor: Ferro-Fibrous
Armament:
    21.75 tons of pod space available

GARGOYLE

Type: Hellbringer
Mass: 65 tons
Chassis: Standard
Power Plant: 325 XL
Cruising Speed: 54 kph
Maximum Speed: 86.4 kph
Jump Jets: None
Jump Capacity: None
Armor: Standard
Armament:
28.75 tons of pod space available

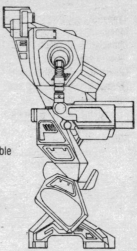

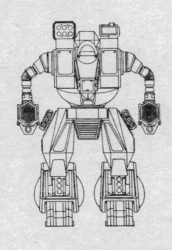

HELLBRINGER

Type: Ice Ferret
Mass: 45 tons
Chassis: Endo Steel
Power Plant: 360 XL
Cruising Speed: 86.4 kph
Maximum Speed: 129.6 kph
Jump Jets: None
    Jump Capacity: None
Armor: Ferro-Fibrous
Armament:
    9.75 tons of pod space available

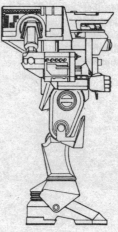

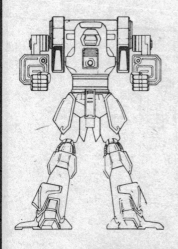

ICE FERRET

Type: Kit Fox
Mass: 30 tons
Chassis: Endo Steel
Power Plant: 180 XL
Cruising Speed: 64.8 kph
Maximum Speed: 97.2 kph
Jump Jets: None
    Jump Capacity: None
Armor: Ferro-Fibrous
Armament:
    16 tons of pod space available

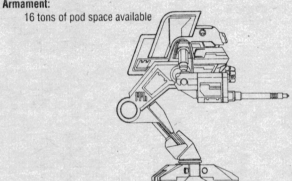

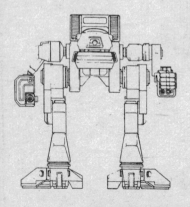

KIT FOX

Type: Mad Dog
Mass: 60 tons
Chassis: Standard
Power Plant: 300 XL
Cruising Speed: 54 kph
Maximum Speed: 86.4 kph
Jump Jets: None
Jump Capacity: None
Armor: Ferro-Fibrous
Armament:

    28 tons of pod space available

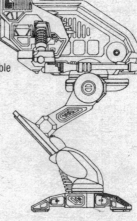

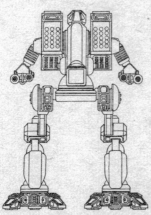

MAD DOG

Type: Mist Lynx
Mass: 25 tons
Chassis: Endo Steel
Power Plant: 175 XL
Cruising Speed: 75.6 kph
Maximum Speed: 118.8 kph
Jump Jets: 6
    Jump Capacity: 180 meters
Armor: Ferro-Fibrous
Armament:
    8.75 tons of pod space available

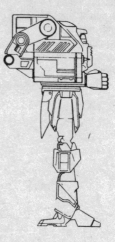

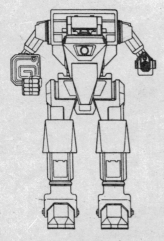

MIST LYNX

Type: Nova
Mass: 50 tons
Chassis: Standard
Power Plant: 250 XL
Cruising Speed: 54 kph
Maximum Speed: 86.4 kph
Jump Jets: 5
    Jump Capacity: 150 meters
Armor: Standard
Armament:
    16.25 tons of pod space available

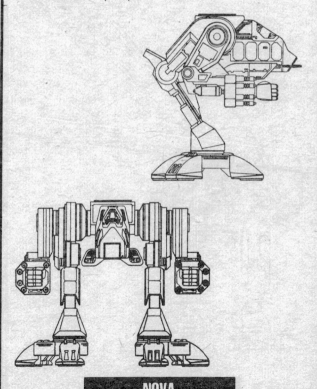

NOVA

Type: Stormcrow
Mass: 55 tons
Chassis: Endo Steel
Power Plant: 330 XL
Cruising Speed: 64.8 kph
Maximum Speed: 97.2 kph
Jump Jets: None
    Jump Capacity: None
Armor: Ferro-Fibrous
Armament:
    23 tons of pod space available

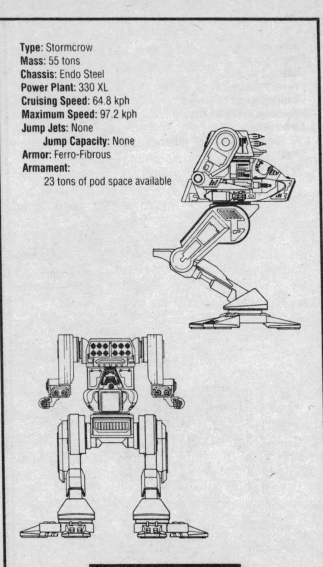

STORMCROW

Type: Summoner
Mass: 70 tons
Chassis: Standard
Power Plant: 350 XL
Cruising Speed: 54 kph
Maximum Speed: 86.4 kph
Jump Jets: 5
  Jump Capacity: 150 meters
Armor: Ferro-Fibrous
Armament:
  22.75 tons of pod space available

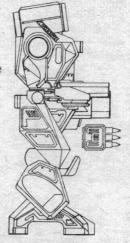

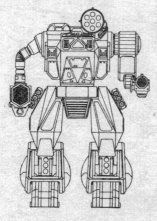

SUMMONER

Type: Timber Wolf
Mass: 75 tons
Chassis: Endo Steel
Power Plant: 375 XL
Cruising Speed: 54 kph
Maximum Speed: 86.4 kph
Jump Jets: None
    Jump Capacity: None
Armor: Ferro-Fibrous
Armament:
    28 tons of pod space available

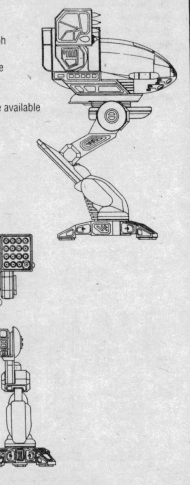

TIMBER WOLF

Type: Viper
Mass: 40 tons
Chassis: Endo Steel
Power Plant: 320 XL
Cruising Speed: 86.4 kph
Maximum Speed: 129.6 kph
Jump Jets: 8
    Jump Capacity: 240 meters
Armor: Ferro-Fibrous
Armament:
    8.75 tons of pod space available

VIPER

Type: Warhawk
Mass: 85 tons
Chassis: Standard
Power Plant: 340 XL
Cruising Speed: 43.2 kph
Maximum Speed: 64.8 kph
Jump Jets: None
    Jump Capacity: None
Armor: Ferro-Fibrous
Armament:
    32.5 tons of pod space available

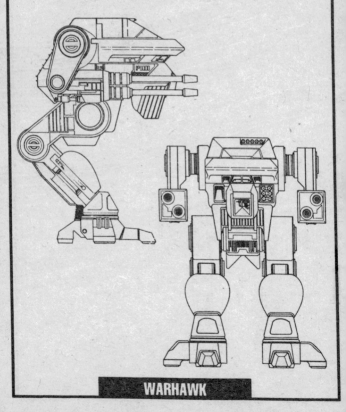

WARHAWK